BELLS IN THE WILDERNESS

DAVID MARTYN

BLUE FORGE PRESS
Port Orchard ✹ Washington

Bells in the Wilderness
Copyright 2025
by David Martyn

First eBook Edition January 2026
First Print Edition January 2026

ISBN 979-8-89439-065-9

For information about film, reprint or other subsidiary rights, contact: blueforgegroup@gmail.com

Blue Forge Press is the print division of the volunteer-run, federal 501(c)3 nonprofit, Blue Legacy (EIN 83-4307421), founded in 1989 and dedicated to supporting artisans marginalized due to race, age, disability, economics or other factors. We strive to empower storytellers from all walks of life with our four divisions: Blue Forge Press, Blue Forge Films, Blue Forge Gaming, and Blue Forge Sound. Find out more at www.BlueForgeGroup.org

Blue Forge Press
7419 Ebbert Drive Southeast
Port Orchard, Washington 98367
blueforgepress@gmail.com
360-550-2071 ph.txt

MORE BY DAVID MARTYN

THE HALL OF FAITH

The Praise Singer: A Disciple of Melchizedek
The Oak of Weeping: The Story of Isaac, Rebekah, and Deborah
The Epistle: A Story of the Early Church

ROBERT CURTIS MYSTERIES

Called Into Service
Soldiers of the King: The Bramshill Affair
Lords and Ladies: The Banqueting House Plot
For God and King: The Deadly Pamphleteer

A LITTLE GOOD BOOK

Huldah and the Last Righteous King
The Hospice of King David
The Annunciation of the Magi

STAND-ALONE BOOKS

The Great Gig Harbor Canoe Caper
A Light in the Darkest Night: Sixteen Stories of Love & Rebirth
The Magi's Apprentice

ANTHOLOGIES

Beacon: When Faith Shows the Way
Enduring: Stories of Unconditional Love
Unnerving Descent
Unnerving Eclipse

WWW.DAVIDMARTYN.COM

IKE CURTIS AND THE BELLS OF WAR

Book 1: Bells of Redemption

Book 2: Bells in the Wilderness

To Lillian Martyn—

*Daughter of an orphaned immigrant mother and an
immigrant father—a gravedigger—she dropped out
of school at thirteen when her mother died and
went to work to help support her family.
A housewife, stay-at-home mother of six,
and PTA president.*

What others would call sacrifice, she called love.

I knew you in the wilderness, in a land of drought.
Hosea 13:5

PROLOGUE

Bells in the Wilderness is the second book in the Ike Curtis series. In the first book, *Bells of Redemption*, Montclair Isaac 'Ike' Curtis, an American Observer, is assigned to the British Royal Air Force (RAF). His Special Unit Reconnaissance (RECON) Squadron supported British Military Intelligence, MI9, British Intelligence, MI6, and the Special Operations Executive (SOE) before and during the American buildup in Britain in the years leading up to the Normandy Invasion.

Ike Curtis, an Army Air Corps Reserve Officer from Washington state, attempts to bury his pain and guilt in the mission of MI9, saving downed Allied pilots and escapees from German POW camps. He led night missions supporting Belgian and French 'helpers,' unarmed citizens who rescued, hid, clothed, and fed Allied personnel, guiding them along escape routes, that they might fight again. His squadron of small planes delivered agents, cash, and radios. The many willing French helpers were at constant risk of betrayal by collaborators, German Military Intelligence, Abwehr, agents, and traitors embedded in the escape line leadership.

A British Woman's Auxiliary, RAF officer, a parish secretary, a vicar, and fellow officers help Ike face his doubts and recover his faith. Bells of Redemption ends with Ike announcing he is staying, as his father would sing, "Stayed on Jehovah," when a staff officer arrives with orders and drives him to his base, RAF Churchstanton.

Our story picks up ten minutes later...

Bells in the Wilderness

David Martyn

CHAPTER 1
ALLIED FORCE COMMAND

The familiar green and rolling Somerset countryside along the short ride from Saint Peter and Saint Paul Church to Royal Air Force Base Churchstanton slid by as Major Montclair Isaac 'Ike' Curtis sat humming to himself in the back seat of a Royal Air Force staff car. *Stayed upon Jehovah, hearts are truly blessed, finding as he promised perfect peace and rest.* The joyful tune, learned in childhood, would not leave him, nor would he let go of it. He exalted in joy, present and past remembered. Joy had been missing in his life since the death of his wife, Linda, five years earlier. He had always blamed himself, his overconfidence landing a seaplane in fog, causing the fatal crash that left his young son without a mother. Everyone forgave him, but he never forgave himself—or God. Where was God that day? Why did he let it happen? But today, his burden was finally lifted. He could love again—he was loved—he was in love! Now the scenery, so familiar, was new. His joy made the fields and pastures greener, the sky bluer, and the sun to shine brighter. Ike saw the beauty of creation. The prodigal son had returned; the stray sheep was back in the fold.

"Lieutenant, any idea what this is about?"

"No, sir. My orders are to escort you to headquarters ASAP."

The RAF staff car turned into the guarded entrance of RAF Churchstanton. Ike Curtis, seated in the back, sat up straight when the car turned right once through the gate. "Where the hell are you going, Lieutenant? The Officers' Quarters are to the left. It will only take me a few minutes to pack a bag. How long will I be gone?"

The young American behind the wheel turned his head and spoke over his shoulder. "Don't worry about your bag, Major. All your belongings are already on the plane."

Surprised, Ike Curtis replied, "All my belongings?"

"Yes, sir. Every arrangement has been made."

Ike settled back into his seat and processed what he heard. *I guess I'm in for a ride. I better be stayed upon Jehovah, after all!*

The car continued down the perimeter road and drove past a hangar. At the end of the taxiway, Ike spied a twin-engine Lockheed Hudson troop transport with prominent white stars of the US Army Air Corps painted on the desert-camouflaged wings and tail. Group Captain Hastings and Flight Lieutenant Marley were standing outside the open door of the American plane.

The car stopped beside the plane. The young lieutenant opened the door for Ike. "Sir, we need to depart immediately." He saluted Hastings and handed him the car keys. "Sir, thank you for your assistance. Shall I pass your regards to General Eisenhower?"

Hastings returned the salute. "Tell the General that Major Curtis is an important member of this Group. We need him back as soon as possible."

"I'll give him that message, sir." He turned to Ike and said, "Major, time to go."

Ike turned to Group Captain Hastings and asked, "Do you know what this is all about? They packed all my belongings!"

Hastings shook his head and said, "No more than you, Ike. No time even for a farewell with the mess." Ike saluted Hastings, then reached out to shake hands. "Thanks for putting up with me. You're an outstanding officer—one of the finest I've served with and a good man."

Ike turned to his Number One, Marley, who saluted him sharply in the exaggerated, palm-up British fashion. Ike returned the salute. "Good luck, Nigel. I know the 545 will be in good hands. Tell the men… tell the men—say they're first rate every one of them."

"God go with you. Skipper."

Ike climbed aboard the Hudson transport and was surprised not to find four seats on either side of a center aisle, but three large seats facing the center, with a table at the rear. As he boarded, the lieutenant, seated in the back, said, "Wherever you're comfortable, Major."

Ike sat down and noticed a command patch sewn to each headrest. Ike had never seen it before. It was a rounded A and a rounded F in white on a red outline against a blue background. "Not your normal transport, and I don't recognize the unit emblem, Lieutenant. And if we are together for a while, don't you have a name?"

"Sorry, sir. Yes sir. Second Lieutenant Johnson, sir. Why, this is General Eisenhower's command staff transport. That's the Allied Force Headquarters patch."

Ike leaned back in the comfortable seat and nodded. "So, how long to Gibraltar?"

Lieutenant Johnson looked askance and replied, "The General has moved his headquarters to Algiers. That's where we're headed. The Jerrys are on the run in North Africa. Sicily is next."

Ike turned and looked forward to the pilot as the engines began to turn over. He scurried forward behind the pilot and asked, "I expect there will be an escort?"

The army captain behind the controls turned his head halfway around and replied, "No escort. We've done this before."

Ike nodded. "To Gibraltar, I understand. But everything I've seen in intelligence says it is still hot over the Med."

The pilot moved forward in his seat and turned around to face Ike. "Major, you're wearing wings. You're attached to the RAF. I hear you're some kinda RECON whiz. Let me ask you, how many planes have you lost?"

"Three. Two in France and one over the Channel."

"The ones in France?"

"Security leak. Our French helpers were penetrated."

The pilot nodded. "Right. "I carry many senior officers to and from General Eisenhower's HQ. We can't afford a security leak. No one knows my schedule but the General."

Ike sighed, "Security didn't help the man I lost over the channel."

The captain replied, "No. But I bet your pilots know the best routes in and out. They know the Jerrys' defenses and routine. How many missions has your unit flown?"

"Hundreds."

"That's a damn good record. Near perfect. I'll take those odds. Now, if you return to your seat, Major, I must get us in the air."

Somewhere over the Atlantic, settled in the comfortable seat, his ear tuned to the hum of the engines, Ike shook his head. *I don't get it. Orders from General Eisenhower? He's leading the fight in North Africa. What would he want with me, a reserve Major, an observer with a RAF reconnaissance squadron? The US Army is well into the war, and the Eighth Air Force is gaining strength. Is he reassigning the remaining observers? He could easily reassign me through the chain of command. Not Eisenhower himself, but some personnel officer well down the chain. No, he shut down the observers last year when he relieved General Cheney. He left me to work with British Military Intelligence, MI9, at Colonel Dansey's request. Have I fouled up? I made mistakes, but no reprimands. Hell, the Brits gave me command of the 545! Why me? Why so urgent?*

Six hours after takeoff, the unmistakable towering gray granite Rock of Gibraltar appeared, bearing about 315 degrees relative. The Hudson came in steep from the Atlantic and touched down on the airfield. The small transport was taxied to the first hangar from RAF Gibraltar Operations. The pilot came back and said, "Major, we'll refuel and wait until midnight. You can have something to eat in the officers' mess, and you can rest in the ready room. Lieutenant Johnson knows the way."

Ike followed Lieutenant Johnson to the Officers' Mess. As he carried a tray of reheated supper to a table, he noticed an RAF officer sitting alone behind an empty dish and a cup of coffee. Ike stopped and said, "Mind if I join you? Just arrived, and I have a few questions."

"Sit down. How can I help you, Yank?"

Ike put down his tray and sat down. Lieutenant Johnson froze, not knowing if he was welcome or if he should find another table. Ike pointed to another chair and said, "Take a load off, Lieutenant."

Ike turned to the British officer and said, "I'm here on a layover, food, fuel, and off again. But there is someone I would like to see before I leave. A British civilian. He works for the MOD. His name is Osbourne, Arthur Osbourne."

The Brit replied, "I can't say as I know him. He's easy enough to find, though. Go to the personnel office in the Rock—they'll point you to him. It opens at 0800."

Ike nodded. "That's about eight hours too late. But

thanks, maybe next time."

The British officer took the last gulp of his coffee and excused himself. Lieutenant Johnson stared at Ike. Ike replied, "It's personal." And they finished supper in silence.

Some two hours later, Ike looked out on the ink-black sky. Occasionally, a setting crescent moon peeked through the overcast, shedding the only light on the sea below. The same eternal blackness that the pilots he sent into Nazi airspace faced. None of them ever complained. They did their jobs and volunteered when called upon to do more. *Why do they do it? It must be more than duty.* The steady hum of the Hunter's twin engines was broken by the voice of the co-pilot. "Keep the curtains closed. Secure all lights. We have a target approaching from the North African coast."

Radar, Ike thought. *Wish they would send some our way.* The plane fell into a dive and right roll, heading low and to the right, and the sea below. *How high were we? IFF must've pegged him as a Jerry. Must be trying to duck under him. God, I hope it works!* Ike laughed to himself. *Am I praying? Yes. And now I know you hear my prayers, Lord.*

In the silent darkness, Ike could hear the copilot. "He seems to be diving as well. Still heading toward us."

The pilot replied, "I'm coming left, leveling off at 500 feet."

"Skipper, the target is matching our course change—closing on us. I should have visual any moment... still closing...."

Ike glanced at the fluorescent face of his wristwatch. 0220. He shook his head when he read the date—May 1. *Mayday! Irony or one of your jokes, God?*

The copilot called out loudly, "There he is! I have visual. He's on fire—the moon is behind him. Yes, I make it a twin-engine, a Heinkel 219. One engine is on fire. Target is sliding left and right... wait, two more targets on the screen. Friends! Closing on target one. Come right and clear the way."

The plane rolled right and climbed. Ike peeked behind the curtain as the HE 219 night fighter burst into flame and began a deep tailspin to the dark waters below. Just before he pulled away, Ike saw two single-engine fighters fly by. The pilot called out over his shoulder. "Well, Major. It's good to see our fighters in action. We should be landing in twenty minutes, that is, if there are no more surprises."

At 0300, a weary Ike Curtis stepped out of the transport onto the tarmac. A warm, moist sea breeze pushed away the chill desert air from Maison Blanche Airport. Two jeeps were waiting to drive Ike, Johnson, and the flight crew to the officer quarters. The driver moved Ike's baggage to the jeep. The flight crew and Johnson picked up the room assignments waiting for them. Ike found an envelope with his name on it and opened it. It read: Major Curtis. Suite A, first floor. Report to General Eisenhower 1000. A driver will be waiting at 0945 in front of Officer Quarters. Ike mumbled, "Nice of him to let me sleep in. I hope I can find my least wrinkled uniform after a few winks and a shower."

Ike opened the door to Suite A, turned on the light, and was surprised to see a fully furnished apartment. A bowl of fresh fruit was on the table. The latest American magazines were neatly arranged. The small refrigerator contained ice, water, juices, sodas, and milk. A night lunch was neatly arranged on a command monogrammed plate. Ike stepped into the bedroom. He saw a large double bed, flanked by two small tables. Beneath the reading lamp on the nightstand on the side toward the separate bathroom lay a Gideon Bible. Next to the bathroom door was an open closet door. Hung on the inside was a pressed uniform with his name tag and ribbons; on the shoulder was a large AF patch of the Allied Force Headquarters, and pinned to each collar was a silver oak leaf indicating his rank as a Lieutenant Colonel. *Well, I guess this tells me everything I need to know about tomorrow.*

Ike stepped out of the Officer Quarters at 0940. A staff car was waiting. A young second lieutenant jumped out, saluted, and, using the polite form to address a Light Colonel, said, "Good morning, Colonel. It's a short ride to HQ."

Ike returned his salute and said, "Good morning, lieutenant. I didn't find my things in the room last night."

"The Colonel's bags were delivered to your quarters in town. The fresh paint needs to dry, and the air needs to be cleared. Expect you'll get the go-ahead this afternoon. Otherwise, you'll spend another night in the Senior Officer suite."

Bells in the Wilderness

They drove off the airbase into the old city. The French Governor's Palace now flew Free French and American Flags. Three flags stood on both sides of the entry. A prominent lower flag between the flags of state was a red flag with four white stars. It was clear to everyone in Algiers that this was General Eisenhower's Headquarters. Ike was led upstairs to a suite. If the four stars didn't tell you, the two guards, standing at ease with M1 rifles, made it clear the wing was off-limits, except by invitation. When the young lieutenant led Ike past, both guards snapped to attention.

Ike entered an anteroom staffed by an adjutant and several aides and furnished with a couch and several comfortable chairs. The adjutant spoke. "Colonel Curtis. Please make yourself comfortable. The General will call for you at his leisure."

The young lieutenant silently slipped away. Ike glanced at the patch sewn to his uniform, the same patch worn by everyone in the room and every American he met since being whisked away. Feeling out of place, Ike's thoughts went back to Churchstanton. *Will I ever see Rose again? I miss her. And Dottie and Hugh. Lord, did you have to pull me away so quickly? I owe them so much—their patience and love. They brought me back like a lost sheep and a prodigal son. Must you put me to the test so soon?*

Ike's memories of Rose were interrupted by the adjutant. "Colonel, the General will see you now." Ike looked at his watch. It was exactly 1000. Ike walked into Eisenhower's office, stood before his desk, saluted, and said out of habit, "Major Curtis reporting as requested."

Eisenhower did not lift his head. "You're either out of uniform or a slow learner, Curtis." The general looked up and smiled. "The uniform is correct, Colonel—I like to congratulate my officers upon their promotion."

Ike replied, "Thank you, General, as one of your American Observers. I see the Allied Force patch on the sleeve. I take it you meant more than congratulations on the promotion."

Eisenhower smiled. "I'm giving you the opportunity to join my senior staff as my RECON officer. The position is slated for a bird Colonel, but that will happen in time. Just keep performing as you have. I've heard good things about your work with MI9. You, Curtis, have a reputation for being right and having the lowest loss rate of any squadron in the RAF, two qualities I can't ignore."

Ike nodded. "Thank you for the kind words, General. You said opportunity, General, permission to speak freely."

"Granted."

"General, do I have a choice? I believe my work with the MI9 escape routes and the ferreting out of a traitor who has infiltrated our network, costing many lives, is not finished. Sir, with all due respect, if it's only an opportunity, I would like to return to my unit, Special Unit Flight 545, where I know I can be effective."

General Eisenhower's stare sliced through Ike's face. Gradually, Eisenhower's smile returned. "I'm not having this from you, too. I rely on the Air Group RECON wing for my reconnaissance, and he is off playing cowboy.

Tried another officer, and he's—well, I'm all for a desire to be effective. But this is a war, and you are an officer of the United States Army. We follow orders. We trust our seniors and do our duty—and I mean effectively as ordered where ordered."

Ike nodded. "Yes, sir. Where ordered, General."

Eisenhower looked down at his desk and picked up a folder. "Colonel, report to RECON. Give this to Colonel Johnson." Ike accepted the folder from Eisenhower.

The General looked back at Ike and said, "Colonel, one week from today, you will report to me with your evaluation of Allied Force Reconnaissance activities and a plan of action to improve results. Our current bombers can't seem to hit the broad side of a barn. Mission after mission, dug-in enemy gun emplacements are untouched. You want to be effective. I want results. Good day, Colonel."

In the outside office, Ike stopped at the adjutant's desk. "Could you direct me to RECON?"

The adjutant handed him a folder. "It contains a map and all the instructions you need, Colonel. Welcome to Allied Force Headquarters."

CHAPTER 2
ALLIED FORCE RECON

Colonel Johnson greeted Ike as he entered the office. "You must be Curtis. Jerry Johnson. Is that envelope what I think it is? It's all yours, Curtis. I stand relieved."

Ike replied, "Hold on, Colonel. You are not relieved until I am satisfied that a proper turnover has been completed. I suggest we sit down, and I hear your brief."

Colonel Johnson pointed to his office and said, "Of course. It's just that I'm a fish out of water here—not my area. I was temporarily assigned when your predecessor was sent packing."

"Where is he? I want to talk to him as well," Ike replied.

Colonel Johnson shook his head. "Last I saw, he was on a plane for Washington. Probably counting paper clips in the Pentagon, knowing Ike's, that is, General Eisenhower's, temper. Gotta give him that; he's not afraid to make a decision—action—he expects it. Don't get me wrong. Ike is fair—good to his staff. He'll hear you out. But he expects results—expects you'll have your facts and recommendations straight before you brief him. That's why I'm happy to see you. My day job is INTEL Officer. I read the RECON and recommend the targeting and RECON sites. We've been getting it wrong. Photographs have been good, and the bombers swear they're over the coordinates but are only making holes in the sand."

"Ike interrupted. "What about the Air Group RECON Wing Commander? Ike said he was playing cowboy."

"That would be Lieutenant Colonel Roosevelt...."

Ike's jaw dropped. "No relation to FDR. I mean, I know FDR junior is with the Eighth Air Force in England...."

Johnson replied, "His younger brother, Elliott. Thinks he is in charge here—I mean, here in North Africa. Does what he wants. Goes off the reservation. If he is called to account, he screams to his mama, Eleanor."

"Not FDR?"

Johnson laughed. "You heard me right. FDR doesn't say no to Eleanor. When you come across him, clear the runway. He got a taste for Special Ops in French West Africa. All hush, hush. Project Rusty, but you didn't hear it from me. We were never there, and we are not at war with French West Africa. Loves to go along for the ride. Rumor—well, truth is he was 4F yet somehow a flyer—officially a RECON Officer, not pilot—but—now off on a gambit stateside. Thank goodness—it keeps him away from Operations Mincemeat and Husky. Give him credit for one thing—he wanted British Mosquitos for RECON, and we got them. Now, if only we knew how to use them."

Ike asked, "Husky, I know—the Sicily campaign.

But Mincemeat?"

Johnson replied, "Part of the Brits' Operation Barclay. Deception for Husky—using Sardinia and Greece as a decoy to draw the Jerries away from Sicily."

"Right. Eisenhower said something about holes in the sand. Let's back up. Start with the situation. I'm new to the operation."

Johnson walked over to a large map of the North African coast, grabbed a pointer, and said, "We've bottled up the Jerrys on the coast trapped against the Bay of Tunis, their bridgehead out through Tunis, Bizerte, here to the north of Tunis, and Enfidiville to the south. We've been pushing back since March. They know they are hanging on by the skin of their teeth, but they're well entrenched. These harbors are critical to Nazi resupply from Italy. The Royal Navy has gained sea superiority, and we've achieved air superiority, but the skies are still contested. Hitler evacuated Rommel in March. General Hans-Jurgen von Arnim now commands the Army Group Africa. He, along with Italian General Giovanni Messe and General Gustav von Vearst and his 5th Panzer Army. Two days ago, the British 4th Infantry was pushed back by von Vearst here, at Cactus Far, and withdrew. The 12th Royal Tanks lost twelve tanks to sticky bombs, that is, Teller anti-tank mines, when they advanced without infantry support. The Jerries have their best in the middle, the Hermann Goring Division and the tanks of the 10th Panzer Division. RECON never found their entrenched artillery and tank positions. General Eisenhower is calling for a new plan, code-named 'Strike.'

We must find those emplacements and break through their line for the kill. No more excuses now that air superiority is established. The goal is to end all Fascist resupply and to block enemy evacuations. He wants to stop the bleeding of Allied Forces and move on to Sicily. We've laid out landing sites in Sicily, but he's lost confidence in the RECON. Can't say as I blame him. He doesn't want to land our boys only to leave them as cannon fodder to the Jerrys."

Ike Curtis took a deep breath. "Eisenhower wants this campaign wrapped up. He made that clear. And he wants it done within a week." He paused. "You can't identify the emplacements? What do the pilots say?"

"As I said, they say they're laying their bombs where directed."

Ike replied, "I meant your RECON pilots?"

Johnson shook his head. "According to their reports, they swear by what they see and report. Their photographs back them up. They go out every day and follow any Jerrys in the open. Tanks and infantry. They confirm the damage that our attack planes inflict. As I said, there is no problem with their photographs. Clear as a bell."

"The best photographs in the world cannot penetrate camouflage. And their night photos?"

"They don't fly at night. They fly high altitude. There's good visibility during the day. We vector the Jerrys' movements to any new night encampments. However, they seem to have dug in for now. Despite our air superiority, Jerry Night Fighters are still active. We must keep losses low. Allied Force has had good results with low losses. We need every asset for Sicily. The Jerrys have a near-equal reign after dark. Truth is, they've become a problem—a real menace to our men in the field at night."

Ike nodded. "I have some experience with their night fighters. Okay, Colonel. I think I understand the situation. Introduce me to the staff, and I will relieve you."

Johnson stood up. "Right. Major Don Shelton is your deputy. This way." Ike followed him out of the office to Major Shelton's office. Johnson knocked and entered. The Major stood at attention. Johnson said, "At ease, Shelton. This is Colonel Curtis, the new AFRECON Officer. I expect you to give him your full cooperation. I want you to gather the staff in the front office in five to meet Colonel Curtis."

Major Shelton replied crisply, "Yes, sir. Gather the staff in five minutes, sir."

Ike added, "And I want you to gather all the RECON pilots for a briefing."

"Yes sir. The daily briefing in the Ready Room is at 1300. The daily mission commences at 1330. Is that soon enough?"

"No. Tell them 1230 today. Tell them the new AFRECON boss will expect a complete debrief on RECON operations and tactics. And as soon as this short staff meeting ends, you'll drop me at the airfield. I want the Wing XO to meet me at the hangar."

"Which one, Colonel?"

"Surprise me. Just make sure the Wing RECON XO

and an operable plane are waiting."

Ike and Johnson left Shelton to make a quick phone call to spread the word before reporting to the front office.

Johnson told Ike, "You're not giving them much time for lunch. Won't make you popular."

"I didn't ask for this job. I was happy with the good results I was achieving. General Eisenhower wouldn't hear it. I'm here to get results. Fast results. He put me on a tight timeline. Popularity is not a priority. Results come first."

After quick introductions to the RECON Office staff. Colonel Johnson called the men to attention, saluted Ike, and said, "Attention to Orders." Ike read his orders, turned to Colonel Johnson, saluted, and said, "Sir, I relieve you."

Johnson returned the salute and said, "I stand relieved." Johnson shook each man's hand and was out the door.

Ike was short. "At ease, men. I know you are dedicated and capable. I'm here to make you effective. There will be changes starting today. You will return to your quarters, get some rest, and report back at 1800 hours. You'll be here all night. Any questions?"

The staff looked at each other and said nothing. Ike nodded. "Good. You're dismissed."

Ike turned to Major Shelton. "Take me to the airfield."

Ten minutes later, Ike stepped out of his staff car in front of Hangar Twelve. A twin-engine De Havilland DH.98 Mosquito, painted in RECON desert pink camouflage, was parked in front. An American Major saluted as Ike stepped out of the car. The Major held back his smile when he recognized the wings device of the Army Air Corps. *At last, there will be changes around here.* The major saluted and said, "Welcome, Colonel Curtis. I'm Fred Engert, XO of RECON Wing."

Ike returned the salute. *That's an accent I've never heard.* Ike said, "Ironic, Major, they put American paint and an American Officer in a British Mosquito. I come here from RAF Special Duty Flight 545. The Brits give away these fast, first-class airplanes while the RAF RECON flies old, slow Expeditors and Hudsons. What I would have given for a couple of these in my stable."

Major Engert replied slowly in his non-rushed Maine accent. "Well, sir, she's a RECON pilot's dream. Fast and high—over 400 mph with a ceiling over 35 thousand feet. With a cruising speed of 300, she has the oomph when needed to outrun any Jerry fighter that may come across her. Haven't lost one yet. Fitted with the best high-altitude cameras, she can really do the job."

Ike smiled. "But she hasn't," he replied.

"Hasn't, sir?"

"Major, the reason I'm here is that your RECON Wing hasn't done the job. Oh, you take good pictures. You don't contribute to the destruction of the enemy. Of course, you know this already…"

Engert thought. *Lt. Col. Roosevelt ain't gonna like this. Maybe this is the guy to get him out of our hair.*

Ike continued, "I'm here to change that. Now, show me around this plane and get me in the air. We have a meeting to get to at 1230 hours."

Ike was surprised by the smooth fuselage and wings. He ran his hand over the sleek surface, absent any rivets. *No wonder they call it the 'Wooden Wonder.' Smooth as glass—aerodynamic.*

Major Engert read his mind. "Wood composite. Alternating layers of South American Balsa and Canadian and American Birch. Surprisingly strong. She slips through the air like an eel through a fisherman's fingers."

In the air, Ike asked, "How long to get us to altitude?" Major Engert pulled back the stick, and the twin engines showed no sign of struggling as the lightweight plane climbed steeply. Ike was impressed with the pressurized cockpit. "Level at 35,000 and photograph Algiers and the airbase. Then take her down to 500 feet and slow to just above stall. I want to know her speed, low and slow."

Major Engert acknowledged and replied, "Sir, the stall speed is 135. With your permission, I'll make our speed 150."

"Make it so, Major."

Approaching the airfield, Ike said, "Take a pass over the city 500 feet and photograph HQ. Then put her back down."

On the ground, Ike said, "Get the film to processing ASAP. I want to view it this afternoon." Ike looked at his watch. "1150. You have half an hour to show me around before the pilot's briefing. By the way, Major, where are you from? Can't say I've heard your accent before."

"Down East Maine. God's country, where America begins."

Ike smiled. "Where America begins. I'll remember that. Take me to your lead camera tech. Do you have infrared equipment?"

Engert replied, "We do, not sure how much. Haven't needed it since we're restricted to high-altitude daylight flying. Master Sergeant Feinberg can answer your questions. Good man—Hollywood film experience. Knows his way around any camera and film."

Major Engert opened a door in the rear of the hangar that read "Camera Shop" and printed below in pencil, "Don't bother to knock; I see you."

Ike commented, "The Master Sergeant has a sense of humor."

Engert sighed, "Not really. If he doesn't want to see you, he won't unlock the door. He can get away with it because he really is that good."

Ike knocked on the door, and it quickly opened. A skinny man in shorts and a T-shirt opened the door. He scrambled to get into a short-sleeved uniform shirt. "Major Engert, Colonel, what can I do for you, sirs?"

Ike said, "At ease, Master Sergeant. I'm Lieutenant Colonel Curtis, your new AFRECON Officer. Tell me, what does the squadron have in the way of infrared cameras and film?"

Feinberg left his shirt unbuttoned, wiped the sweat from his brow, and replied, "Finally, we're going to catch the Jerries in their sleep! Colonel, I've got ten unopened infrared cameras and cases of film. Look, I know our high-altitude cameras are good. They're great for fixed targets, but a mechanized force moving across a roadless desert at night—it just ain't gonna work."

Ike smiled. "We're going to get along well, Master Sergeant. How many can you install by 1800 tonight?"

"My boys are green regarding infrared. I'll have to show him how it's done. With luck, half a dozen."

Ike replied, "Break them out, inspect them, and lay out the work. Major Engert will get you the list of planes within the hour."

A smile broke across the beard-stubbled face of the Sergeant. "Yes, sir. We could save some time if I started with the XO's plane. I mean, you havin' no objection, Major."

Major Engert nodded. "No objection. But tomorrow morning, I expect to see you here, showered, shaved, and in uniform. And in case you've missed the point, not hung over, I expect your equipment will be driven hard and put away wet in the next few weeks."

Walking to the ready room and the waiting assembled pilots, Engert said, "1800 tonight? That's an aggressive schedule, Colonel. I can't remember the last time these men flew at night."

"We have to start somewhere, sometime. Tonight is as good as any. But I agree, we'll ease them into it— somewhat." Ike stopped and faced Engert. "One thing I missed, Major—Radar. I've heard your wooden wonders can be fitted with Radar. How many in your squadron?"

"Only two, but we're promised more. When they arrive in theatre."

"That'll have to do for now. Let's meet your men, Major."

Twelve pilots stood at attention when Major Engert led Ike into the ready room. "At ease, men. This is Lieutenant Colonel Curtis, our new AFRECON Officer. He requested a briefing before today's mission and will lay out some operational changes. Colonel…."

"Thank you, Major Engert. Seats gentlemen. General Eisenhower pulled me away from my Special Unit Flight to be your new AFRECON Officer. The General is unhappy with the reconnaissance he's receiving. He put me on a tight schedule to identify what's wrong and to fix it. I don't need to tell you why he is unhappy. The bombers—if they drop their bombs at all—are just making holes in the sand. Now, Major Engert has introduced me to your Mosquitoes. I'd have given my eye teeth for your planes in my unit. I can't imagine a better RECON plane in the Allied Forces, heck, any air force in the world. You've got the tools, so what's wrong? That's what we're going to find out and correct. Now, you've all heard of the immensely successful introduction of the fast, high-altitude RECON, which led to the most successful bombing raid to date in Norway. What was the lesson learned? Anyone?"

A hand went up. Ike said, "Speak up. And state your name. I want to get to know you."

"Captain Lewandowski, everyone calls me 'Ski."

Ike smiled. "Glad to meet you, Ski. Go ahead."

"Well, sir, it proved high altitude RECON was feasible and offered a distinct game-changing tactic over the old 'low and slow' tactics that were a carryover from WW1."

Ike asked, "Game-changing. How so?"

"Well, sir, with new freezeproof cameras and better optics and control, we can collect clear, high-resolution photographs at high altitudes."

"Right, and why is that better than low-altitude high-resolution photographs?"

"Sir. If you install the new cameras on a fast plane capable of high-altitude flight, it greatly reduces risk to the plane and the pilot."

Ike nodded. "Major Engert has shown me the climbing ability and the speed of your planes, not to mention a pressurized cockpit. It must be comforting to know you can outrun Jerry fighters. Everything considered, you have the advantage of flying a low-risk mission. And be sure that General Eisenhower appreciates lowering the risk to his men and equipment. So, with everything going for you, why is your RECON effort worthless?"

The room was quiet. Ike looked around and counted the pilots. "I count twelve pilots here. Am I right to assume twelve Mosquitos?"

A pilot replied, "Yes, sir. And the Lysander retired from artillery spotting, or so Lieutenant Colonel Roosevelt says."

"You have a Lysander? Is it fitted out and in flying condition?"

"Yes, sir. But we haven't used it on a RECON mission. It's an easy target in daylight, slow. We're talking snail slow."

Ike considered what he heard. "We'll talk about the Lysander later. Let's talk about flying experience. You trained for the Mosquito—how many would have preferred the attack variant, guns that can rip through armor and bomb in close support? Who flies the attack and bomber variants?"

"The Brits, sir."

"Yes, the Brits. They have experience. They've been in the sights of Jerry fighters and survived. Ski, tell me how many flight hours you had when you came here?"

"Twelve hours, sir."

"And in the Mosquito?"

"One hour, Colonel."

"One hour. And how many at night?"

"No night hours in my Mosquito yet."

Ike looked around. "Have any of you had night hours in your Mosquito? Any night hours in any RECON plane?"

One pilot raised his hand. "First Lieutenant Anderson, sir. I flew the commercial Lockheed Super Electra—in the Air Corps, a Hudson, and the Twin Beech Expeditors at night. And came in once after sunset in my Mosquito."

"Anderson, I'll have something for you. Now, the rest of you, that will change tonight. Look, it doesn't take a genius to figure out that the Jerrys know your pattern; they know when you will fly, they wait hidden beneath camouflage, no one coming or going until you pass. Your vectoring is little more than a guess. Camouflage can defeat any photograph, high altitude or low. Known fixed emplacements can be mapped at any time. Infrared can penetrate common battlefield camouflage, such as silk netting, day or night. I know of factories back in the States covered with painted residential neighborhoods on plywood. In these cases, friendly agents are our best source, but lacking that, nighttime infrared can capture and recognize traffic—trucks, tanks, and even men on foot can be seen entering and leaving. Today, you will be given a baptism by fire in new tactics and night reconnaissance."

A pilot asked, "Colonel, let me get this right. You want us to fly at night, and it appears, low—won't we be sacrificing our advantage of speed at altitude?"

Ike stared at the young pilot. "What's your name?"

"Jenkins, sir?"

"Thanks for asking the question your squadron mates didn't have the guts to ask. Yes, there is more risk. But you do not lose your speed and high rate of climb. And while the Jerry night fighters are radar-equipped, we can counter that risk with a radar-equipped plane flying high cover. Risk mitigated. Reward—getting our night attack fighters and bombers over the target."

Ike paused. "Wake up. Remember why you're here. I came here in an unescorted, unarmed staff transport. It's how the General moves his senior staff. The pilot knew the Jerrys' routine, just as the Africa Corps knows yours. And even when the unsuspected Heinkel night fighter did find us—well, I'm here because the cavalry—our night fighters—sent the Jerry to rest at the bottom of the Med. Great reward, small risk. Now, here's today's mission plan.…"

Chapter 3
Second Guessing

Ike returned to his office in AFHQ. Major Shelton greeted him at the door. "Colonel, I have the photos from your morning flight and an envelope with your keys and passes."

"Thanks, Major. Don, can I call you Don?"

" You're the boss. Don is fine."

"Don, show me the German positions and our recent RECON photos."

Ike followed Major Shelton to a large table map showing INTEL's charting of Nazi and Allied forces identified by unit and estimated strength. Don looked over the map and said, "I've updated it today based on yesterday's RECON and field reports. Not much change since the pushback on 30 April."

"Show me the photos. Lay them out according to the map."

Shelton said, "I'll start with where we withdrew on the 22nd, the central approach to Tunis. The day before yesterday—southeast of Medjez el Bab—photos of targeted areas. You'll notice the slightly different hues and gloss over the target areas. INTEL determined it to be camouflage."

Ike picked up an eyepiece and scrutinized the photos. He put it down. "I concur. The targets appear to be camouflaged areas."

Major Shelton handed him another batch of photos. Ike didn't need the eyepiece to see the craters in the rock and sand. Standing up with his head tilted back and a distant gaze in his eyes, Ike thought. "Don, it's all a matter of knowing your enemy—their routine, habits, and proclivities. The Jerrys can set their clocks by our RECON missions. That's going to change. Without night RECON, they are free to reset the battlefield. Move if necessary—it hasn't been necessary lately, but they can and have set up decoy sights. Without infrared, we can't even detect camouflage. I hope our pilots are fast learners. We need to catch the Jerrys quickly before they can adjust tactics."

Don Shelton smiled. "It's about time! So, the night RECON begins tonight. But what about this new infrared I've heard about? Rumors say you've proven it in France. But our planes aren't outfitted...."

"Master Sergeant Feinberg tells me he can have six mounted by 1800."

"Just Tunis or...."

"I want to hit both Fascist Armies—send them reeling and open up opportunities for Allied Armies."

Don smiled, and then his eyebrows tightened. "So, Bizerte corridor, too. This is a big change, and it's only your first day. Do you want to submit your plan for approval up the chain? There is risk. A bold change without training."

Ike inhaled and exhaled deeply. Finally, he said, "Get on the horn with Air Group. Tell them we will need fighter coverage beginning at 1800 and through the night. Tell them we will maintain high cover with radar-equipped planes over Tunis and Bizerte, where they should be looking for Axis night fighters and supply drops."

Ike turned to Shelton and said, "Eisenhower wants to wrap things up. He made that clear. I'd rather be judged by my results than second-guessed by his staff. If I'm wrong…hmm…if I'm wrong, we're no worse off. Now, I'll try to get something to eat and rest. I need to be back before 1800. By the way, Don, this morning—I haven't seen a salute that crisp since I left the RAF. Where did you learn that?"

Don smiled. "ROTC drill team at MSOE."

"Where?"

"Milwaukee School of Engineering."

Ike's face radiated confusion. He said, "Never heard of it."

Shelton laughed. "No one has, outside of Wisconsin—make that no one has outside a two-mile radius of the campus. But I assure you I know a wingnut when I see one."

Ike laughed. "See you at 1800."

Shelton's voice turned serious. "I'll get Air Group on the horn ASAP. You'll need the envelope on your desk. Map, keys, pass. I'll send for a driver."

"How far are we talking?"

"Less than two blocks. The staff are all billeted less than 5 minutes from HQ."

"Then, the map will do."

Don smiled. "Glad you're here, Colonel."

"Ike. My friends call me Ike."

Ike stepped out of HQ and looked down at the map. Tapping the address with his finger, he walked down the steps to the boulevard and turned left. The cool Mediterranean Sea breeze drifted down the street between the tall buildings. *This isn't the North Africa I envisioned.* The sunny May sky did not beat down on his head. It gently warmed him. It reminded him of summer in Gig Harbor. The temperature couldn't have been much above 70 degrees. *Balmy, not hot.* He came to the seaside promenade with stately French Colonial buildings on one side and large palm trees standing guard against the endless advance of waves spilling on the beach. *Palms. No, I'm not in Gig Harbor or Churchstanton.* The thought chilled him. *Rose. Hundreds of miles away. Stranded—no, safely at home. She has no idea where I am. She will wait patiently, confident of my return. She is my rock. I miss her, and yet I gave her no thought all day. Lord, remind me, please, Lord, I owe her better.*

Ike came upon the address in the middle of the block. He stared at the café before him, then looked again at the address. A waiter was clearing a table. Ike walked over to him and pointed to the address on the map. He asked in slow English, "Is this...." The waiter pointed up. Ike stood and stared. The waiter did his best. "Must go up," and showed him to a door. He opened the door and held up three fingers. Ike nodded and climbed the stairs to the third floor. The high ceilings of the third floor surprised him. Then, he remembered a friend's description of Paris. *Yes, like Paris, shops on the first floor, the shopkeeper's family and warehouse on the second, and the bourgeoisie on the third, above the noise and smells of the street.*

There was only one door. Ike tried the key in the lock. Before he could turn it, the door opened. An olive-skinned middle-aged woman bowed and greeted him. "Colonel Curtis, welcome. I hope your stay here will bring you peace and rest from the heavy burdens of your duties to rid Africa and the world of fascists. My name is Justine..." *Such deep blue eyes, penetrating and even mysterious—her hair and skin dark, but her features sharper than many Europeans... Striking!* "I am your cook and housekeeper. Your things have been delivered. I have put them away. Let me show you your apartment."

Ike stepped into the spacious salon, furnished with very French carved pieces covered in fine silk. Drapes billowed beside three French doors opening to a small balcony. "I keep them open until sunset. The air is fresh but cools after dark. Your bedroom is the first. You will find another balcony overlooking the sea. Next to it is another—a very fine guest room. My room is all the way in the back. You need not go there."

Ike found himself mumbling in reply, "No, of course not." He turned and smiled at Justine. *It is very fine indeed. But I need to sleep. Can you wake me at 5 PM? I need to go* back to work. I will work all night."

Justine nodded. "A warm meal then? Before you go?"

"Yes, thank you. That would do me well."

Justine replied, "I will knock on your door at 5 PM, Colonel. I will leave you now."

Ike opened the door to the bedroom. The closet door was open. His uniforms were freshly pressed and hanging neatly. A chest of drawers against the wall had each drawer pulled out three inches further than the one above, so all its contents were visible. Everything had been laundered and folded. Ike smiled as he pushed each drawer closed. He removed his Air Corps blouse (a waistcoat), his necktie, and his shoes and fell back into the bed. He closed his eyes and sighed. He gave no thought to closing the balcony door. The sounds of the breeze and muffled voices from the café below brought peace. He turned to his right and saw his framed picture of Rose on the nightstand. He smiled and fell asleep.

An hour and a half later, Ike's now restless body jolted—a dream. *"You have your orders," General Eisenhower said. Inexplicably, Ike found himself in the same Allied Force transport. The same crew manned the aircraft. Ike was sitting silently in the same seat. He watched as Gibraltar disappeared behind them. His eyes closed, his head nestled in the headrest, and a photograph of Rose in his hand. Lieutenant Johnson tapped Ike's shoulder and whispered. "Colonel, I thought you would like to see the last of Europe. If you look now, you can see Fastnet Lighthouse off the coast of Ireland, the last land sighting until Thule, Greenland."*

"No!" Ike shouted as he shot up from the bed.

Moments later, there was a light tapping on the bedroom door. "Did you need something, Colonel Curtis?" Justine asked softly.

Ike replied, "No, Justine. Thank you. I'm sorry. It was just something I remembered I needed to do."

Justine replied, "Dinner is waiting whenever you're ready."

"Give me fifteen minutes to shower and change clothes."

The shower water soothed his still weary body and cleared his mind. *Am I pushing too hard, too fast? Should I have briefed the staff on my plan? If it all goes south, will Eisenhower exile me like the last guy? Am I risking what I had and still want at RAF Churchstanton? I can't afford to lose Rose.*

When Ike left the bedroom, the spicy aroma of traditional North African cuisine led him to the table set for him. Justine was waiting. "There's only one setting," Ike said.

"I'm the cook and housekeeper, not your guest."

Ike nodded. "Yes, I know. I come from a working family. It will take me some time to become accustomed to your service. And I'd like to get to know you, and you me. It will make our time together easier. Please, if only this one time, join me."

"Well, maybe this one time." Justine went for

another place setting. Ike called out, "You can start by telling me what this dish is. It smells great!"

"Kamounia. It's our traditional lamb stew, though some use beef liver. Onions, garlic. Olive oil, parsley, tomato sauce, and spices. It's the many spices that make it special. I serve it with rice. It goes farther that way and tastes wonderful."

Ike took a bite and waved his mouth. "Good, hot, and spicy. I'll need water with this."

Justine smiled. "Colonel, you Americans have no taste for spices! And I made it extra mild." She set down her plate and spooned a small amount on it.

Ike swallowed and said, "Ike. Please, not Colonel. Yesterday, I was a major, and today, I am a lieutenant colonel. I'm not used to these perks of rank. I come from a small fishing village. My family ran a ferry boat. I joined the Army when they promised to cover my university costs. Four years of education in return for my service as an officer. But what about you, Justine? Your English is excellent."

"You do not need to know my past. It is a burden I carry alone."

Ike smiled. "You wear a cross. Are you Christian? Catholic perhaps? Our Christian faith teaches us to bear one another's burdens. I would like to hear your story. I'm told that I am a good listener."

Justine looked down at her plate and took another bite of dinner. She said nothing. Ike ate silently, alternating each bite with a drink of water. She discreetly wiped her eyes and looked up. "My husband, I fear—I don't know—I hear nothing from him. I pray he is not dead. I would know if he died, would I not? I hear women in the market. They say they know—a wife knows if her husband or child is alive or dead. Is this true?"

Ike sighed. "I've heard that, too. I don't know if it is true. Tell me about your husband. Perhaps I can help—ask the right authorities."

"He was with the resistance here in Algiers and then joined the Free French Army– or that was his intent. That was three months ago."

Ike nodded. "Write his full name and the date he left. I will make inquiries." Ike looked at his watch. I must go soon. Thank you for dinner."

Justine jumped from her chair. "Yes, at once. I must write his name for you."

Ike returned to the bedroom to collect his hat. He glanced in the closet, then went in and grabbed his flight jacket. Justine met him at the door and pressed a piece of paper into his hand. She squeezed it and said, "Thank you. God keep you safe, Colonel Ike."

CHAPTER 4
INTO THE NIGHT SKY

The last rays of the setting sun crept through the street, leading him west, one block from the sea. Ike stopped for a moment to admire the dimming golden sparkles on gentle waves. He took a deep breath of determination and glanced at his watch, *1740. Sunset in two minutes.* He walked briskly to AFHQ. Don Shelton was waiting for him. "Don, I'm hoping the first run made it back okay. When will the sunset sorties return?"

Major Shelton replied, "The first of three patrols, three birds, including one radar-equipped RECON, was back an hour ago. The film is being processed. The second patrol of three should now be over the targets. Expect them back in an hour and fifteen minutes. The second Radar bird will linger off the coast. The first refueled and will fly with sortie three at 1800."

"Any unusual enemy response reported?" Ike asked.

"None. Seems the Jerrys are sitting tight. Fat, dumb, and happy dug in in their camouflaged positions."

Ike nodded. "Drop me off at the squadron and bring me the photos as soon as they come in."

Ten minutes later, Ike joined Major Engert in the squadron ready room. "What do we have so far, Major?" Ike asked.

Fred Engert turned from the OPS board, saluted Ike, and said, "Welcome, Colonel. From the pilot's reports—much the same as yesterday. Minor vehicle traffic and visual indications of a new, false target."

Ike nodded. "Good. They've grown complacent. With any luck at all, we should catch activity tonight. How many cameras did the Master Sergeant manage to install?"

"He's still here, working last I heard at six. He's already installing cameras on the returned birds. Should have all ten up and running sometime tonight."

"Take me to him. I want to run something by you for tonight."

Engert smiled. "A fourth patrol? I'm all in."

"Are your men up to it?"

"I haven't seen this much adrenaline flowing since this wing was formed. They're up for it, Colonel."

"Ike. Call me Ike, Fred, not to be confused with Eisenhower, but in my presence. 'You ever fly a Lysander? I can get Lieutenant Anderson."

Fred replied, "There are no cameras on the Lysander. What's the plan?"

Ike smiled. "Let's ask Feinberg."

Feinberg's team was busy at work under the three Mosquitos that returned from the first sortie. Feinberg looked up from beneath a plane and said, "Kinda busy,

Colonel. Forgive me if I don't salute."

"As you were, Sergeant," Ike replied. "Where are we?"

"These are the last. Another hour and all ten will be installed."

Ike smiled. "Well done, Master Sergeant, to you and your team." Ike paused. "You wouldn't have squirreled away back in your workshop a handheld infrared, would you? I'd like to take a predawn sortie, low and slow, over the targets in the Lysander, just to see if the Jerrys have gotten the message and scramble."

Feinberg slid out from under the plane. "Now, if you had a first-rate cinematographer and cameraman aboard that Lysander, a personal camera might be found."

Ike chuckled. "You know, that little Lysander is slow, and I mean to make passes. Who's to say the Jerrys won't be so rattled as to break out searchlights and anti-aircraft guns? Hell, small arms might be enough."

Feinberg nodded. "And I expect we may get a little sand on the bottom. Give me this ride, Colonel, and you'll always have whatever you need."

Ike said, "What do you think, Fred? Can you outfit the Sergeant for a 0230 mission?"

Fred nodded. "He's awfully scrawny. If he were a lobster, I'd throw him back, but we can find something to fit him."

Feinberg, out of character, or perhaps not, shocked Ike and Engert. He jumped to attention and saluted the officers. "Master Sergeant Feinberg will report to the ready room at 0130 for flight duty."

Ike returned the salute, and Engert said, "As you were, master sergeant. Get some rest. I'll see you in the ready room at 0130."

The early evening RECON photos arrived. The sortie caught the Germans setting up camouflage tents on a ridge half a mile from the previous night's position. More activity was noted in wheat fields behind a ridge of stone and sand closer to Tunis. Ike scrutinized each before handing them to Shelton and Engert. He tapped his finger on the map. "So far so good. They confirm the Jerrys haven't moved. They are staying with their decoy tactic. The infrared should catch them napping. When the first night sorties return at 2300, jump on developing. Urgent. Get the pictures to AFINTEL, Field HQs' INTEL, and Air Group ASAP. Don't wait for clearance. Send them on. If the artillery acts quickly, they can pull the fangs from the Nazi beast even before the bombers are in the air. Bomber and strike squadrons can follow up and catch them on the run."

Major Shelton asked, "Kinda going out on a limb, Colonel. You're asking on your authority for our ground pounders and artillery to attack. What will Eisenhower's staff think? You know you are expected at the morning brief at 0800."

Engert added, "Eisenhower is not one to criticize success. It's ballsy for sure, but I like it."

Ike smiled. "I am providing them urgently needed

intelligence. I am not telling them what to do with it. If they're aggressive Commanders, they'll know how to act. And I don't mind facing the music in the morning brief. That is, if Fred and I make it back alive in the Lysander."

Don Shelton looked up from the map. "I'll get on the horn now and give them a heads up. Hot RECON on the way."

Fred Engert pointed to the map. "Give me tight coordinates to this area. I'll need them. Unlikely we'll see the infrared photos before we leave. Tight. Have them to me by 0130."

When Ike and Engert returned to the RECON squadron, the Lysander was parked in front of the hangar. The ground crew was just finishing the pre-flight check. The tanks were full, and the engine was warm. Major Engert told Ike, "You know, she only has two seats, Colonel."

Ike laughed. "Two seats but room for five. I know how to stack 'em, Major. I'll let you take the pilot seat. You know the area. I'll sit comfortably in the back seat while Feinberg can lie on the shelf between us. It gives him easy movement in any direction."

Engert asked, "Out of curiosity, where did you put the other two?"

"Standard SOE loading. Pilot in front, two in the copilot seat behind, one on the shelf between, and one on the floor."

Engert snorted a *Hmmph*. "Not exactly regulation. Things are wrapping up in North Africa. Any chance you can hook me up with the Special Operations Executive? I like how they operate: wit, deception, and surprise. No mother may I."

Ike smiled. "Initiative is encouraged, yes, but SOE is not without risk. But first, let's hope we can convince Eisenhower we've solved his RECON problem."

The returning night sortie began arriving. Master Sergeant Feinberg was in front of the hangar, barking orders to his men. As Ike approached, Feinberg saluted smartly. "All cameras installed and functioning. Film processing being expedited, sir!"

"Very good, Sarge. When you're through here, report to the ready room to be outfitted and briefed on our mission."

Twenty minutes later, when Feinberg reported to the ready room, Ike and Fred Engert were bent over the first infrared photographs that had been developed. Engert had a pointer on the decoy tent. "Clearly, nothing inside," he said.

Ike replied, "They did a good job on tanks and manned camouflaged emplacements, but they're very bright and blurred."

Feinberg stepped between them. "Wrong shutter speed. Too much exposure. I can compensate. I won't make the same mistake with the handheld. I can readjust as I shoot. It might be the film as well. I'll get on it as soon as we return."

Ike nodded to Feinberg. "I like your optimism. These were taken at altitude from a fast plane. We'll be making repeated passes from different directions to make sure we get them all and look a little closer. I want to know what is under every one of those camo sites. I'm saying very low and very slow, over and over. Gear up, Feinberg. You'll be riding the shelf. We can strap you down, but I think that would cramp your filming. Can you go, cowboy, and ride bareback?"

"I've filmed from every conceivable position and contraption. Just throw me in, and I'm good. Mind if I lay out the courses to the target? I wanna get the best angles."

"The Major Engert will get us there. You can call it over the targets. I'll handle observation and communications with our radar plane. But I'm in command. You will obey my orders."

The ungainly Lysander was in the air at 0200 and flew east toward the Tunisian coast. A radar-equipped Mosquito made lazy circles overhead on guard for German or Italian night fighters. Almost two hours passed before Major Engert banked right and descended into the clear night sky over the coast just above Tunis. The first sweep was to establish a precise location and orient to the targeted areas. Ike was surprised by the lush coastal land and grain fields beyond the coastal range. As they passed low over the center of the enemy's line, Fienberg called out, "Got it! We're good, Major. Swing around and come back on 120 degrees relative."

Engert replied, "Returning on one-two-zero relative. 300 feet."

Ike's head spun from the ground to the sky above.

The radio was silent. It appeared they had the sky to themselves.

Feinberg said to himself, "That's it, baby, come to Papa. A couple of degrees to the right, Major."

Engert replied, "Steady on one-two-two relative."

He mumbled, "You certainly are bright. One hot machine or many? I'm about to peek under your skirt, dirty lady. You'd better be wearing knickers."

Engert spoke louder, "Armored vehicles, maybe two dozen, Colonel. We'll be able to count them on the film."

"Take us to the second target, Major."

Sites two, three, and four were all confirmed as artillery sites. Ike called out, "There must be more, many more tanks, armored personnel carriers, and transports. And the barracks, where are the tents or barracks? Major, has INTEL reported caves in this area? They can't be this well dug in."

"Not caves, but mines and an old archeological dig near the ridge. This area has been settled by Carthaginians, Romans, and Berbers for millennia."

Ike barked, "Pass beside that ridge at 50 feet. Feinberg, find me some light or heat. There's no need to dig if it's already been done for you."

Engert repeated the order, "Skirt along the ridge at fifty feet." He reminded himself softly, "Careful of the shelf."

Ike retorted, "Shelf? How high?"

"Varies. Sixty-five to eighty feet."

"Stay under it. A little off to the side is Okay.

Feinberg, you know where to look.”

The sergeant was pointing his camera towards the ridge. “Got it, Colonel. Heat or light under the shelf. Wo! There we go! A whole line of chimneys or exhausts, and I can make out doors, large doors.”

Ike directed Engert. “Note the position. Can you find it on the map when we return?”

“I’ll know.”

“How are we on fuel? Do we have enough for a flyover of their Bizerte positions?”

“One low pass before we head home.”

Ike replied, “Good, one very low pass. Feinberg, you know what to look for. Major, any digs or mines at that position?”

“Could be. As I said, the whole area has been inhabited forever.”

Fifteen minutes later, the noisy, squat, and ugly little Lysander, lights out, approached the center of a German Army position as if coming in for a landing. Engert began to swerve back and forth, but Feinberg insisted he stop and allow him to establish targets. “Hold course, I’ve got something.” Just then, a bullet ripped through the fuselage and passed between Sergeant Feinberg’s legs.”

Ike called out, “Evade and take her home.”

The plane was already climbing and banking toward the sea. Engert replied, “Everyone okay? We can go back for another run if you’re up for it.”

Feinberg replied, “Came close to another circumcision, but I’m good.”

Ike sighed, "That's what one man with a rifle can do. That's enough fun for one night. Let's go home." *Thank you, Jesus!*

Feinberg mumbled, "Hey, it did go through my pants. I got me a great souvenir!"

CHAPTER 5
REPORTS

Ike's presence at the Commander's brief drew stares and a few introductions. Brigadier General Walter Beddel "Beetle" Smith, Eisenhower's Chief of Staff, entered before Eisenhower. "Curtis, you look like hell. Is this how you present yourself to your Commanding General on your first brief?"

Ike replied, "My apologies, General. I came straight from a night RECON mission. I've had less than three hours' sleep since I arrived two days ago."

"Mission? You're supposed to be our RECON officer. You're not here for flight duty."

"General Eisenhower expressed some urgency in identifying deficiencies in RECON. I took the initiative, and I believe the General will…."

Eisenhower came through the door with Colonel Johnson, the AFINTEL Officer. Beetle Smith called, "Ten Hut." The gathered officers stood. Eisenhower replied, "Seats, gentlemen. Where's Curtis? There you are. Get a shave when we're through. And some sleep. You look like something the cat dragged in. I've been reviewing some

RECON photos. I'm informed they've already been forwarded to my field commanders. I'll let that slide this time, Curtis. But don't make it a habit. And these last ones, Johnson tells me from a slow Lysander—you've uncovered most, if not all, of the center corridor to Tunis positions. He tells me you flew below the ridge at what, 50 feet? This is the second time you surprised me, Curtis. Well done. You're excused, Curtis. Get some rest. Report to my office at 1700, clean and looking like an officer of the US Army. Now, Colonel Johnson will begin with Operation Mincemeat."

Outside the briefing room, Ike stuck his hand in his pocket and pulled out the crumpled paper with a single name on it. *Where do I start? I promised. Why couldn't I wait a day or two? I must write to Rose, and I am exhausted. I can't show up again like this. I must slow down—pace myself. But first, I must make a start—personnel? A liaison officer of the Free French?*

Major Shelton led Ike to the French Liaison office, where Ike asked the duty officer, "I am Lieutenant Colonel Curtis, AFRECON officer." He pulled the note from his pocket and continued. "I need to find a French soldier. Former resistance who joined the Free French Army a couple of months back—name's Jacques Samson du Rochelle."

"Colonel, with respect, we do not chase down missing persons for wives, girlfriends, or family. Later, all will be accounted for. Tell his mistress to use proper channels."

"This man has skills critical to RECON and INTEL

here at AFHQ. I am meeting with General Eisenhower at 1700 hours to report on changing RECON tactics. Shall I tell General Eisenhower that an aide to his Free French Army Liaison is holding things up?"

The junior officer, whose rank was unknown to Ike, came to attention. "*Non!* I shall see that it is passed to our headquarters at once. I shall deliver a report personally. Is there anything else, Colonel?"

Ike nodded. "That is all. Thank you, er, *merci beaucoup.*"

Stepping out of the office, Ike mumbled. "I probably crossed the line on that one."

Shelton asked, "Do you know this Frenchman? Do we need him?"

Ike stopped and turned to Major Shelton. "Keep this between you and me. The Frenchman is my housekeeper's husband. I promised her. But there is more to her story—something about her." Ike paused and considered the woman he barely knew. "Anyway, if he was French resistance, as she claims, and now Free French Army from here in Algiers, and she—most unusual—I think is mixed North African European, maybe Berber, but with an aristocratic air—hey must be of some value to us."

Shelton shook his head. "Colonel, you really know how to spin things up. Initiative is one thing, but do you ever stop pushing? Sooner or later ... ,"

"Yeah, I know. Eisenhower liked what we gave him this morning. It should be worth one get-out-of-jail-free card. By the way, I'm supposed to be sleeping. I see him again at 1700. And get with Fred Engert on the mission schedule he and I set up. Tell him to proceed as planned. I'll let you know if anything changes after I meet with Eisenhower. Try and get some rest yourself."

"Boss, before you go, I've set up a new watch schedule for round-the-clock office operations. We won't need you until 0600, which gives you time to study the night's RECON before the 0800 brief. Of course, that's not to say we don't need you—we'll call if anything interesting develops." Shelton exhaled a sigh. "Sir, your body needs rest. Good sleep can make you more effective."

Ike directed his weary body out of HQ, into the cheerful morning sun. The boulevard was busy with morning traffic. He sensed an air of hope in the faces of the French citizens. The few Berbers that passed wore more stoic faces. It was just another day of occupation.

Justine met him at the door. Ike cracked a weary smile. "I may have overstepped my authority, but our Free French Liaison is searching for Jacques's whereabouts. Look, I'm very tired. I am going right to bed. Wake me up at 4 PM. I have a meeting at 5. Afterward, we can talk. I hope to go on a regular schedule, up at 5 AM and out the door at 5:45."

Ike was surprised when the silent Justine ran and kissed him on the cheek. "Thank you, Colonel. God bless you. Yes, up at four. Haven't you eaten today? No, I thought not. Have a meal before you go. Yes, to bed. All will be well."

Shaved and in a clean and crisp uniform, Ike sat in

General Eisenhower's fully staffed outer office. Promptly at 1700, the General's aide picked up the phone and quickly put it down. "Colonel, General Eisenhower will see you now."

Eisenhower was signing documents. Without looking up, he said, "Have a seat, Colonel. I'll be with you in a moment."

Ike glanced around the room. Everything he saw told him that this was the domain of a very organized man. Nothing was out of place. There wasn't so much as a smudge on the polished desk. A wooden box marked "For the AFC" was to his left, and another marked "From the AFC" waited to his right. On a blotter before him, Eisenhower was signing the last page of a document in an open file.

The General closed the file, put it in the box to his right, capped his fountain pen, and looked up. "Tell me, Curtis, how did you solve my RECON problem so quickly? What did you see that the others missed? They were bright men. I know Roosevelt can be difficult, but were they truly incompetent?"

I have to be diplomatic. How do I tell him he has a messaging problem? "No, sir, I don't believe they were incompetent. Haven't met Colonel Roosevelt and heard little about the others. I can't speak for them. The men I have met are very competent. What I can say is that I observed two tactics—Army doctrines, that were, how shall I say, well, not misapplied but inappropriate to the situation."

"No need to be diplomatic, Colonel. Be straight and specific."

"Yes, sir. Air Group RECON Wing has been provided with the best RECON planes in the world. Mosquitoes. Fast and maneuverable, with the most up-to-date high-altitude cameras. When used with support, they can safely photograph areas of interest in daylight."

"So I've been told. Go on."

"Well, sir, this tactic comes with some tradeoffs. The enemy has observed and adapted to our routine: staying put during the day and making movements at night. Since April, those movements have been conducted under cover of darkness and primarily as decoys. They have our artillery and bombers chasing empty decoys safely away from their dug-in positions."

"Yes, yes, so you went to night missions. Go on."

"Not just night missions but infrared cameras able to penetrate—to see through their silk camouflage, but even better, to find more."

"Like the cave beneath the ridge."

"Yes, sir. And there are still more to be found. There is far too little visible for the estimated size of the force, both at Tunis and Bizerte. And, I should mention, a slow, low-flying British Lysander found the caves—Lieutenant Colonel Roosevelt brought it here from artillery spotting. It was able to get beneath that shelf, too risky for a mosquito."

Eisenhower sat back. "You mean from his days with Project Rusty. You went old school. So, there are still more positions to be found."

"There always will be, especially in Bizerte, where the Nazis are also quartered in town. And I'm told the whole area is riddled with caves and digs—camouflaged digs. Penetrating silk is one thing, but earth and wood are another. The best we can find is heat from exhausts or sloppy darkening, most likely at night during movement. But if I could offer a recommendation, General, some artillery or bombing against what we have found should stir things up and get them moving."

Eisenhower asked, "These infrared cameras were available in Algiers. Why weren't they used before?"

Ike inhaled and took his time. "Well, sir, as I said, the high-altitude tactics have proven effective elsewhere, Norway being notable. And I found in AFRECON a strong desire to minimize casualties before the Sicily operation. There is still a Nazi night fighter presence in the night sky. Everything my predecessor heard told him he could meet the mission and preserve assets by daytime high altitude RECON."

"You're saying my desire to reduce casualties led RECON to play it too safe."

"I didn't say that. They went by the book, General, but sometimes the book doesn't apply to the situation in the field. If I may, General. I first saw you with General Arnold, leaving the office of General Cheney in London. I was leaving Claude Dansey's office, carrying orders for my assignment to MI9. He knew Cheney was leaving. He told me something I never forgot: "Initiative—expected of

Generals; better to learn it as a major."

"Good advice. My wife, Mamie, was fond of quoting from Paul's Bible letters: '*We are all parts of one body—different parts, but all necessary.*' A good staff needs all those parts as well. Even those who question doctrine and take risks. I'm glad you're on my staff. But I want to be kept informed."

"I will, sir. About my request to shake things up?"

"Colonel, your job is to provide RECON, not strategy. You don't have the full picture. I have others—notably my field Commanders to advise me." Eisenhower smiled and shook his head. "It will help you to know—I want more on enemy positions—always more on enemy positions. You will get your artillery tomorrow, and the redeployment of our forces. If the artillery doesn't convey the message, massive bombing and a full assault will. And soon, we'll be chasing Mussolini and his Fascist friends from Italy. I'll need your best efforts over Sicily. That will be all, Colonel. Keep up the good work. Give my regards to your men. But remember—no more surprises."

Ike stopped by his office and checked in with the duty officer. "Give me a quick update. What have we seen so far today?"

For once, Ike took his time. He listened carefully to the thorough report. "So, Captain, what do you make of it? Has what you told me led to any conclusions? Do we hold to the mission schedule, or do you recommend adjustments?"

The captain paused to look Ike in the face,

unaccustomed to being asked his opinion. He collected his thoughts and replied, "Well, sir, I'm more accustomed to organizing the RECON than interpreting it, but as you ask, I would skip Tunis tonight and concentrate all our efforts on Bizerte. Seems they've hunkered down in Tunis."

Ike nodded. "We certainly have been more successful in Tunis, but what if I were to tell you the Tunis caves and known artillery position will be hit heavy tomorrow with our artillery?"

The young officer stared at the map. "Well, sir. We will certainly see more of Tunis after the strike. I would still prioritize Bizerte tonight."

"Approved. Make it happen. Is the Lysander in tonight's plan?"

"Yes, sir, Anderson and Master Sergeant Freiberg are off at 0200."

"I don't want them over Bizerte. Tell them there is more to be found in the central corridor to Tunis. Have them take another look—a longer peek under that ridge. And remind them I expect them back. We need them and that plane. If there is any enemy fire, they are to abort and return to base. Is that clear?"

"Restrict mission to west Tunis ridge, in case of enemy fire, evade and return to base. Yes, sir. I'll make sure they understand."

"Good night, Captain. You know where to reach me. Oh, and pass the word to the men, General Eisenhower's compliment on their good work."

The beaming staff officer replied, "Thank you, sir.

Good night, sir."

Outside in the cool evening sea breeze, it occurred to Ike. *Time. I've time to write Rose. My sweet Rose. He wants to keep me on staff—but for how long? When will I see you again, sweetheart?*

As he rounded the corner and walked along the peaceful shore, another thought emerged from the past, from his youth: a Bible verse: "I know the thoughts I think towards you saith Jehovah, thoughts of peace, and not of evil, to give you hope."

Ike hurried along the way. *Thank you, Lord. I'm stayin'.* As he approached the small café restaurant and heard the subdued voices of people, he said to himself, "Ike, you need to find a Bible."

CHAPTER 6
JUSTINE

When Ike went through the door, he was surprised to see the balcony curtains drawn back and a table set before the open doors. A candle flickered in the breeze, its light dancing across delicate crystal and fine bone china. Silver serving dishes and a wine carafe were on a fine-wheeled cart. Standing on the balcony, Justine, in a delicate gown and a single strand of pearls, turned and smiled. "I hope you will forgive my intrusion, but you have given me hope and a reason to celebrate—unless of course...."

"No, no, I'm surprised, not angry. You gave me something to eat before I left—but this?"

"Earlier? Mere appetizers. A good meal should be enjoyed—never rushed. In a proper house, nothing disturbs dinner, and one learns to linger over dinner and enjoy conversation with the best food and wine."

And she comes from the best of families. "I have time tonight. I have so many questions."

"Then please sit while I bring the first course. I have it warming. I will only be a few minutes."

As Justine flowed past him to the kitchen, Ike asked, "Can I help?"

With a smile in her voice, she replied, "You can open the wine. We'll start with the white."

Ike uncorked the wine, and as he poured two glasses, he inquired, "Smells great, what is it?"

"You smell the lamb. But we will begin with anchoiade: anchovies and capers, topped with garlic and olive oil, on toast. Simple yet delightful. I can make Salade Nicoise if you prefer."

Ike inhaled the aroma and smiled. "The Anchovies sound good. I can't wait to try it." Ike watched Justine as she plated the starter. "It's been some time since I've had a good meal in the presence of a lady. And it is quite clear that you are very much a lady, Justine, not a housemaid. This is your apartment, your art, fine furnishings, and a well-stocked pantry. Who are you, Justine? Who is Jacques Samson du Rochelle, and why do you need my help finding him?"

Justine brought the first course from the kitchen and set it on the table. Ike pulled out her chair. She sat, smiling at the candle-lit table and gazing out into the cool night breeze. "This is such a treat. I haven't enjoyed a table set before my balcony since before the war."

Ike sat down and smiled.

Justine lifted her wine glass. "A toast: to finding answers and the end of occupation!"

When she set down her glass, Justine continued. "Please eat. I know you are hungry, and I shall answer all your questions. Yes, this is our apartment. Jacques is my husband. His family owns Corsair Shipping Company here in Algiers. His father arranged a position for him in the American Consulate. Jacques used his position for access to—how shall I say? Information beneficial to the family business. Please don't misunderstand; he wasn't a spy—he never sold information. Jacques enjoyed his work at the consulate more than the family business. He got on well and was a frequent aide at diplomatic functions. That is how we met."

Justine looked down at her plate and poked the food with her fork. Ike could read her pensive, semi-smile, which spoke of bittersweet memories. She looked up and asked, "Where was I?"

Ike smiled warmly. "You were about to tell me about your first meeting with Jacques. You were at a diplomatic function. Isn't that unusual in Colonial France?"

"Not always. My family—my grandfather—was Muhammad VI al-Habib, Bey of Tunis. My cousin is the current bey, Ahmad II ibn Ali. They enjoyed the American functions—quite unlike the French and British with their Colonial superiority. They felt safe bringing us to their parties."

Ike interrupted, "Excuse me, Justine. Did you say the Bey of Tunis is your cousin? It must be well known in the French ministries, and yet they will not answer your inquiries after your husband?"

Justine nodded. "As you say. But it is complicated, you see. First, my cousin is aligned with Germany, a sad position forced on him to preserve his rule. The French hypocrites, who acted the same, seem unwilling to act on behalf of any in their family. Not that the bey would take my case to them since I have converted to Christianity. Then there is the problem that I am not recorded as my husband's next of kin, and so I am denied in my requests to find him."

"Not recorded? Surely there is documentation? A marriage certificate?"

"Yes, of course. But Jacques signed papers—we argued. I did not want him to join the resistance. I pushed him away—we were hurting, but he was stubborn, pigheaded, I hear you Americans say. Yes, most determined, he joined the special squad—assassins and saboteurs chosen for the most dangerous missions— suicide if necessary. Only men without families were recruited. As I say, he signed—he told them we had separated, and he no longer called me his wife."

Justine sniffled. Her eyes were red and tearing. "I love him so much. He is a good man, brave but stubborn. To God's glory, Jacques survived. When he joined the Free French Army after the Germans evacuated Algiers, I believe he signed the same papers. I am told an army has a great need for men with his skill."

"I don't understand. How do you know he joined the Free French Army? Did you see him again? When?"

"No, a comrade, a neighbor who served with Jacques told me. He came and said he had a message from Jacques: 'He is well and has joined the Free French Army.

He says he is sorry for the argument and the worry he has surely caused. He tells you: Please forgive me, my love, Jacques.'"

"Did he say where he saw Jacques? Where were they when Jacques gave him the message?"

"Only that he needed to return to Tib-Harine, a small farming village in the Atlas Mountains. About 80 kilometers south."

"Farming in the Atlas Mountains, aren't they dry? I mean 50 miles inland."

Justine smiled. "Tib-Harine means garden terraces in our Amazigh language. There is a priory there that built a pool to water the new, fertile, terraced fields. French colonists also settled there and took the best land from our people."

After they finished their dinner, Ike said, "Justine, this has been a delightful evening, and your company has been wonderful. But I must beg your pardon. I have letters to write."

Justine smiled. "To the lady in the picture on your nightstand—your wife?"

"I hope so. We will marry if I survive the war. She is English, and I will not leave her the widow of a wartime romance with a yank."

"Go! Go! You must write to her. You have not stopped working since you arrived. Tell her you are safe. She must know you are well."

Ike could hear Justine singing softly to herself as she

cleared the dishes. He pulled out a pen and paper and wrote:

Dearest Rose,

I have missed you so much and feel terrible for not writing sooner. So much has happened. I have been transferred—I can't say where, but I hope it is not for long. I am determined to return to you soon. I am safe—more so than even back there. But war is never without danger or surprises. I tried to look in on your dad at a stop in my travels. Hopefully, I will be more successful on my return. You can reach me at the return address via the Army Post Office. Drop it off at the base. They will make sure it gets to me.

Send me letters! I will always have time to read your letters. How is Uncle Hugh? Tell him I miss his sermons, advice, friendship, and our time with his Kentucky friend, good American Bourbon. And how is Charles recovering? And Dottie, is she through with her European wandering? Tell me everything. I'm kissing your picture goodnight. Pray for me, Rose. I know he hears our prayers.

All my love,
Ike

The next morning at the Command Staff Brief, Ike was happy to hear that an all-out bombing assault on the Axis positions was scheduled for May 6, the following day. With the information provided by RECON, there was a sense of optimism that the war in Africa would soon be over. The Germans and Italians were trapped with no hope of escape, and all that awaited them was merciless bombing and artillery barrages. Surrender was inevitable. As they got up to leave, Beetle Smith stopped Ike and said, "General Eisenhower wants to see you in his office. Now, Curtis."

Ike's footsteps echoed on the stone floor as he hurried to Eisenhower's office. *I wonder what he wants. It's too soon for congratulations. Have I missed something? Should I have focused more on Sicily? Is it some special RECON mission?*

"Go right through, Colonel. General Eisenhower is expecting you," the aide said as Ike stepped into the anteroom.

Inside Eisenhower's office, Ike was surprised to see the back of the head of a French Senior Officer seated facing his Commanding General. "Take a seat, Curtis. General Giraud has questions regarding your interest in a Frenchman named Jacques Samson du Rochelle. It seems, Curtis, you have a rare gift of stirring the pot."

Giraud eyed Ike coldly as Eisenhower continued. "You used my authority to find this man. Why? Who put you up to this? Let's hear it."

Oh, Lord. What have I gotten myself into? Ike

coughed and began, "Well, sir, his wife…."

Giraud replied in his thick French accent. "He has no wife. It is in his record. Who is this woman who claims to be his wife?"

"She claims to be Justine Samson du Rochelle. She claims her husband hid their marriage when he joined the French resistance and the Free French Army. He was determined to accept the most dangerous missions where men with wives were spared."

Giraud shot back. "Nonsense! She is, at best, an old mistress or perhaps his whore."

Ike replied, "She is no whore. She is a refined and sophisticated woman of the royal blood of the Bey of Tunis."

Eisenhower interrupted. "You are in Algiers for five days, and you are acquainted with a Berber noblewoman?"

Giraud followed up, "The Bey of Tunis harbors our enemy's army. He has made a pact with the Nazis. At best, if she is of the royal house, she is a spy."

Ike replied, "A contract made under duress—for survival. No different than the French in North Africa. As for her loyalties, she has no love for the Germans or the French colonials—but for her husband and her people. She converted. As a Christian, she is no longer accepted by her family."

General Giraud put his hand under his chin and thought. After a few moments, he took a breath and slowly exhaled his irritation. "The man served as an agent in the resistance, penetrating the Abwehr. He now provides similar duties for Free France. He is in France. There will be no communication from him. Tell this woman, this Justine, he has not been reported dead or missing, but his posting cannot be shared, and she should expect no mail. And find out more about this woman. I want to know her true loyalties."

General Eisenhower's eyes bored into Ike's. Eisenhower shook his head and said, "That will be all, Curtis."

Chapter 7
Victory in North Africa

Just before dawn, the airfield east of Algiers came to life as squadron after squadron of bombers took to the air. Days before, the Allied fighters and attack planes had relocated to RAF Bone, halfway to Tunis. Awakened by the unbroken drone of powerful bomber engines, Ike sat up. His feet found the floor, and he hurried to the French doors, pushed away the curtains, swung the doors open, and stepped onto the balcony. The squadrons formed over the sea before flying southeast toward Tunis. Ike gazed as the flying armada gathered, a swarm of angry hornets waiting for the call to attack. Ike closed his eyes and said a prayer. *Lord, protect our boys. Bring them home safely—is it wrong, Lord, to pray for victory? For the deaths of many Germans and Italians? Can I pray for victory and for the comfort of the families of the men that our victory would bring? You know what I mean, Lord. Your will be done.* He shaved, had breakfast, and walked to AF Headquarters. He stopped at his office and checked in with Don Shelton. Without so much as a good morning, Ike asked, "What's the latest? Any response by the Luftwaffe?"

"Morning, Skipper. No sir. The fighters have cleared the way. Only artillery awaits them."

Ike smiled. "And our RECON squadron?"

"All accounted for. Finished their last pass ahead of the bombers. They will refuel at RAF Bone and stand by for artillery support.

"Do you need me here, or is all under control?"

Don flashed a smile at Ike. "Nope, just the routine. Seems they have more than enough eyes on the target this morning." Don paused a moment, then ventured, "You don't need my permission. Go ahead, sit in on the action in the OPS room. But I expect a good report from you later."

"Lunch. I'll stop by for lunch and give you the full scoop." And Ike was out the door.

Ike entered the Command Operations Room and found a seat. Men with headsets posted reports and moved little pieces with unit identifiers across a flat topographical map. Operation Strike, the final Allied assault on the Axis's last foothold in North Africa, unfolded before him. Ike smiled when Eisenhower's promised artillery barrage and massive air strikes drove the stubborn Panzers from their dug-in position in the ridgeline between Medjez and Goubellat. Four hundred Allied guns fired 16,000 shells in two hours. The German Commander, General von Arnim, could do nothing as the center of his line, the proven Hermann Goring Division and the 10th Panzer Division guarding the west approach to Tunis, retreated and were decimated by the Allied artillery and more than 2000 Allied air sorties.

With the British 8th Army facing little resistance streaming north around Enfidaville, Eighth Army veteran units, the 7th Armored Division, the 4th Indian Division, and the 201st Guards Brigade reinforced British General Horrock's IX Corps in the center. The American II Corps, commanded by Major General Omar Bradley, began its drive to the high ground east and west of Chougui, and on to the Tebourba and Djedeida river crossings, with its objective Bizerte. By mid-morning on May 7, spearhead units reported scattered resistance.

Ike kept his promise and ate a sandwich with Shelton. "Don, we took the western approaches. Eisenhower promised artillery, and boy, did he deliver. The Tenth Panzer and Herman Goring Divisions folded like umbrellas. Hard not to pity the poor bastards. Heavy bombers too—took a hell of a toll on the Jerries in retreat. Look, I hate to eat and run, but it's happening—happening so fast, I need to get back."

By early afternoon, British units were in sight of Tunis. The 6th Armored Division moved to cut off a futile German attempt to form a new defensive position across the Cape Bon Peninsula. British Admiral Arthur Coningham's control of the sea made any escape by sea impossible. Ike watched with excitement as the First Derbyshire Yeomanry and the 11th Hussars reached the center of Tunis. By 4 p.m., the British First Army Commander, Lieutenant General Anderson, reported that Tunis had been taken.

Ike called Don Shelton. "Don, drop what you're

doing, and get over here. It's all but over!" Shortly after Don came in, a cheer went up as American troops entered Bizerte. With Tunis and Bizerte secured and no new defense line across Cape Bon, Bradley moved the US II Corps to surround Enfidaville and its 80,000 mostly Italian troops. With no further enemy action, all that remained was the surrender.

Ike joined Don Shelton, Fred Engert, and the staff and pilots of AFRECON at the Officers' Club for a drink. But no one stopped after one. The party went on long into the night. When Ike stepped out into the quiet darkness, he inhaled deeply the clean, fresh air. The floral and sea-scented night air cleared his mind as it filled his lungs. *What now, Lord? Will you help me get back to England—to Rose? I guess I'm praying again and trusting that you're listening. I should be ashamed of myself for asking God to send one lonely American to his girlfriend. So many dead and wounded. And prisoners, there must be well over one hundred thousand. Hugh. Hugh would tell me you want to hear our wants. God knows our needs. But if you love me, Lord, don't forget the desires of my heart. I do miss her so— and little Earl. It must be hard for him. I never went without my dad nearby, loving me and helping me grow into a man he could respect. A sign. Lord. A sign would be nice.*

Eisenhower waited for the formal surrender. On 12 May, German General Hans-Jurgen Arnim surrendered. Italian Marshal Giovanni Messe delayed, asking for an honorable surrender. Eisenhower refused, demanding nothing less than unconditional. On 13 May, with 240,00

German and Italian prisoners, North Africa was under Allied control.

With the Allied Force Command staff busy processing the surrender of a quarter million enemy soldiers, Ike saw a reprieve from the tyranny of the urgent. Sitting at his desk, he wondered: *What is Justine's story? Should I believe her? Everything tells me she is credible. Such devotion would be hard to fake. Is she a German spy? I can't believe it. She has never once asked about my work and is certainly no honey trap. Her husband, Jaques, is the real mystery. What's his story? A Frenchman who penetrated the Abwehr? Really? Whose side is he really on? Everything about him screams outsider to me. There's a reason they take only single men—one less relationship to be threatened and used to turn him if he is discovered. The double agent game is high-risk. How do I handle this with Justine?*

Justine was in the kitchen when Ike returned. He greeted her as he entered and said. "Good evening! Such a beautiful day. Perhaps you will join me tonight. I have time. I thought we might eat on the balcony and enjoy a peaceful sunset. Peace is such a precious thing. The war will be moving on and..."

Justine thought, *Of course, he will be leaving soon.* She interrupted, "Yes! I will make it happen. We will toast to peace in North Africa. You go, wash up, and change while I finish preparing." *How soon will he leave? What about my Jacques?*

When Ike came out, the small table was set in front of the stubby balcony. The sun was low, gilding the sea.

The evening breeze carried its salty sea scent into the room, and the gentle waves provided a soft counter beat to the hum of conversation from below.

Ike smiled at Justine and stepped onto the balcony, where he gazed out to sea. "It's like I finally have time to see, to breathe, and take my time. Look at what God has given us. Our world is so rich in variety. So abundant, so full of life. What have we done to it, to each other, to ourselves? Stewards. He called us to be His stewards. I can't believe he will abandon us or ever permit us to destroy His creation. What does it say in Genesis? *'And it was very good.'* Very good, indeed."

Ike turned to Justine. "Hope. Do you still have hope? I'm sure you do. We must never lose hope. I've been meaning to speak more with you about Jacques…"

Justine nodded. "Yes, please sit." She motioned him to the table. "I will tell you everything. Sit, please. You are my hope. News. Is there news about my husband? When must you leave? I hope not soon. You must help me before you leave!"

Ike assisted Justine into her chair before sitting down. "I don't know how long I will be here or where I will be sent. But I have some time—so many prisoners to be processed and sent who knows where. And so many more are dead. Their bodies must be collected—if they can even be found in the desert and wilderness. Of course, I want to help you. Tell me about the village—the one where the neighbor saw him—in the Atlas Mountains."

"Tib-Harine. What is there to say? A small farming

village. Most of the French have evacuated."

"A monastery—you mentioned a monastery." *Dottie's Charles was hidden in a monastery in France. Many Allied airmen were hidden. The Nazis always trod softly on their searches—never pushing the monks or nuns to aid in the search, so as not to betray their 'civilized' occupation.*

"You speak of the Priory, the Priory of Our Lady of the Atlas. It was the priory that built the ponds and terraced the hillsides, which became gardens. The monks shared their skills with the locals. But success only brought French colonists, and soon the village, the region, was owned and farmed by the French—Amazigh, sorry, Berbers, now labor on their former land."

Justine lowered her head and closed her eyes momentarily before continuing plaintively. "I do not fault the French farmers. They intend no harm and treat our people well. They bought the land. They could pay a higher price. Wealthy Berbers sold to them. But it is still an injustice to our people."

"Does Jacques feel the way you do? You seem an odd couple, you, Berber, and French, with a heart for the Muslim Berbers but a confessed love for Christ—Jacques French, a colonizer. How does Jacques feel about the Berbers and his faith?"

"Jacques is French, but as a protestant from an aristocratic family long persecuted by the French government, he feels like an outsider among his fellow French colonials. We did not worship in the Catholic Church, though we admired the monks' acts of mercy and goodness at the priory. Before the war, we worshipped with protestant English and Americans, and yes, even the Germans he met through the consulate. So, that made us look suspicious to the French authorities."

"Suspicious, yes. Add his access to small ships and knowledge of smuggling, and he is useful to each side—a prime candidate for a double agent. The trouble with being a double agent is that neither side trusts you completely. You are very expendable."

Ike cast his gaze inward, then exhaled a deep sigh. "Do you have a recent photograph of Jacques—and this neighbor who delivered his message? His name and perhaps a photograph of him as well."

Justine stood and walked toward her room. "Yes, yes, I think I have one of them together, taken at a celebration before the war. Let me look for it now. I remember his name. Andre. Andre Batten."

Ike greeted Major Shelton at the office. "Good morning, Don. What do you have for me?"

Shelton replied, "Good morning—and not good news. Lieutenant Colonel Roosevelt has returned from his stateside boondoggle—from California. Who knew we had a war on? He's starting to shake things up at Air Group. Listen to this: he's bragging he 'bought' the next generation RECON plane from Howard Hughes—telling stories at the O Club about all the Hollywood honeys he partied with, winking it went further."

Ike shook his head and chuckled. "Talk is cheap."

"Wait, it gets worse. No sooner was he briefed by Major Engert on the Infrared photography and night patrols and our breakthrough than he put the wing in for a unit commendation medal and a commendation for himself."

"Well, Engert's men deserve it. When do I meet with him?"

"Major Engert's RECON Squadron, yes, but the whole wing?" Shelton sighed. "He hasn't asked. Either he doesn't want to face you for putting himself in for what is rightly your medal, or he honestly doesn't give a…look; he's never been one to concern himself with others. It's only about him."

"I hear you. Their success is his success, even in his absence. Don't let him get to you. Anything new on Sicily RECON or planning?"

"We're following through with night and infrared surveillance coordinated by our friends on the ground."

Ike stood before the chart table. "What do you have for me to see?" Ike studied the latest photos and reports. "It looks like Operation Mincemeat is working. I don't see any build-up in Sicily. Now, let's look at Sardinia and the Peloponnese. Oh, yes! Lots of new Axis activity. The nazis have taken the bait!"

Don Shelton came alongside Ike. "INTEL believes Hitler bought it hook, line, and sinker, but Mussolini still argues Sicily makes more sense."

"Tell me more about Mincemeat. I know it's a decoy, but I haven't seen any indication of Allied Forces feigning an attack on Sardinia or Greece."

Shelton looked up. "You never got the brief?"

"Twice when Colonel Johnson was to brief, I was excused from the brief for other duties."

Major Shelton smiled. Sit down, Ike. You're gonna love this! British Special Operations Executive, SOE, deception operation. It seemed bizarre, but apparently, it worked. The Brits took the body of some tramp, dressed him in a Royal Marine Officer uniform, and gave him an identity card, a wallet full of backup, and documents from a couple of British generals discussing Allied invasion plans for Sardinia and the Greek mainland—Sicily would only be a feint. The body was dropped in the sea near the coast of Spain, where the Spanish would likely find it. Apparently, our neutral Spanish friends did as Churchill expected and passed the information on to the Nazis before turning the body over to the British embassy. It seems the wizards in the SOE labs could determine the letters were read and resealed before the body was returned."

"And Hitler bit over Mussolini's objection. Who needs advisors when you're the all-powerful Führer? I believe Hitler's ego will prove one great allied asset in defeating the Nazis."

Ike stood and walked to the map table in the center of the room. "Static. Nothing is moving while the prisoners are shipped off, and the invasion transports get underway. I think I have time for a side trip. With North Africa secured, Don, is there any reason I can't take the staff car for a day? There's a Priory nearby, in the mountains, that I would like to visit."

Shelton replied, "You mean the Priory of Our Lady of the Atlas. I won't complain. I can cover for you, no problem. You sure you don't want to take along some armed help—just in case?"

"No, I'm good. But I must see every Hollywood starlet's dream man, our bold and daring Lieutenant Colonel Eliott Franklin. See if he can find room for me on his busy schedule the day after tomorrow."

"Day after tomorrow. Will do. Ike, is this little excursion about Justine and her husband?"

"If anything does go wrong, Don, you never asked."

Ike stared at the map, focusing on Trib-Harine. Looking up, he asked, "Do you have a road map I can borrow?"

CHAPTER 8
THE ROAD SOUTH

Ike was amazed that Justine was always just inside the door when he arrived. Was it her sixth sense, or had she established some sort of early warning system? Ike greeted her. "Good evening, Justine. I need to make it an early night tonight. I'm off at dawn on a RECON patrol."

Justine stared at his flight bag. He never brought it home before. "Yes, I can do an early dinner. I see you have a staff car parked in front and now a flight bag. I never heard of a flying car. You're driving somewhere—into the interior, the mountains? Can I ask why? Have you heard more about Jacques? But why the flight suit? Where are you going?'

Ike scowled, "You've never asked about my work before. Why now? And how did you know about my staff car while we're at it? And why are you always at the door when I arrive? Are you spying on me?"

"Colonel Ike, you know why I ask. This is different—out of your routine. But yes, you caught me. The maître d at the café rings me when you arrive so that I can meet you at the door. It is a trick I learned from my father's servant."

Ike chuckled and sighed in relief. "And you caught me, as well. I'm driving to Trib Harine, to the priory, to ask after Jacques. I felt I would appear less out of place in my flight suit and carry my weapon. My mission, if asked, is to follow up on RECON of Nazi stragglers and deserters."

Justine protested, "Your danger will not be German deserters or Italian stragglers, but bandits. Yes, Berber bandits will exploit the power vacuum in the countryside. And you do not speak their language. Why, you cannot even speak French! I am coming with you. Now, what is your weapon?"

Ike's brow furled. "Like most American pilots, I carry a .45 caliber semi-automatic pistol."

Justine nodded. "Springfield model 1911 ACP, no doubt. Yes, good stopping power at close range and a nine-cartridge magazine. How many magazines did you bring? Never mind. I will bring my scoped hunting rifle, a box of cartridges, and good binoculars. And if we are stopped, I will speak for you. Wait, I will be right back."

Ike stood pondering Justine's knowledge as she walked off. Moments later, Justine returned with a rifle case. She opened it, carefully removed the rifle, worked the action, and handed it to Ike. "Bandits only send a recruit to stop the vehicle while they wait in the hills above. We will need this. It is far superior to anything they carry."

Ike took the extravagant but deadly product of French craftsmanship in his hands. He was surprised how light it was, perhaps six or seven pounds, and 40 inches long, perfect for Justine. Ike mumbled as he examined it.

"Doubled-barreled, rifled—I've heard of Circassian walnut—beautiful and the blued, engraved silver receiver. And a scope like I have never seen. It's lightweight and can bring down big game! How can anything so deadly be so exquisite? It must have cost a small fortune!"

"It is a Chapuis Armes. Father wanted me to have something to stop any animal I encountered in the mountains. Hunting with my father and uncles is one of my fondest memories."

"But can you hit anything? Never mind. I know the answer." Ike cocked his head and smiled. "Okay, you can ride shotgun."

"This is no shotgun…."

"Just an American expression for ride alongside."

Justine stared. Ike explained, "Like on a stagecoach, the driver and the shotgun… never mind."

"Good. We will eat, then I will prepare food to take along tomorrow. How long will we stay? Should I pack a bag?"

"We should be back tomorrow night."

A faint golden light in the east announced the coming sunrise. Birds in the trees along the seashore chirped merrily, singing songs of hope for the new day. Ike carried a basket of food and several water bags to the car, while Justine transformed from a European Colonial to a traditional, no, an upper-class, royal Berber. Her robe and head scarf were fine white linen that breathed through the heat. The matching headscarf was casually, yet serenely, wrapped around her neck. The scarf opened around her face just enough to reveal delicate gold earrings. In defiance of conformity, she wore a simple cross around her neck. When she was satisfied with her appearance, she picked up her rifle, locked the front door, and went downstairs. Ike was waiting by the car. The country gentleman in him prompted him to step to the passenger door and open it for Justine. Justine paused.

"It would not be right for a Berber woman to ride in the front seat with a man not her husband. But if I sit in the back, I relegate an American officer to my servant."

Ike smiled. "Is it right for a Berber woman to wear a cross? Sit in front. I can't tell if you are dressed as a Berber or as a nun."

For the first time, Ike heard Justine laugh. It was the sweet laugh of a young girl devoid of sophistication. She looked at the wooden cross she chose and giggled. "A nun? Yes, I suppose so. Me a nun?"

Her smile left as quickly as it came when she sat down in the front seat, and Ike gently closed the door. When Ike came around and sat in the driver's seat, he noticed her now stoic expression. "Any second thoughts, Justine. I can do this alone."

She turned and faced Ike. "No. No, I want to do this. I need to go. I was just thinking about what you said. It occurred to me I have become a nun, a nun living outside, yet alone with only my prayers to support me."

Ike smiled warmly. I know what it is to be an outsider, alone. But you have one advantage: your faith has remained strong. I had to be rescued and brought back. I thought by saving others I could save myself, but....”

Justine's blue eyes studied Ike. “The girl, the English girl, you plan to marry after the war. She brought you back from a heart of darkness.”

“Yes. She and her family. They brought me in and loved me. They helped me find my faith.”

Ike started the car and drove south. At a checkpoint outside the city, a guard saluted Ike and let him pass unquestioned. Ike resumed the conversation. “Your faith seems strong for one who converted for marriage…”

“Oh, you misunderstand. I was a Christian before I met Jacques. A silent Christian, but faithful, nonetheless. I could not tell my father; honor would force him to disown me, to cast me out, or sell me as a slave. Yes, a slave—the practice continues even under the eyes of the French.”

“Really? I never considered. How?”

“There is one great advantage to Islamic tradition. Women are protected, yes, like property, but also free to speak among other women. There was another woman, older, yes, very old and very wise. She spoke of Jesus. She taught me that Jesus was more than just a prophet. A prophet like no other—a king and the very Son of God. He did not come to condemn me—I knew that I was condemned, Islam taught me that, but the message of surrender, of inadequate payment, hoping for mercy, provided me no assurance. But the message of Jesus—he came not to condemn me, but to love me and forgive me, to make me righteous, not in my sinful inadequacy, but in His righteousness. What a wonder that God loved me, that

Jesus died for me. I still sin, but I pray for forgiveness, and I have hope—yes, hope that I am His forever."

The car was silent as they both watched the sun rise above the hills. Justine's eyes still looked forward to the road ahead. "So, of course. Like my grandmother, I mean, my elderly friend—please tell no one I said my grandmother."

"No. Of course not. I would not put her in jeopardy."

"Thank you. As I was saying, I kept my faith secret outside the court of women. But she taught me...."

Justine smiled. "So, when I was permitted to attend functions among the Christians, out of earshot, I would ask questions. I enjoyed how the men treated me. They were not brutish infidels, but charming men. That is how I met Jacques. Oh, Jacques was charming, but he, too, was different. I could tell. So, I sought him out and spoke to him whenever our paths crossed. He slowly opened up to me. I thought I found my soulmate."

"You say it was your grandmother, not your French mother, who taught you about Jesus. She must be your paternal grandmother. Does your father know of her faith? And what about your mother's faith?"

"My mother has no faith in any God. She worships fine things—a luxurious life. But my father, yes, he knows. He was not surprised when I told him I wished to marry Jacques—that Jacques would never convert."

Justine chuckled and turned to face Ike, who caught her smile and returned it. "Father hugged me and said he was both happy and sad. He said I am his mother's daughter. She is a faithful Christian and a loving mother, not like my mother. My father said he was charmed by my mother's beauty and her taste for fine things. When she agreed to convert and marry him, he was ecstatic, only to find she was shallow and unloving. He keeps her happy but finds more comfort with his mother, daughter, and hunting with his many brothers. He held me tight, and I saw tears in his eyes. He said honor requires him to disclaim me, but I must remember he will always love me. Unbeknownst to anyone, he gave me gifts, money, and things to remember him when I left."

"Like your fine hunting rifle?"

"Yes, but best of all, I saw him hiding in the church, behind the organ stall, at my wedding. Grandmother was crouched beside him. A sign of their love that I shall never forget."

They drove on in warm, silent companionship. The road carried them over a ridge and curved into a narrowing descent, following a dry riverbed. Justine's smile gave way to concern. She picked up binoculars and scanned the hillsides, top to bottom. "The road ahead is perfect for thieves and bandits. We will soon descend to a narrow pass, no wider than the road itself."

As she spoke, a bright flash appeared on the ridge ahead of them. "As I feared," she snorted. "Slow down, gradually. Pull to the side."

Stopped along the side of the road, she said, "I want you to take the map, get out of the car, and study it as if you are considering where you are. Stay close to the window. I want to take a closer look."

With Ike out of the car, Justine slid low across the seat, head down. She set the binoculars low in the open window, sheltered close against Ike's side. Lying down on the bench seat, with only the top of her head, behind the black binoculars visible through the window, she whispered, "Now, move a half step forward." She scanned. "A little more." Again, she scanned.

Ike fought the urge to look. Unable to look, he listened. There was no traffic noise, not another car or beast-drawn cart for miles. He could taste the dust and hear nothing. No sound carried in the still breeze. Ike flinched when the screech of an eagle shattered the silence and echoed through the canyon.

Justine's whisper calmed him. "Now, move back, yes, that's right. Ah! I've got you, my friend! The spotter. How many of you are there? Where are the others? Ah! Two more on a trail to the bottom. Just the two? No, three. All moving down. Yes, three."

Her voice sharpened. "Ike, fold up the map and get back in. Drive slowly as if nothing happened. They will have someone to stop us at the bottom, at the last curve before the narrow pass. Get in, let's go."

Ike drove off slowly. He watched as Justine opened her gun case, pulled two cartridges from the silver cartridge case filigreed in gold. Her movement was natural. Experience. *What is it with the aristocracy and the wannabes that they desire such beauty and luxury in weapons? As deadly as they are beautiful—the Chapuis Armes rifle, and Justine.* Satisfied she was ready for what awaited, Justine set the rifle down low and out of sight.

As they rounded a curve at the bottom of the valley, just as Justine predicted, a car blocked the road with its hood up. "Do not get out. Make him come to us. We need him. I will translate. Call him over," Justine commanded.

Ike stopped ten yards from what he made out to be an old Citroen barely recognizable through thick layers of sand and dust. A man dressed in robes stepped out of the Citroen, waved, and called out in Amazigh. Ike shook his head. Cupped his hand behind his ear and waved for the Berber to come to him. The setup man took two steps and called out again, this time in French. Ike waved for him to come closer, vigorously shaking his head. The bandit paused, looked up the hill, then back at Ike. Hesitant at first, he walked increasingly fast to the prey in the waiting car.

When the man approached the driver's window and bent over to speak to Ike, he saw a 45 handgun pointed at his face. He froze. Justine said calmly yet firmly in Amazigh. "Do not move. Do as I say, and you may live to see your loved ones again. Do you understand?" His face shaking in fear, he nodded. "Speak up. Tell me you will do as I say."

"Yes, yes. I will do just as you say. Let me live, and I am your servant."

Justine smiled, but not in a friendly manner. "Good. And remember, my American friend is most proficient with his pistol. You will not survive if he shoots. Now, turn around. You will feel his gun in your back. If you step away, if he cannot feel your back against his gun, he will shoot. Now, call the others down. All of them. When they come within earshot, tell them that the driver is injured and cannot get out. Tell them the other is a wealthy lady fleeing the British and Americans with all her treasure."

Ike could feel the young Berber shaking as they waited. Even with his arms waving, he kept his back pressed against the barrel of Ike's gun. They waited.

An eternally long five minutes later, a distant shout could be heard from the hillside. "Bring them to us," Justine translated.

"He cannot get out. He has an injured leg. Come. All is well; a rich woman fleeing the war travels with him. She carries money and jewels. Come. We will all be rich." Again, Justine translated.

The shout back came from closer. "Do not let her go. We are coming!"

Justine balanced her rifle on the window just in front of the frightened robber. Figures appeared from behind rocks, not twenty yards from the road. "Don't just stand there, search the car. Gather what we have come for and be on with it," A man, apparently the leader, commanded.

"I cannot. She is an important lady, Amazigh, like us. She carries jewels on her body. I will not be the one to violate her."

The bandit chieftain started forward. Justine called out. "Not another step." She raised the rifle where it could be clearly seen. "Stand where you are, Ahmed. It is you. One of Jacques's smugglers."

Ahmed chuckled. "Yelli-n-Teydemt, daughter of Justice. It is a pleasure to see you again. So, the French are onto you. But I am sorry, times being what they are, I must insist you give what you carry, and I shall let you continue your journey."

"One step and you are a dead man, Ahmed."

"I know your rifle. Oh, yes, a weapon of great beauty, but you have but two rounds, and there are five of us. You will die, and your wealth will be divided between us."

The young Berber began to shake again and shook his head vigorously. Justine laughed loudly, "Don't be a fool, my friend, the American Officer has his 45 in your young friend's back. His magazine carries nine bullets. We have more than ample ammunition. You and all your men will be dead in a heartbeat. Give the order. You and your men will put down all their weapons."

Ahmed sighed, then laughed. Do as the great lady says. Put your guns on the ground."

"And your knives and swords. Every weapon." Justine insisted.

"Knives, swords, all of them. Do it."

Ahmed laid his pistol and several knives on the ground. His men followed suit. "You too," Ike said to the trembling young man. Justine translated softly and gently.

Justine tisked at Ahmed. "What has become of you? An accomplished smuggler, now a common road bandit?

And a not very good one at that. The Citroen? Is that a company car? My husband's and father-in-law's car? Close the bonnet and clean away the door so I can read what is written."

Ahmed shrugged. "When I returned from my last run, there was no one to meet me. So, I took what was owed to me. I am sorry to tell you, but your father-in-law is in prison. His ships and boats were commandeered. They are safely anchored in Bizerte. I heard you and Jacques joined the liberation. I have never been political. I only wish to feed and care for my family."

Justine replied, "Take your men and leave, drive north."

Ahmed laughed loudly as he walked to the dirty Citroen, slammed the hood, and drove out of the way.

Chapter 9
The Garden in the Atlas Mountains

Justine gazed out the passenger window in silence. Nearly ten minutes passed before Ike spoke. "The liberation, not the resistance? Both of you? What other lies have you told me?"

Turning to Ike, Justine barked, "Yes, the Amazigh Liberation. But it is not what you think. Jacques is with the Free French. He is missing…"

Ike scolded, "Spying for the Liberation. And now you know what I think? I trusted you. I went out on a limb. General Eisenhower warned me not to get involved, but like a fool…." Ike stopped the car. "The French General, Giraud, knew Jacques. I bet he has the book on you, too." Ike looked at the rifle lying across Justine's lap. "Are you going to use that on me as well? The great hunter? Or more likely an Amazigh Liberation assassin. Does Giraud suspect you of the assassination of Admiral Darlan? Who's your next target? Am I your hostage? A bargaining chip to get your father-in-law free?"

Justine's eyes teared up, and she cried. After several sniffles, she sobbed, "Yes. I confess. I have withheld from you, but what I told you is true. Jacques and I want to see Algiers, Tunis, and all of North Africa free from colonial rulers. It is plain to see that the Germans and Italians are no better, yes, even worse than the French. They say, 'Choose your enemies.' At least France calls us citizens. Now, France needs us, needs the liberation movement. We are armed and trained."

Ike snorted. "You believe that. Or is it just wishful thinking?"

"Jacques approached the Free French. He asked them—insisted he would only work for them if Free France would remember and reward those who serve in the war against the Nazis and their Fascist friends. They swore that France would reward all who served, French and Berber. And Free France will not forget those who conspired with the Nazis, French and Berber."

Ike shook his head. "So, suddenly, the enemy of my enemy is not my friend? Your uncle, the Bey of Tunis, saw an opportunity with the Germans. Hasn't he determined that the Germans would leave him in control of Tunis after the defeat of the French? A puppet, maybe, but with wealth and status?"

"Not all are entrapped by wealth and status. They see behind the words of the Nazis. They look at those beneath the Fascist boot. They see—we see—we decided that fighting for France, well, the French would owe us. And with all of France needing men to rebuild, French

North Africa could become autonomous if not fully free. So, yes, the liberation, then the resistance. Jacques' diplomatic connections made him a valuable asset as an agent. He was groomed to infiltrate the Abwehr. I traveled among the tribes, urging them to support the French, not the Germans. I speak the people's language, I carried letters from my father, who is still regarded among the beys and sheiks."

Ike stared at Justine, not knowing what to say. Justine finished. "And I do enjoy hunting. I am my father's daughter. But I am not an assassin. It seems a most un-Christian thing to do."

Ike started the engine and drove on. "I'd like to start at the priory."

Trib-Harine was a small, quiet village with a tropical feel, bathed in bright sunshine. The small main street was lined with trees. Their leafy green boughs hung lazily, shading the dusty road. Ike stopped the car and looked around. The only sound he heard was the water fountain in the center of a small plaza. A sudden feeling of release overcame him. *Peace, what is it that makes me feel so at peace? It feels as if time has forgotten this village. A hellish war raged only miles away, and yet I feel peace.*

A chorus of bells interrupted the silence. "That would be the priory," Ike said.

"Yes, it is there, high on the hillside above us." Justine pointed to the right. "Let me out here. I will speak with the locals, Berber and French. Perhaps they can tell me something. You go to the priory. When you are finished, return to the plaza, and I will meet you there."

Ike nodded. "All right. I shouldn't be long. We can have a meal before returning."

Justine jumped out, closed the door, and stuck her head back in the window. "There is a small dirt road just ahead to the right. It will take you to the priory." Ike nodded and looked at the hunting rifle back in its case, lying on the back seat. "Maybe we should put that in the trunk. We don't want to send the wrong message."

"Good idea, but not here, up ahead, out of sight of many watching eyes," and Justine walked off.

Ike drove off slowly. *So many watching eyes. Is any place truly peaceful?* Ike found the dirt road, which was more like an oxcart path than a proper road. Around a bend out of sight of the town, he stopped and put the rifle in the trunk. The going was slow, between ruts, rocks, and switchback turns. When he rounded the last turn, he saw a barefoot monk sweeping the dusty trail toward him. Ike stopped and greeted the monk. "Good morning! Please, may I speak to the prior? It is of some urgency, but no one is in danger. The war in North Africa is over. Please. I am an American seeking information on a missing friend, well, that is the husband of a friend. You may know them."

The monk kept sweeping. Ike looked down and saw boot prints. He was sweeping away boot prints—prints showing studded soles. *German.* "I won't keep you from your work. I will go to the priory and ask again."

Ike walked up the path to the gate. The monk finished his task and joined him. "I am Brother Paul. I am permitted to leave the priory and speak with visitors, pilgrims occasionally, and villagers more often. I will tell the Prior, Father Michael, you are here."

Ike waited in a small room, seated on a bench opposite the nave, which featured a sculpture of Mary, the Lady of the Atlas Mountains. A crucifix was prominently mounted above it. A door opened. "I am Father Michael, Prior. I will hear your request."

Ike entered the prior's study and took a seat when Father Michael pointed to the chair. Ike began, "I am Ike Curtis, Major Curtis, though rank is of no matter to you. I am here looking for someone."

The prior smiled. "And why do you come to me? We live apart from the world in a strict routine."

Ike held back a smile. "First, because he was seen in Trib-Harine, and second, well, second, because I have experience finding men trapped in enemy territory. I help them escape. My experience in France taught me that most monasteries and abbeys shielded and protected allies from the Nazis. The husband of my adjutant was tended for wounds and sheltered for nearly a year. It is a great service that men and women of God do for others."

"Who is this man you seek?"

Ike presented the photos of Jacques and Andre Batten. "This is the man. Jacques Samson du Rochelle. The other, his friend, Andre Batten, visited Jacques' wife, Justine. Andre saw Jacques here some months ago and reported that Jacques is with the Free French but cannot contact her. I am Justine's tenant and determined to help her."

Father Michael sat back in his chair. "Justine Samson. Yes, I know her and Jacques. They have been here on pilgrimage. Protestants, but passionate in their love for God. I do not know where Jacques is. It is true that he and Andre passed through. I do not ask where they come from or where they go. Is Justine with you? She must be. She is a most adventurous woman. Tell Justine I will pray for her."

Ike got up to leave. "Father, Trappists go barefoot. Not every boot print that finds its way to your gate can be swept away. The war in North Africa is over. My car will be parked in the village plaza. Any man wishing to return from hiding will be safe. German soldiers, a quarter of a million, are being sent to safety. Prisoners of war, yes, but safe from harm and safe from Nazi authorities who may not wish them good health. I tell you this in confidence that they are going to America. They will be well fed and cared for; the Red Cross will see to that. We are not fascists; we are not animals. They can heal. They will find work in the fields alongside American farmers and wait out this hellish war."

Father Michael smiled. "I have answered your questions, Major, now you must answer mine. Why have you come? Yes, you seek Jacques, another life to be rescued, like the men in France. But you did not need to go here. You knew Jacques had moved on. You knew he would not say, and I would never ask where he goes or what he does. Why are you really here? You come as a pilgrim seeking answers, not as a soldier or a friend of

Justine. We have time. Sit and tell me what troubles your soul."

Ike turned to the priest. His face drained of confidence, and he sat down. "I don't know why I came. As you say, I knew he had moved on. Yet, I needed to come. Perhaps Justine, in the village, may hear something, but I needed to come here. It's strange, ironic really, when we stopped the car in the village, it was silent and peaceful, and then I heard the bells. Church bells spoke to me in the past—a year ago, in another small village, Churchstanton, England. God put me there. He put me with good people—faithful to him and loving." Ike paused and lowered his chin into his fists.

"They sound like godly people. They helped you."

"Yes. I had lost my faith, and they brought me back. Patiently and lovingly, they showed me I could love God and trust him again. They understood the difference between happiness and joy, as well as the distinction between relaxation and genuine comfort. They showed me how my obsession with saving others was my way of coping with my own lost faith. Guilt. I carried so much guilt. The vicar, Uncle Hugh to my friends and me, patiently taught me the power of prayer and faith." Ike stopped. "Hey, is this a confessional?"

"Confession is good for the soul. Even Anglicans know this."

Ike chuckled. "Yes, that's true. Funny thing, when I finally recovered, I went to tell Hugh, the vicar..."

"Yes, you call him Uncle Hugh."

Ike smiled. "I went to Hugh and shouted, 'I'm staying—stayed on Jehovah, never to leave our Lord again.' I know it is He who never leaves us, but while I was there, a messenger came from General Eisenhower, and I was on a plane for Algiers within the hour."

"God has a sense of humor, but it is his way to grow us spiritually. He moved you for his purpose and your growth. Do you remember the baptism of our Lord Jesus by John? God's voice spoke from heaven: *'This is my Son in whom I am well pleased.'* What love, what joy! What glory! And what did Jesus do? He went into the wilderness to be tempted and tried for forty days. When God calls—when you accept the claim he has made for your soul, he does not leave you in ecstasy. No. He spurs you to do his work in the world. We have our reward—yes, in heaven, but here on earth. Hope and assurance. A comfort that a sinful world cannot overcome."

"What you say makes sense. You would like Uncle Hugh. But if what you say is true, why are you and so many other monks still hiding in the wilderness?"

Father Michael replied, "Hiding is not a good word. A bit harsh and a little judgmental. Our Savior commanded us not to judge, lest we be judged. Now, as to your question, there are many reasons we remain in the wilderness, but I assure you, we are not hiding. If I were to mentor you, I would begin with the wilderness stories in the Bible. Some you might not consider wilderness, but God always has a purpose for sending us out of our comfort—into the wilderness."

Ike looked up. *Mentor me?* Father Michael gazed at the crucifix on the wall behind Ike. "Call me a steward in the wilderness, not a steward to the wilderness, rather to those who wander there."

Ike sat motionless. The prior stood. "Come back. Go, find Justine, and return. We will talk over a meal, and I will say a mass for Jacques, and for you as well."

Driving down the narrow road, Ike's thoughts bounced with every rut, hole, and rock. *Why did I come? How did he know? What does he know about me? And Justine—the woman is a mystery wrapped in a riddle, deceitful, no, careful yet somehow authentic and compelling. Why did she come? Lord, I don't know what to pray for— wisdom? Discernment? Open my heart and mind, for you sent me here.*

Ike parked in the plaza near the fountain. He sat listening to the fountain water splash melodiously into the basin. It was only the opening of the passenger door that interrupted his daze. Justine jumped in and said matter-of-factly, "Nothing. Nothing new. The Free French, the resistance, and liberation have all moved on, though there are rumors of a stranger staying in the priory. Ike, are you listening? Did you learn anything up the mountain? Ike?"

Ike turned and smiled at Justine. "Sorry, no. I mean, yes. There is someone up there. I believe, a German soldier. I saw his boot prints. The prior, Father Michael, remembers you and Jacques. He expects us for lunch. Said he wants to talk to both of us over a meal."

Justine sat back in her seat and gazed up; a smile

grew on her face. "He asked you a question. After listening to and addressing your questions, he went deeper and asked—deep within, you knew what he was asking. He asked you why you came. And now you wonder why I have come as well."

Ike said nothing. Justine turned and said, "What are you waiting for? We have an invitation we cannot turn down. It should be a most enlightening meal."

Brother Paul met them at the priory gate. "This way. I will take you to the table set for you." Ike and Justine followed silently to a small room. Brother Paul said, "Here. The prior will join you soon," and he closed the door behind him. Three chairs encircled a small round table set simply, yet inviting—with a basket of baguettes, a pitcher of water, a bottle of wine, fruit, and cheese. An open rear window invited in the sounds of creation: chirping birds and rustling leaves. Fresh air carrying the sweet fragrance of flowers and grass drew Ike's eyes to the beauty of the priory garden. "Idyllic," he said to no one. "But there must be more than creation's beauty that keeps them here."

The sound of Father Michael opening the door drew him back to the company of the others. "Please, sit," Father Michael directed with a warm smile. "Anywhere is fine. There is no precedence in a circle. We are all friends, brothers and sister in Christ."

Ike and Justine each found the nearest chair. Father Michael took the last. "It is a blessing to see you again, Justine. On your last visit, you struggled with your duty as a disciple of Christ to pursue justice as you saw it. Justice for your people, Amazigh and French. Christian and Muslim, and the war—Nazi and Fascist against the French and their European allies. You came without the traditions of European Christians. An open mind and yielding heart."

"Yes, Father. And you showed me that my questions were not new. That many, even the great thinkers, Doctors of the Church, struggled to reconcile our Lord's commands to love our enemy with His warnings to be wary of evil, to protect, and when necessary, to fight back, justly. How satisfying it was that an African Bishop, Saint Augustine of Hippo, led Christians through this issue, using simple questions to guide us."

Father Michael smiled. "Yes. He outlined four conditions under which war is justified. Do you remember them? The first is that the damage done by the aggressor must be lasting, grave, and certain…"

Justine replied, "Yes. In my mind, both France and Germany are aggressors, bringing grave and lasting damage to our land. And the second condition Saint Augustine proposed was that all other means of putting an end to it have been ineffective or impractical. This is a hard one. Have all other means been attempted? Petitions to the governor? The voices of the people made loud, but unheard? I think yes, but maybe not completely. And revolt itself has failed in the past."

Father Michael continued, "Which leads you to the third condition—is there a serious prospect of success? Past wars have failed, and now there are two aggressors, or are there?"

Ike interjected, "You and Jacques have determined the Nazis a greater evil, and now he fights for Free France and hopes for better treatment by your rulers after the war is won."

Justine nodded. "As you say, and more. Saint Augustine set a high standard for success. He taught that using arms must not produce evils graver than the evils eliminated. The French have been unjust, but our beys and sheiks have joined with them. They may be unjust, but they do not kill or imprison without good cause."

Father Michael broke the momentary silence. "You see, then, morality requires reason and intentions within God's love even for our enemy. War is never to be taken lightly, and when fought, it, too, Augustine teaches, must be fought with equal reasoned and discerned morality. Even more so as we have brothers and sisters among our enemies—do we cease loving them? No. Nor do we cease loving our enemies—even those outside the body of Christ. Even war must be fought in love. It is a very hard thing."

Ike closed his eyes and sighed. "Father Michael, I know of a man-a true man of God. A pastor and lover of widows and children, who returned from safety in America to fight Hitler in Germany. He is determined to see Herr Hitler dead. He refuses to escape from prison and continues to plot against the Führer. Do his actions—motives align with historic teachings of the Church?"

Father Michael replied softly, "Only God is our judge. He judges the heart. Saint Augustine's and now church doctrine provide guidance, not permission or endorsement. We are each held to a standard, and we are all sinners. Perhaps that is the best test of our intentions. Am I, an unjust sinner, one to bring action against another sinner?" Father Michael nodded and smiled. "A good discussion, but that is not why you come here. Our Father in heaven has sent you both into the wilderness to find answers. That is why you come—to learn God's lessons taught in the wilderness."

The room fell silent. Father Michael waited patiently. Justine stared out the window at the garden scene. Ike sat with his head down and his eyes closed, his chin resting on his left hand. He sighed. Father Michael continued, his voice still soft but louder. "Ike, may I call you Ike? When we spoke this morning, you mentioned the bells and how they called you and led you to Father Hugh and his family. And how you sensed a similar calling here. In England, Churchstanton, if my memory serves me, your faith did not return in an instant. It took time. Trust takes time and love even more. You laughed when you spoke of God's timing. On the very day you affirmed your faith, you determined to stay the course. You spoke of an old hymn your father sang, 'Stayed Upon Jehovah,' that very instant you were called away. What you found ironic was in no way so. You spoke of how peace and joy overwhelmed you. It was God's blessing poured out to overflowing. His love for a son…."

Both Justine and Ike were focused on Father Michael. "Ike, this morning I told you the story of Jesus being tempted in the wilderness for forty days and nights. I tell it first because it provides hope. And as you go from blessing and joy into trial in the wilderness, you are reminded that Jesus knows the trials you face and promises his presence to comfort and guide. But other wilderness stories can be more troubling. I've made a partial list for you to study. Read them and ponder the lesson, to the Jew under the law, but also in light of God's promise through Jesus. Ask yourself questions. For instance, the baptism of Jesus, why? He, without sin, needed no cleansing. He publicly obeyed the Father, and what happened? The dove, the Holy Spirit descended on him, and the voice of the Father in heaven all proclaimed who he was and is. Jesus fulfilled the law in every way, and God blessed him. What does that mean for us? But be warned. After a great blessing to men, they fell into sin and wandered in the wilderness. And so he has called you and sent you, like his Son to be tried. You will fail. You will sin. But you will learn to trust him and put your burdens on his shoulders. You will prepare, like an athlete for the race he has set before you, and you will become more like him."

Father Michael turned to Justine. "My daughter, Justine, has heard this lesson, and yet she struggles. Why do you struggle, child? Did you expect your trial to be easy? The world is at war. Your struggle is not unique, but your hope is so much stronger. Perhaps you should recall the story of Mephibosheth, driven by fear to hide in the wilderness of Lo Debar, while all the time, King David sought to bless him and restore him for the sake of his father, Jonathan. You do not need to tarry here. Seek your strength from the Lord and go where he leads you. Remember, he led David to set his table in the presence of his enemies. What did David say? '*He restored my soul.*'"

The Prior sat back away from the table. "You must go now if you wish to cross the mountains before dark." He paused and gazed at them warmly. This priory is not the wilderness. We are an oasis for those who wander—for those belonging to the Kingdom of Jesus coexisting in a wilderness of a fallen world."

Ike and Justine stared at each other. Their eyes joined their hearts, minds, and souls, reckoning a journey ahead, separate but somehow together.

CHAPTER 10
LETTERS

Ike and Justine were in different worlds as they walked together to the car. Eyes ahead, but looking inward, neither noticed the boot prints on the ground. Nor did they notice the head of someone in the back seat. Only after opening the car door did Ike see him —a small, sunburned young man with blonde hair, wearing a desert khaki short-sleeved shirt and shorts. His billed khaki hat, emblazoned with the Luftwaffe device, was on the seat beside him. There was a tremble in his voice as the soldier said in a heavy German accent, "Father Michael says if I go with you. I will be safe."

Ike scanned the inside of the car. He saw no weapons, no bags. The German brought nothing but the shirt on his back. "Yes, I can take you. You will become a prisoner of war. You will be treated well in accordance with the Geneva Convention."

"America. I want to go to America, away from the Gestapo, away from the SS. They cannot find me."

Ike asked Justine, "Check the trunk, the boot. I will keep an eye on our guest. I don't believe we are in danger, but to be certain…"

Justine went around to the trunk and opened it. "Just my case, Ike," she said. She slammed the trunk shut and got into the front passenger seat.

Ike reassured the frightened young man. "You are my prisoner. I make no promises to you other than delivering you to the American prisoner detention camp. But you will be safe. The Germans and Italians have surrendered North Africa. The war here is over. What is your name?"

"Ernst Schmidt, corporal. Fallschirm-Panzer-Division."

Ike nodded. "That's the Goring Division, correct? They suffered heavy losses in the battle for Tunis."

"I do not know this battle of Tunis. Please. Do not take me to them."

Ike studied the young man. "I see no wounds. You either became separated from your unit or deserted."

Corporal Schmidt nodded. "Ja."

"Ja—yes. I was separated. I was the only survivor of an attack on my outpost. I made no effort to find my unit. I hid until I remembered the priory on my map. I took the rations of the dead and made my way here."

Ike started the car. "We have a long drive. You can tell us your story on the way."

They drove down the mountain in silence. Passing slowly through the village past the square, the gentle sound of the fountain was a natural sigh of relief to the trio of travelers. Corporal Schmidt spoke softly. "I am no Nazi.

It is the truth, so help me God! I despise everything they teach; I abhor the lies. It is all about hate. Blame others—France and England at Versailles. The greedy Jews—sub-human beasts. I was to become a pastor. Not in the Nazi state church. Do you know that Hitler is the head of the state church? Can you imagine the Nazi flag has replaced the Cross over the altar? Anathema! I curse him! I stood with those who would not put Hitler between the people and God. I found like-minded brothers and sisters in the Confessing Church. Have you heard of it? Probably not. Can I tell you? Can I explain how I came to be here?"

Ike looked into the mirror and saw the prisoner's earnest face. "As I said, we have time. We will listen."

Seminary. The Confessing Church established a seminary—underground, of course—in Finkenwalde, on the Oder River near the Polish Border. There were twenty-seven of us. Our teacher, Herr Direktor, Bonhoeffer..."

"Dietrich Bonhoeffer?" Ike asked.

"Yes. You have heard of him?" Ernst replied.

"Yes. I know of his work, and I carry his book, 'The Cost of Discipleship.'"

Ernst asked, "His work? Is he safe? He had gone to America."

Ike sighed, "He is in Berlin. Tegel Prison. He prefers pastoring in prison to the escape offered to him. Continue your story, and then I will tell you what little I can."

"And all this time, I thought him fortunate to have left before the Gestapo discovered us. And so Herr Doctor Bonhoeffer is arrested, along with all the others: Martin

Niemöller, Karl Barth, and Martin Gruber. All boldly opposed the Nazi Church. But not just our leaders, all of us at the seminary. We were given the choice of the Wehrmacht or a concentration camp. I prayed. I meditated on the Lord's command: "Go. Make disciples of all men." Right or wrong, I do not know, but I chose the Luftwaffe. I believed I would stay in Germany, close to my family, a private, servicing warplanes. I did not know of Göring's Division, paratroopers, and air assault. Tanks, in the Luftwaffe? Once the war began, we were sent to France and from there to North Africa."

Ike glanced at him in the mirror and replied, "It's been four years since Hitler began his attacks. You chose to desert; that is what you did in the sight of the Geneva Convention. By your own words, you willfully hid and sought asylum in the priory."

"I do not deny my guilt. I acted on principle, on my faith. The guilt of killing brothers, yes, brothers in league against Hitler. I am willing to fight alongside Americans or the French, if you will have me. I tried to make disciples. My words fell on deaf ears. How long do I kill the good while the bad do not listen? If they heard my words, they were too frightened to act or acknowledge in public. There were too many true Nazis. Vindictive devils. Rats ingratiating themselves with the Gestapo and the party. It was more than seeking promotion upon the lives of fellow Germans; it was an unholy dedication to Hitler. My Sergeant was such a man, a beast. Hate. Filled with hate, he lived to kill, if the foreign enemy, so be it. If, in his eyes, a traitor to Hitler, even better."

Ernst exhaled his anger and stared out the window as they drove toward the narrow pass. Ike broke the silence. "And now he is dead?"

"Yes, and God will judge him. But I could not return. So here I am."

"A prisoner of war in the hands of the Americans."

Ernest's eyes lit up. "No! I am in the hands of God! Whatever happens, his will be done."

Justine caught the smile that formed on Ike's face. "You speak like a true follower of Christ, but who is this Bonhoeffer you both speak of?"

Ike joined in. "The Seminary. Tell us about his seminary. I know he is a theologian, a brave Christian and beloved pastor, but the seminary I did not know."

Ernst smiled broadly. "It was almost like heaven. He brought us close to God and each other. It was unlike any other seminary in Germany. Herr Direktor Bonhoeffer's heart was to train pastors, not scholars. He found no value in debating abstract religious constructs. Three pillars—at Finkenwalde, we focused on three pillars: the Bible, prayer, and confession. However, the seminary wasn't about learning but about doing. We were expected to practice what we learned. Assignments were to study Scripture, to meditate, and to pray. He challenged us—how can we pastor others unless we are grounded in the Word of God and are men of prayer?"

Justine commented, "It seems more like a monastery than a seminary. Bible, meditation, and prayer."

"No, there was more. The Bible and prayer are the grounding and a lifestyle. The third pillar, confession—confession was the curriculum. By confession, I mean the confessions of the Church. The fundamental teachings handed down from the apostles as interpreted by the fathers. The Apostles Creed, the Nicene Creed, and the Augsburg Confession. Herr Direktor Bonhoeffer taught from his ragged, bound copy of the Book of Concord, which unfolds the depths of the confession to the Christian. It is these three pillars that the Nazi church has abandoned: the Bible, humble prayer, and the confessions and creeds of the Church. No, Finkenwalde in its brief two-year life was not a wilderness escape. Germany is the wilderness. The Wehrmacht and the Luftwaffe are in the wilderness. You are returning me to the wilderness."

Ike slowly exhaled. "Bonhoeffer's words still haunt me: 'When Jesus calls a man, he bids him come and die.' An honest man. A faithful man—he has chosen to stay, to pastor, and if God wills, to die."

Ike stopped the car and turned to face Ernst. We will soon come to the checkpoint. I do not know what will happen to you there. I expect they shall take you in custody. What can I…"

"We," Justine added.

"What can we do for you, Ernst?" Ike finished.

"A letter, letters. Would you see to it that my letters are sent? I have some that I wrote while at the priory and… and can I write one now, telling of my capture?"

As Ernst fished his letters from the pockets of his

trousers, Ike reached for the small notebook and pen in his breast pocket. Ike tore off a few pages of notes and traded the notebook and pen for the letters. "It is better that you are not found with my notes. And addresses, where should I send them? Are there others I should notify?"

Ernst did not reply. He was busy scribbling a letter to his wife and young children. After a few minutes, he paused, looked up, and said, "I tell them that my Redeemer has brought me out of the desert. I will follow him wherever he leads, but he is not finished with me, and I am not coming home soon. I tell them to pray and to find strength in His Word and prayer. My love, share my deep love with our children. Do not cry but rejoice, for the Lord is my strength, my shield, and my defender."

Ernst handed the notebook and pen back to Ike. A soft sob escaped his lips, and tears fell from his eyes. "Thank you, my friends, for listening, not judging, but with open hearts. It is a blessing more than I deserve."

Ike scribbled his name and address in the notebook, tore out the page, and gave it to Ernst. Please contact me. I have written that I am your captor and promised to notify your family personally. Take it."

Justine took off the cross she wore. "Take my cross and wear it. Let it be a reminder of the cross of your redemption and that you are marked by his blood forever. God bless you, Ernst."

They drove on in silence, each with a smile and tears in their eyes. Ten minutes later, they reached the checkpoint, where the guards took custody of Ernst. Ike was asked to write a statement on the capture. When Ike finished, he asked the guard, "Where will you take him?" "To Tunis," he replied. From there, likely the U.S. The harbor is filled with Liberty Ships to transport the prisoners."

"One last request," Ike asked. "We want to say goodbye."

The guard stared at Ike. "You want to say goodbye to a prisoner?" The surprised guard scratched his head. "Well, there's no regulation saying you can't."

Ernst was brought before them. Ike and Justine, in turn, hugged him. Remembering what he witnessed in church, Ike put his hand on Ernst, bowed and prayed, "Lord, bless this your servant Ernst Schmidt, keep him safe, reunite him with his family, and keep him in the palm of your hand as he follows the path you lay before him. Amen."

Justine added her amen. The guard, bewildered by what he witnessed, also drew upon his Christian faith and added the final amen.

When Ike returned the staff car to AFHQ, he stopped by his office and found Don Shelton working. "Don, I didn't expect to find you here. What's so urgent?"

"They have us doing double duty. They want us to intensify RECON on Sicily but also support maritime patrols over the Med. Subs. Only one or two can wreak havoc on convoys of Liberty ships."

"Can I stay and help out?"

"Thanks, boss, but I am just finishing up. By the way, it looks like the Army Post Office finally caught up with you. There's a stack of letters from home on your desk."

Ike gathered up the letters and headed for the door, hiding his eyes still red from crying. "Good night, Don."

Don couldn't help but notice Ike's face. "You haven't even opened them yet."

"I don't have to. They are letters from home. Love letters. It's enough."

"Good night, boss. Happy dreams."

CHAPTER 11
ORDERS

Ike trudged up the stairs to his apartment. The day's events played through his mind. Everything changed, yet his brief conversation with Shelton and the familiar staircase were the same. The contrast, or was it a new perspective? His time with Father Michael, the questions—*it's like he knew me—his teaching, his wisdom, and his prior discipling of Justine and Jacques, and Justine's skills, undoubtedly honed by the Liberation movement, but her faith, strong and honest, and then there is Ernst and his connection to Dietrich Bonhoeffer. A strong Christian, yet an enemy. What does it all mean? It weighs on me to do something, but what?*

The apartment door was unlocked, but Justine was not standing inside to greet him. Ike saw her sitting at the table, staring out into the night. The curtains were pulled back, gently ruffling in the breeze, but no one noticed. Justine wore the same clothes, her headscarf lay on the table. She clutched a drink on the table with both hands. Not turning her head, she said, "I need to talk. Please, sit with me. I need someone to listen, to help."

Ike dropped the letters and his hat on the table and sat down. "Me too. So much to…to work through."

Justine opened up. "Ike, I can't stay here. And if what you say is true, you, your army will soon leave Algiers and North Africa. Father Michael would say I'm being called to move. I know it's time, but where? And do what?"

Ike put his hand on hers. "Justine, we are in this together."

Justine looked up and smiled. "Yes, together. I like that. Friends on a journey, what is the word? Pilgrim? Yes, two pilgrims on a wilderness road."

Justine's vacant stare fell on the pile of envelopes. She squeezed his hand, sighed, and said, "Letters. So many letters! I must not keep you. Enjoy them—I'm sure there must be one or two from your sweetheart, and from home…"

Justine sniffled. "Home, how I miss having a home."

Ike and Don Shelton were bent over the maritime RECON photos. Don said, "Nothing. Nothing for three days." Ike picked up a photograph and scanned it under his magnifying glass. "I don't see anything, let alone a sub. What's the altitude? They're too high to pick up a white cap, let alone a ripple."

Don double-checked the report and replied, "Ten thousand feet."

Ike glanced at Don. "Ten thousand feet? Engert knows better than that…"

"Roosevelt's standing orders to the squadron.

Wants to preserve assets for Sicily. He doesn't see any need for low-level RECON."

Ike shook his head. "Idiot. Draft an order to AF Airwing RECON Officer. Conduct two low-level night maritime flights, Tunis to Gibraltar at 0000 and 0230. Two planes per flight utilize infrared photography. Altitude 1000 feet. Presence of U-boats is the highest priority. Continue until further instructions."

"Roosevelt isn't going to like this…"

An officer stepped into the room. "Isn't going to like what? I'm Colonel Roosevelt. Who are you to cross swords with me? Don't think you can take me on."

Ike turned, smiling, and offered his hand. "Lieutenant Colonel Roosevelt, my name is Ike Curtis, glad to meet you. My deputy and I were just going over your maritime RECON photos…"

"I heard Eisenhower brought in some cowboy while I was gone."

Ike's smile broadened. "Guilty. I've been waiting to meet you—must've finished the O Club circuit briefing for your Hollywood holiday."

Ike didn't wait for a response. He held up a photograph. "Too high, you're not going to pick up a snorkel or periscope at that altitude. No. From now on, you'll be conducting maritime RECON at night, infrared cameras at 1,000 feet. Even if you are smart enough not to surface in daylight. Don't thank me. There will probably be another medal in it for you. Just promise me Engert and his boys are recognized—first-class men, all of them."

"You got balls, Curtis. I know your type, smart ass. Don't cross me or…"

"Or Momma Eleanor will see I'm out of the way. Get out of my office, Lieutenant Colonel, you'll receive your orders soon enough."

Half an hour later, the phone rang. Shelton answered, his eyes widened, his face drained of color. He turned to Ike. Only seconds later, he replied to the caller with a sharp, "Yes, sir. Immediately," and hung up.

Ike, concerned, waited for Shelton to speak. "Ike, Chief of Staff's office. Beetle Smith wants to see you now, not ASAP, now. Ike, there was no courtesy at all. Beetle Smith is coming after you."

"That was quick," Ike said as he straightened his tie, grabbed his hat, and headed for the door. "Beetle Smith, Eisenhower's hatchet man. Well, I never expected to be here long."

Ike quickly marched down the Commander's Corridor to the office across the hall from General Eisenhower's. The door was open. The aide looked up. "Colonel Curtis, the General will see you now. Go right in." *He must really have a bee up his bonnet, not even a knock first.* Ike opened the door and came to attention before General Smith's desk. Beetle Smith pushed his chair back, looked Ike in the eye, and said, "What the hell were you thinking? As if I don't have enough problems to solve, but when it gets to Ike before me, someone has to pay."

Ike stammered, "I'll apologize to Lieutenant

Colonel Roosevelt…"

Beetle Smith interrupted, "What's 'Randy' Roosevelt got to do with this? If he is involved with the Justine Samson woman, I'll get his ass on the carpet beside you." *Not Randy Roosevelt? Justine?*

Ike regained his wits. "Pardon, General. You said this is about Justine, my landlady?"

"You and Miss…"

"Mrs. Samson, General."

"Have it your way. The two of you delivered a German POW captured at, where? Yes, the priory at Tib Harine." General Smith looked up, pushed his glasses back up against his face, and said, "General Eisenhower himself commanded you to have no relationship with this woman. The French suspect her of espionage. What do you have to say for yourself before I put you on a plane out of here?"

"General, may I speak freely?"

Beetle Smith sighed. "Sit down. Tell me your story."

"Well, to begin with, Justine, that is Mrs. Samson, is my landlady and housemaid. She cooks my meals, and she keeps a room in her apartment. It's pretty hard not to develop some relationship. Yes, General Giraud was in Eisenhower's office when the direction you mentioned was given. But…"

Smith interrupted, "But? But what? You're digging yourself a hole. This better be good."

"Yes, sir. But Mrs. Samson had already confided in me about her husband's service for the Free French, and his history of, of well, espionage. She only wanted to find her husband, to know he was alive. The French—they knew but would not answer her questions. Something about their requiring agents to sign a document that they have no spouse or children."

"Go on."

"Well, General, my experience with British…"

"I'm aware of your relationship with MI9 and SOE."

"Anyway, Mrs. Samson opened up to me about their past and a recent sighting of her husband at Tib Harine, and, well, we decided to follow up on it. Sir, my experience with monasteries and convents in France—their sheltering our downed airman—well, it convinced me that the priory at Tib Harine would be a perfect shelter for passing agents or stranded soldiers."

"And you found the German deserter there."

"Yes, sir, and more. Mrs. Samson told me about her past service to the Berber Liberation movement. She and her husband decided to trust in a promised French reward for turning their fight toward the Nazis. Her husband, Jacques, is planted in the Abwehr. But Justine, Mrs. Samson, well, I can only say, she is a skilled agent, savvy, bold, and a good shot. She is more than capable. We could use her, Sir."

Beetle Smith sat back and stared out the window. After a long pause, he turned back to Ike. Eisenhower asked me to find something else for you, Curtis. He wants to reward good work but not empower any more cowboys. Patton and Montgomery give him enough grief, and he is saddled with babysitting young Roosevelt. What to do with you?"

"If I may offer a suggestion, General, I would like to return to my Special Flight Unit in Churchstanton. I have unfinished business there."

"Back to your English girlfriend. No."

"No, sir, the pursuit of a traitor—one of ours who has cost the lives of many agents and downed fliers. I was close when I left."

"If General Eisenhower believes what you say, with your successes here, he will want to keep a hold on you. Let me see what I can do. You're dismissed, Colonel."

Ike stood, saluted, and turned for the door. Beetle Smith spoke, "And Curtis, don't worry about Colonel Roosevelt."

Ike returned to his office. Major Shelton stood up, the look on his face asking, silently, "Well, what happened?"

Ike smiled. "I still have a head on my shoulders. It seems our work results are noted, but…"

"But what? Come on, Ike, spill the beans. Do I send the orders to Roosevelt or not?"

"By all means, send them ASAP. Beetle wasn't interested in Roosevelt. I was called on the carpet for something else," Ike sighed, "going off the reservation despite a warning from General Eisenhower, himself."

"Let me guess, Justine. Your gambit to Trib Harine."

"Bingo. Somehow, Justine's statement on the capture of our German POW was flagged and made its way to the Command Corridor. Seems the French have been watching her. I told you about her husband's connection with Free French Intelligence. Well, it's complicated. Anyway, I mentioned my problem with 'Randy' Roosevelt…"

"Randy?"

"Per General Smith. However, I will be reassigned. I asked to return to my Special Flight Unit in England. I doubt it will happen. Beetle suggested that Eisenhower wants me where I am available. I don't know if that is a good thing or not. Anyway, I'll do my best to put you in the job. Now, Operation Husky. We have good intel on the airdrops that will precede the amphibious landing. We are about to witness the largest amphibious operation in the world; over seven divisions will board twenty-seven hundred ships and large landing craft. All these ships are gathering near Malta. The Brits, Admiral Cunningham and General Tedder, control the sea and the air. Commercial traffic is returning to the Med, but I still worry about U-boats. A single wolfpack, I know it would be suicidal, but one wolfpack could wreak havoc. How many remain? Is the Strait of Gibraltar impenetrable? How many are hidden in France, Italy, and Greece?"

"I'm with you on that, Ike, but isn't that INTEL's job?"

"Don, INTEL uses what we, all of RECON, give them. INTEL can tell us what to look for and where to look, but they don't tell us how to look and finding Nazi U-boats during the day from 20 thousand feet won't cut it. That's why you are needed here. If Elliot Roosevelt can't see that, someone else must steer him back to effective reconnaissance."

Justine was humming a happy tune when Ike came home. *It's been only two months, and coming here to Justine feels like coming home. But Rose is back home in Churchstanton, and young Earl is home in Gig Harbor. Can I really feel at home in three places? Three families? Is Justine family? A friend, yes, maybe a sister. Should I feel guilty?*

"Bonjour. You're back early, Ike. I was thinking, we never go out. I enjoy cooking for you and our dinners on the balcony, but in all your evenings in Algiers, you have never enjoyed the nightlife."

"You're right, I've avoided the throngs of soldiers losing their troubles in wine and women. I suppose we could try the Hotel Aleti. It is restricted to field-grade officers and above. Officers can be just as randy as any soldier, even the women, from what I've heard. But in the club, there must be some level of decorum."

Justine laughed. "In the café and bar, yes, but if you ask the barman, he will send you upstairs to the madame who runs the bordello. No, Ike, let me choose where we go."

Ike sighed. "I'm glad you suggested a night out. I had a meeting today. I won't be here much longer. It seems I've upset the apple cart once too often. They say my work is good, but..." Ike paused. "Do you remember when I promised to inquire after Jacques? Well, I was warned not to get close to you. Somehow, our visit to the priory and your statement when we turned over Ernst at the checkpoint made their way to the top. I believe General Giraud still suspects you or perhaps maintains an interest in your activities. And there is the normal jealousy and personal vendettas inherent in staff operations... Simply put, I'm leaving, but somewhere General Eisenhower can quickly pluck me back. I've already told you too much."

Justine's cheerfulness was gone. "I feared as much. It's time I leave."

Justine smiled and took both of Ike's hands into hers. "But tonight, we celebrate our time together. Half an hour. Give me half an hour. Have a drink, and I will show you how we celebrate in Algiers."

Thirty minutes later, Ike stood in a clean uniform with crisp, creased pants and sleeves, drink in hand, staring off into the last golden flashes of sun on rippled waves. Justine entered and announced, "Well, Ike, what do you think? Tonight, I am French!"

Ike's jaw dropped when he turned and saw her. Her black hair flowed in gentle curls, framing her radiant face and falling softly on her bare shoulders. Her femininity was unveiled in a blue silk gown. A perfect match for her enchanting, deep blue eyes. It was little more than a slip, yet exquisite in its journey of discovery, that drew his eyes down the curves of a truly stunning woman. Ike's attempt to lift his eyes to her eyes paused at the waterfall of large pearls falling from her neck between the twin mounds of her soft breasts and buried deep in her decolletage.

After an eternity of seconds, Ike smiled, his eyes finally locked on hers, and said, "Stunning. Justine, is it polite to call another man's beautiful wife stunning?"

"Thank you. I hoped it would please you—from Paris. Jacques enjoyed hearing others compliment my beauty. I know it was his vanity, displaying me as his trophy. Do you know he travels with a woman? It is true. His pretend wife is his lover. He took his mistress with him! Still, he is my husband. We made a covenant before God, and I will honor it."

As quickly as her smile faded, it returned. "I am not ashamed of my beauty, nor am I afraid to use it to my advantage. My beauty is a gift from God, and not my only or greatest gift. But tonight, I want to honor you, my good friend. This may be our last evening together. I want to make a memory that I can carry with me in whatever lies ahead. Memories of two souls—yes, you cannot deny that our lives have intertwined."

Justine smiled and kissed Ike's cheek. Her gentle kiss delivered a light tingling to Ike. It grew into a wave that carried through him from the top of his head to the ends of his fingers and toes. His eyes caught the sway of her breasts as she moved. His trance was only broken when she said, "Come. The taxi is waiting."

The driver delivered them to an unpretentious canopied doorway of a fine apartment building in the quiet, leafy neighborhood of Algiers' French upper class. The maître d greeted them. "Madame Justine, how good that you can join us tonight. Come, I have your table waiting. Of course, the Champagne is already on ice."

Ike was the only American officer in the club. He noticed several senior French officers. *I hope General Giraud doesn't hear of this.* Couples sat around small tables with shaded lights, which provided the only illumination in the room. A single stage lamp beamed down on a singer, the band accompanying her from behind.

The war was forgotten. Lost in each other's company, they sipped champagne and tasted fresh oysters. They chatted and laughed; their voices shielded by the music. They danced. Ike's shoulders and arms melted into Justine's soft body. His nostrils could not get enough of her scent, enhanced by a sweet, but fresh perfume. She was unlike any woman he had ever known, mature, exotic, her will as strong as case-hardened steel, her body soft and inviting, and her heart gentle and comforting.

The evening passed all too quickly. The band had packed up, and the other patrons were gone. The Maître d walked quietly to the table and smiled. Justine nodded, and he walked off. She reached across the table and put her hands on Ike's. She smiled a sweet invitation. "We must be going. But the night doesn't have to end here."

Ike stood, came around the table, and helped Justine from her chair. His mind spinning, he thought, *what is she saying? I want her so much. My body is screaming for her. Wait! Where is this going? Justine is special, I am captivated, and I do care for her. I am so drawn by her beauty and her…Yes, I do love her, but there are others.* Ike bent down and kissed the back of her neck. "Justine, we have tonight. We have memories, and I want you in my life. It is true we are, as you say, intertwined, but…but there are others. Jacques and Rose. We must remember our love, our commitment to them. We mustn't complicate any hope of a future. Friends. Yes, truest of friends, but not lovers."

Justine stood, tears in her eyes, and said. "Of course. Can a friend have a hug? I desperately need a hug."

CHAPTER 12
CHANGE OF STATION

Ike was up early, careful not to wake Justine down the hall. He slipped out into the predawn darkness. With little sleep, he looked to the night sky to confirm that the moon, Venus, and the stars had indeed continued their preordained nocturne journeys. He grabbed a quick cup of coffee, a slice of toast, and a sticky fig bun at the Officers' Mess before checking in at the office. Don Shelton greeted him. "You're up early this morning. Couldn't sleep?"

"Something like that. Are the night infrareds in yet? I need something good before my fate is sealed."

Shelton replied, "Nothing in the early night. They're on the desk. The 0200 mission photos should be delivered any minute now. Of course, the last flights won't be in for a couple of hours."

Ike scanned the photos one by one. "Nothing. I hate to give Elliott Roosevelt an 'I told you so.'"

Don reassured Ike, "That's only one early night mission. It doesn't prove anything. The tactic is sound. We both know it."

"Yeah. Even so...." Ike looked at his friend and

inquired, "Don, I'm an open book to you, but you never say anything about yourself. You're married, tell me about your family, your wife, Bonnie, right?"

"Not much to tell. Bonnie was my high school sweetheart. We married after I graduated. Her dad, a preacher, insisted that I have a job and security before he would give his blessing. And since she insisted that he officiate the wedding at their small church... well, she was worth the wait. Bonnie was in nursing school when the war broke out. Like you, an ROTC officer, I was immediately called up. We thought it was best to wait until after the war to start a family. She is home in Milwaukee. Nurses are still needed back home as well. So, we write, we pray, and we wait. So far, our hope remains as strong as our love."

Ike nodded. "That's a plan worth sticking to. Don, don't do anything foolish. No crazy volunteer madness. Enough good men are dying. You're providing a great service here on the staff. Promise me."

Don chuckled. "Thanks. I know. I won't forget who is waiting for me back home."

They were interrupted by the courier delivering the latest RECON photos. "They're here. Let me spread them on the table," Don said as he undid the string around the envelope flap. Before they were all down, Ike shouted, "We got'em! One U-boat off Malta...two more in this photo. The Jerries have set a perimeter west of Malta and another below Sardinia." Ike continued down the line of photos. "Ten, I count ten boats on or near the surface charging batteries or dragging radio antennas. Not exactly an armada—get these to INTEL and Admiral Cunningham's staff via the Commanding General's office, ASAP. Tell them more coming in three hours."

Don replied, "I'm on it. You know, Ike, someone needs to get your tactics out. AFC could use a RECON tactics development and training command. Every RECON and INTEL officer, every RECON pilot, and camera officer should receive training. Think about it. Someone needs to stay ahead of the curve. First, Norway and high-altitude cameras; then night-field infrared; and now maritime night infrared. There is sure to be a next adjustment."

Ike replied softly, "Tactics and training, hmm. Special Ops, poor sots on the inside, they need this as well. Structure. Organization. Looking to what's next. Thanks, Don, thanks for putting the pieces together for me. I'm flattered by your nomination, but I'm not sure I'm the right guy."

"Well, if you don't put your hat in the ring now, you can be sure Elliott Roosevelt will chase it and fail us all."

After the morning brief, General Smith asked Ike to remain. As the last of the staff filed out, Beetle Smith said, "Take a seat, Curtis." Ike pulled a chair from the table and sat down. Smith followed suit and said, "As I said yesterday, Eisenhower wants to reward your work, keep you close, but not in the AFRECON job. He doesn't have time to deal with interference from Washington. So, I have a proposal. I've already started the paperwork. I'm putting together an Allied Force Inspection Team. You'll lead the RECON section. The team will visit subordinate commands to evaluate performance, gather lessons learned to share across the Command, and direct corrective action as required. It will take a couple of weeks to assemble and update new inspection guides. The team can start in England—something you desired—in about a month."

Ike replied, "May I speak freely, General?"

"Let's hear it."

"General, inspection teams serve a great purpose in evaluating subordinate commands, and I agree that the inspection guideline must be updated based on lessons learned. If I may offer an alternative, General, much of what I have learned came from my experience working with the Special Operations Executive. SOE has great resources that allow them to adapt quickly and develop equipment and tactics they are reluctant to share. Sir, rather than me hopping on and off transport to spend a few days at a base, I think I could be more effective and deliver faster results by establishing a training Command at RAF Churchstanton. I will continue to support SOE, apply the latest RECON tactics, and train RECON officers. And not just RECON officers, but pilots, camera shop NCOs, the whole gamut. General, I would be fully available to General Eisenhower, get away from Colonel Franklin, and bring Allied Forces the latest developments in the tactics lab that SOE has become."

Both men sat silently. Ike waited. Beetle Smith sat silently. Finally, Beetle Smith spoke, "Claude Dancy wants you back. This could work. Let me run it by General Eisenhower."

Ike added, "General, I can write a mission statement for the AFRECON Training Command, and as for staffing, I would like Major Engert and Master Sergeant Feinberg, both of the RECON Squadron, assigned to the unit. They are both first-class, adaptable, and capable. And…"

Beetle interrupted, "Don't push your luck, Curtis."

Ike continued, "And I recommend Major Shelton remain on your RECON staff. He knows his business and will guide Colonel Roosevelt without being a threat to his, well, his ambitions."

Beetle Smith stood. Ike knew this meant the meeting was over. "General Smith, I would like a short out-brief with General Eisenhower before departing Algiers."

"I'll arrange it. Good day, Colonel."

Ike nearly skipped back to his office. Things couldn't have gone better. With General Smith's support and Eisenhower's direction to reward Ike, he was sure to be back at Churchstanton and Rose soon. *I didn't want to push it with Beetle Smith, but I think I can convince General Eisenhower to bring Justine to England with me. Jim Langley and MI9 will surely sell her skills to Colonel Z. Justine will be away from General Giraud's suspicion and closer to finding Jacques. SOE will soon see her skills put to good use!*

That evening, Ike was whistling, something he hadn't done in years, only his respect for the uniform stopped him from skipping boyishly down the street to his apartment. He took the stairs two at a time and tried the handle. The door was locked. "That's strange," he mumbled as he knocked on the door. No answer. He knocked again as he sought the key buried somewhere in his pocket. *First time I've had to use the key.* He fumbled with the European lock for a few moments until at last the tumbler clicked and the door opened.

The apartment was quiet. Everything was in place. The French doors were opened to catch any breeze. The table was not set, and the kitchen was clean with no evidence of any meal preparation. "Justine, it's me, Ike, where are you? Is everything okay? Justine...." Then Ike noticed an envelope on a silver tray on the small ornate table by the door. Ike picked it up. It was addressed to Lt. Col. Ike Curtis. *Seems terribly formal.* Ike opened the letter and read the exquisite feminine hand; a calligrapher could do no better:

My Dear Friend Ike,

Thank you for everything, for your kindness and warmth, and all your help and support in my search for Jacques. At risk to your position and office, you have given me more than assistance, you have renewed my hope. But it is clear that some in authority still question my loyalty, or perhaps it is something Jacques or I may know—you know this to be true. I fear I am in danger and do not want to entangle you any further in my troubles, so it is time for me to leave here. There could be no goodbyes. Why put each other through any more grief? It is better that you do not know where I go. What a sweet blessing you are in my life. I will remember our dinners on the balcony, our spiritual retreat at the priory, but most of all, I will treasure our time together last night. True friendship is a rare gift. It has energized me as I must journey on. Truly, I am bound to you as my one true friend for the rest of my life. I wish you and your sweet Rose all happiness and a long future together. Pray for me, Ike, as I pray for you.

I sign simply as your friend,

Justine

P.S.: When you depart, please leave the key with the Maître d' downstairs.

Ike sat down and stared. His mind offered no thoughts, no intuition, only melancholy and an empty loneliness.

During Ike's departure call with General Eisenhower, there was no mention of Justine Samson du Rochelle, just a warm handshake, congratulations, and the General's challenge, "I gave you everything you asked for. Now I expect AFRECON Training Command up and running quickly. We need the best men, equipment, and tactics in the operating theatre ASAP. This war waits for no one."

A week after Justine's disappearance, Major Fred Engert, Master Sergeant Feinberg, and the development team of admin and supply officers joined Ike on the Allied Force Command transport. At Ike's request, there would be a one-day layover at Gibraltar. Ike looked down at the calm Mediterranean below him. He saw no threats, pulled the shade, and fell asleep. Ike's last glance at Algiers did not see the MP guard walking the halls of a POW barracks. A tall, wide-shouldered, and squared-jawed sergeant tapped his billy club in the palm of his hand as he stopped in front of a bunk. "Corporal Ernst Schmidt, stand up. If you want it, pick it up and take it with you. Personal items only. You won't be coming back. God help your Nazi soul."

"I'm no Nazi!"

The burly sergeant ignored the comment. "Jonesy, when he has his things, cuff the little Hitler's hands in front."

The approach gave Ike his first view of Gibraltar in the daylight. The famous rock loomed from the sea, rising from a thin, low peninsula like a giant fist wearing a gauntlet of granite, all the while hiding a labyrinth of tunnels and a face pockmarked with guns that gave Gibraltar its deadly punch. After landing, the Hudson transport rolled to a stop in front of a small terminal. The sign read: Arriving personnel Check-in." Once Ike checked through, a small man, a civilian, approached him. "You're Montclair Curtis, I presume. I'm Rose's father, Arthur Osbourne."

"Mister Osbourne, I'm happy to meet you at last," Ike said, extending his hand.

Arthur Osbourne stared at Ike's outstretched hand and replied, without shaking it, "You came here to get my blessing to marry my daughter Rose. I'll say this once, Yank, you might as well get right back on that plane. You will never have my blessing."

Before Ike could reply, Arthur Osbourne turned and walked away.

CHAPTER 13
RAF CHURCHSTANTON

Ike recognized the familiar coastline as the sea gave way to the Somerset countryside. The spring blossoms were but a memory, and the fields were a verdant, undulating green, as a healthy crop promised autumn grain for a hungry army. As Churchstanton came into view, Ike smiled to see the bell tower of St. Peter and St. Paul Church. But the airfield—Ike was surprised to see that the number of hangars had doubled, and several more were under construction. Rows of Spitfires, Hurricanes, and Mosquito light attack bombers lined the taxiways. It was no longer a sleepy outpost of the RAF. Ike openly asked himself, "Has RECON been pulled? Where are the Expeditors? The Hudsons? My Lysanders? How do I train RECON pilots without RECON planes? Even the Mosquitos are rigged for bombing."

Ike turned to see Major Engert's shrug, asking, "Where are the RECON planes?"

Colonel Z must be behind this. What's he been up to since I've been gone? Ike shook his head and hunched his shoulders. The small Lockheed Hudson transport made its approach and touched down smoothly on the runway. It was a short taxi to Group Headquarters, where Group Captain Hastings stood waiting with Nigel Marley, his friend and former Number One. Ike grinned when he noticed Nigel was now wearing the stripes of a Squadron Leader. *It's about time, my friend! If you're here, so are the Lysanders, Expeditors, Hudsons, and that sweet Spitfire of yours! And Hastings! He knows a good man when he sees one. I'm glad to be back—back? You've had my back too many times—all spit and polish, a proper Brit with a heart of gold.*

Ike scrambled to be first off the plane. He strode forward and saluted Hastings. "It's good to be back, Group Captain." He turned with a grin and returned Nigel's salute. "Congratulations, Squadron Leader." And Ike extended his hand. Hastings replied, "And congratulations to you, Lieutenant Colonel. Deja Vous. I'm directed to be your landlord once again. Those new buildings, including two hangars and offices, are your training command. The engineers have been working around the clock. My orders are to give you everything you need. Come to my office where we can talk."

Ike nodded and turned to the cadre of officers standing behind him. "My staff." Hastings nodded. "Welcome to RAF Churchstanton. I am Group Captain Hastings, RAF Air Group and Base Commander. That lorry will take you to your quarters. You may leave your bags here. They will be brought to you. Colonel Curtis will fill you in after our meeting. You are dismissed."

Ike followed Hastings and Nigel to the Group Commander's HQ. Inside Hastings' office, Ike noticed a British Officer with one empty sleeve pinned up to his shoulder below a Cold Stream Guard Insignia. Ike grinned. "James Langley, never one to say hello in public. Always lying in ambush with a new assignment."

Langley laughed. "Welcome back, Ike. Congratulations! Lieutenant Colonel, no longer a need to waste time with salutes. I see you wrangled—that's the right Yank word for it…"

"Wrangled works," Ike replied.

"Yes, wrangled your way back into MI9 now safely protected by Eisenhower. Eisenhower wants more than RECON training from you. You're his mole in MI9 and SOE. Colonel Z has his own reasons to want you, an unofficial, back-channel connection to the Allied Force Commander. How do you feel about being used?"

"It's just as I intended. It got me back to Churchstanton and doing the work I'm called to."

Langley chuckled. "And, of course, there is Rose Osbourne. You should marry that girl and put an end to the mystery. I heard you got religion, Ike, so now it's a calling? Don't get too comfortable; there is work to be done before your Training Command receives its first trainee. Stop by the club after you're settled in for a drink. Oh, right, you'll be off to sweet Rose."

Langley stood up to leave. "You can find me at Otterhead House. Your access pass is still good. By the way, Colonel, will you tell Rose about your Berber girlfriend?"

"You mean Dorothy's counterpart, an agent searching for her husband? Yes. She could teach you a thing or two about underground operations."

Langley smiled devilishly. "Otterhead House midnight." Langley walked out whistling.

Nigel asked, "What was that all about? A Berber woman?"

"It's a long story, an innocent story. It can wait. Speaking of stories, where are the Lysanders, the Expeditors, and the RECON Hudsons? I see new Spitfires and Mosquitos, fast light attack bombers. But no RECON?"

Hastings spoke. "Right. Let's get down to business. Nigel can brief you on his Squadron later. You will be provided with two Spitfires, two Mosquitos, and more on the way, two Lockheed Hudsons, four Beech Expeditors, and two Lysanders for training and other authorized missions. The Spitfires and Mosquitos are here. The Lysanders and Expeditors arrive this week—castoffs, they needed maintenance to fly here. Based on Langley's little speech, he'll try to throw you into the breech quickly. You have flexibility. Don't let him push you too hard. Now, Ike, I will support you as best I can, but as you can see, I've got a full plate—many squadrons…"

Ike replied, "You're busy. The air station is busy. I get it. I'll do my best not to trouble you."

Hastings continued, "We had a good relationship in the past and I expect that to continue."

"Yes, sir. And I still intend to support you any way I can."

"First request is running flight schedules through my office. I need flexibility on training flights, combat has precedence, as do emergency landings, and Nigel's RECON. I know you understand. Now, I'll let you go. I've taken the liberty of scheduling a welcome aboard party for your command. Saturday night at the officers' mess. Bring the lovely Rose Osbourne. I'll let you see to your staff."

Ike stood. "One last question. Where is Dorothy?"

Nigel spoke. "I'll tell you what I can on the way out. Jim Langley will fill you in tonight."

Outside, Nigel spoke softly. "MI9 is acting on a tip about the traitor, *Adder*. An eyewitness description. All right, you didn't hear this from me, but the eyewitness is Charles Barclay, Dorothy's husband. She's in France now."

The Oak Tree traitor, another Nazi snake—like Cobra. Ike shook his head, exhaled a deep breath, and replied, "Not again."

Nigel answered, "She's a big girl. You're not going to stop her, or her husband Charles, for that matter."

Ike chuckled. "That she is. I want you to meet my XO, Major Fred Engert, and I brought along an expert cameraman, Hollywood credentials, Master Sergeant Feinberg. Get them acquainted with your staff."

Marley nodded. "Already in the works."

As they walked toward the Officers' Quarters, Nigel asked, "Berber girlfriend?"

The summer sun was low in the sky when Ike turned up the gravel lane towards the stone cottage hidden on ten acres in the middle of the Otterhead House estate forest. Ike noticed ripening peaches and green apples on the orchard trees, leafy peas, beans, and root vegetables, as well as rows of tall corn in the well-tended garden. *Marge Olson's northwest variety corn seeds have done well. Am I wrong to surprise her? Should I have called first?*

The sound of tires crunching gravel alerted Rose. The front door flew open, and Rose, seeing the staff car, rushed outside. When Ike opened the door, Rose squealed joyfully and ran to Ike. She flew into his arms and kissed him. Happy tears fell on her cheeks. Needing to get even closer, Rose pounced onto Ike, wrapping her arms and legs around him. There was hunger in her kisses and joy in her soul.

Ike fell against the car, then straightened and lifted her firmly. He cupped both hands under her firm, round bottom. He could feel her small, strong, yet soft body around him. Each of her excited breaths pounded through him, bringing her closer. He slid his hands up her back and squeezed her tightly. His reasoning succumbed to sensation as her femininity penetrated his chest and loins. He was at once weak, yet his embrace, firm. He did not want to let go. Their tongues probed through wet, enticing kisses. His senses fueled his emotions, overwhelming any reasoned thought.

"That's enough, Rose! Put her down, Ike. You had your welcome-back kiss. And come on in. We held supper for you," Hugh called from the door.

Rose opened her eyes and grinned at Ike. "You

came back. I am the happiest woman on earth.”

Rose’s uncle Hugh, the vicar of St. Peter and St. Paul, replied before Ike could speak. “I think we got that from your little demonstration. You looked like a cat in heat. What would your father think?”

I know exactly what he would think. If he had a gun, he would shoot me. Ike gazed admiringly at the petite Rose, wearing her white silk blouse, always a bundle of energy, and replied, “I’m the happiest man in the world. You look wonderful…”

“In these old clothes? You just wait and see, mister.”

Rose took Ike’s arm and led him to the door. “Uncle Hugh, a cat in heat? Really? I’m a woman in love and don’t care what others think. Never have and never will. God doesn’t make mistakes.”

Hugh stopped at the door. “Say, Ike, you didn’t bring along our Kentucky friend, did you?”

Ike laughed. “I’m tied up right now. But if you look in the car….”

Hugh raced to the car for the bourbon while Ike escorted Rose inside. He could smell her good country cooking. He felt at home. Rose gave him another kiss out of view of Uncle Hugh before walking over to the oven. “I must confess, Nigel Marley rang me up and said you arrived. I had just enough time to put on this blouse—our blouse. I’ll never forget when the infrared flashlight did its trick.”

“Nor will I. Who knew Churchstanton’s quirky parish secretary could play the vixen?”

"Only for you, mister, and don't call me quirky. I'm just happy being me. I won't be constrained into Churchstanton's mold for young women." She paused to smile. "It's one of the things I love about you, Ike. You don't try to change me. You love me as I am. We're a team. We've proved it. We work together, finding strength in each other. Trust. Our love is built on trust."

Trust? How do I ever tell her about Justine? How do I not tell her?

Ike forced a chuckle. "I fear the Vicar would appreciate some semblance of decency and self-control on our part." He took her hand and said, "I am so happy, Rose. So very happy." Ike sighed, "The garden looks great. And Uncle Hugh looks well..."

Uncle Hugh returned with the bottle. "Fit as a flea, Ike. Rose sees to it that I'm fed and watered like the garden, and...and I'm hungry, Rose. When do we eat? I'm pouring a drink, Ike. Care to join me?"

Rose laughed. "Go ahead. I'll get supper on the table."

Ike accepted a glass from Hugh and asked softly, "I hear Dorothy is out of the country again."

Hugh swirled his whiskey before tasting. "I'm afraid it's true. With Charles' blessing, I might add. There is no convincing them otherwise. It's their mission, almost a calling."

Ike whispered, "That squares with what I've heard. Charles, even in recovery, is training or at least employed behind the scenes in the escape route campaign. But she worked so hard to find him, and now they are willing to give up their future, a long life together."

Hugh looked to see if Rose was listening before whispering, "A true tragedy. Charles confided in me that the doctors don't believe he will ever father a child. That future has already been taken from them, so they live to serve."

"Does Rose know?"

Rose stepped out of the kitchen with a steaming dish. "Sit down. It's time to eat!"

The sentry saluted as Ike drove to the gate. Ike reached for the pass in his pocket. The guard said politely, "No need for that, Colonel Curtis, welcome back."

The moonlight danced on golden toes, the lake its grand dance floor. The weeds and brambles along the shore were discreetly hidden in the shadows. Two dim lights marked the path to the door of Otterhead House. The grand house wore its nightly makeup, hiding the stains of clogged gutters and the rusty drool of the gargoyles. *This place must have been grand in happier times. If only I could promenade Rose in pearls and a fine evening gown for a gala party with old friends. Smitty remembered me. I mean, it's only been two months, but it feels like ages since I left. So much has changed, yet, except for the new hangars, Churchstanton seems the same.*

A sentry stepped from the shadows. "Good evening, Colonel. Colonel Langley is expecting you in the briefing room."

Langley was waiting, seated behind a pile of folders, his pipe clutched in his teeth. "Sit down, Ike. You've got a lot of catching up to do." Langley paused for a rare grin. "Hate to take you away from your lady friend. Couldn't be helped. We're in play tonight. I need you here. How did you get yourself back here, anyway? Yes, initiative, you always had it. And now you're in play for both Eisenhower and Colonel Z. Smooth—well, enough small talk. First, the good news: we eliminated Cobra, the traitor who derailed the comet line. Belgian, Jacques Desoubrie, aka Captain Jacques."

"That is good news! How?"

"Michelle Dumon, you may know her as Agent Lily. Powerful observation skills—one of the best. It seems she first met Desoubrie in Paris last February at the Comet line meeting. He was using the name Pierre Boulain. His polka dot necktie caught her attention. She remembered something her father once said, 'Beware of someone in a garish dress, it may be a signal. During a brief police custody in March, she met a fellow Comet Line helper. When she asked who betrayed him, he said Pierre Boulain. Collette passed the information to Jean de Blommaert and Albert Ancia of MI9. She realized Boulain was the same man as Jean Masson, the man who cost us Belgian leadership and over 100 *helpers*. Her timing could not have been better. MI9 was about to give him five hundred thousand francs to establish a new escape line in Belgium."

Ike replied, "And you say Cobra, this man Desoubrie, is dead."

"Ancia requested the resistance group, the French Forces of the Interior, to execute Cobra. We received the coded response "Gold Tooth" only five days later. It seems his garish dress wasn't his sole distinguishing feature. The man had a gold front tooth."

Cobra is dead. All the efforts and it's over. It's strange, I feel—I feel nothing.

James Langly continued. "Now the bad news…"

An aide popped his head through the open door. "Colonel, they're over the target. You asked me to call for you."

"Right! Langley looked at his watch. "We'll have to continue this conversation later, Ike. It's time to join the others in the OPS Room."

Ike followed Langley out. *The bad news?*

Chapter 14
Pitching Tent

The silence of the familiar, darkened Operations Room was shattered by a broken voice over the squawk box. "Approaching landing zone. Ground lights lit. Signaling Quebec…"

Ike saw Nigel Marley sitting near the squawk box and sat next to him. The pilot's voice came back. "Received response, X-Ray, repeat, X-Ray, wave off. Ground air search lights bright—count six search lights and small lights all around the field. Taking small arms fire as I climb. Wave off successful—returning home. Night owl one out."

Langley shouted, "Damn it! How many infiltrators are we dealing with? If not Cobra, who? Adder? Cole? Harold Cole is still on the loose. The worst kind of a traitor, a Brit, one of our own." He sighed and said calmly, "I want radio checks with Night Owl 1, 2, and Night Hawk every fifteen minutes until they've landed. I will be in my office."

Ike spoke up. "Did Night Owl One have infrared cameras operating? Did he circle first? Do any of them have a handheld infrared? I want a close look at the ground signalers and our team—every bit of the welcoming party.

Who were they? How long were they there? And any RECON of the area before the mission. Oh, and request the Night Hunter follow the Jerries out. That should shake things up."

Langley nodded. "Make it happen. Give Colonel Curtis everything he asks for," and headed for the door.

Nigel Marley got on the radio and calmly directed each of his pilots. Night Owl Two, an Expeditor, was to conduct another RECON sweep and look for the ground team, while Night Hawk, a Maritime Spitfire, was to follow the Jerries. Night Owl One, the Lysander, was to return to base.

Night Hawk radioed back, "Night Leader, Night Hawk permission to strafe."

Marley answered, "Permission granted. Break off at first sign of anti-aircraft fire or Jerry night fighters."

Ike followed Langley back to the office. "I assume this wasn't the bad news you mentioned before. It's not like you to go off in public. Can I ask about the mission?"

"Yes, it was wrong for me to react. Keep calm and carry on, and all that. It was supposed to be a pick-up. Airey Neave and two French agents—talks with London."

They entered the office. Langley's desk lamp was the only light. James sat at his desk, closed the file in front of him, and threw it to Ike. "First, the Comet Line fell. Oaktree is on its last gasp. Ray Labrosse is working hard to pull together what's left. He insists it will still work, but infiltration by the Abwehr is rampant. Airey was escorting two French agents, Georges Jouanjean, head of Paris

Mithridate, and leader of the Pat O'Leary Line, and Guy Lenfant, a Free French Intelligence Mithridate agent who established the Cockle Network in Britney. We have confirmed that Val Williams is in Frenes Prison in Paris. As an escaped prisoner before, he will be sent to a German concentration camp. But Ray, God bless his soul, keeps us informed. Risks, he takes too many risks, but he won't return until our airmen sheltered in Brittany are safely on their way home."

Ike scanned the top file. "Airey Neave in France, not room 900? He's Crockatt's right-hand man."

"Norman Crockatt saw the need for someone close, someone he trusted and knew the whole operation of SOE in France to observe, correct, and report back on countering Abwehr's infiltrators—fresh eyes. I agreed."

"But Airey Neave? That's a huge risk. Many of the French helpers he has worked with have been arrested. What if he is given up? Imagine what the Abwehr would do to turn him."

"Airey knows the risk, and he knows the Abwehr routine. He's been captured before. No, it was the right decision. Geo Jouanjean is well-tried and trusted. Lenfant, also a Mithridate agent and a former French Officer, has proven himself in Brittany and Algiers. Experienced and capable. These men are vital if Oaktree, or any sea escape route from Brittany, is going to work."

Ike nodded. "And how do Charles and Dorothy Barclay fit into this?"

"Charles is at Room 900 with Crockatt. He provided

information on the Abbey's and medical support helpers from the Comet and Pat O'Leary lines. Dorothy accompanied Airey to France. She is to remain in Brittany, establishing new connections and routes to French Abbeys with the medical helpers. Barclay's a good man. One of us, an escapee. He won't rest until there is no man left behind."

Ike nodded. *Just like Dorothy.*

Langley continued, "Keep the file. I need you up to date. Things are moving quickly." He grabbed his hat and headed for the door. "I'm off to London. Get your staff ready for your RECON Training Command while I'm away. You asked for MI9, you're working for MI9."

Ike called after him. "Aren't you going to wait for a report? We don't know if Airey and the two Frenchmen made it out."

"I'll be halfway to London before we know. Besides, it won't change the fact that the Abwehr has penetrated deep into our operations."

It was a short night for Ike. His staff was gathered at 0800 in Group Captain Hastings' conference room. Fred Engert shouted, "Ten-hut!" The men stood at attention while Ike walked to the head of the table. "Seats, Gentlemen, we have a lot of work to do. General Eisenhower expects results, fast results. Unfortunately, I have collateral duties that may occasionally require my attention. Of course, Major Engert has complete authority in my absence. Initiative is what I expect, and that's what this Command is all about: 'Carpe Oportunitas.' That will be our motto. Officially, we're a training command. We are tasked with training RECON pilots in the latest tactics and equipment. That makes us both initiators of new tactics and collectors of them from throughout the allied RECON forces and units. Our authority comes from Allied Forces Command. AFRECON will be our link to AFHQ. Most of you know Major Don Shelton. He's our liaison to move things through AFHQ. We're not here to play catch-up with Jerries. I expect you to keep us not one but two steps ahead, as they adjust to our tactics."

Ike looked down at the folder that Engert had set before him. "We'll begin with reports."

After the briefing, Ike closed, saying, "You all know what's expected of you. We'll have a daily debrief at 1600, until further notice. Go to work."

Ike stood and said, "Major Engert, with me." Alone, Ike said, "No one asked the obvious question. Are they slow or being careful?"

Engert replied, "You mean, where are our pilots? We have planes but no assigned pilots. They trust you to handle it." Fred paused. "How will you handle it?"

Ike looked over his shoulder. "Last night, James Langley came down heavy that I'm here to serve MI9. As much as Group Captain Hastings can help, he can't supply pilots, and he can't be caught in a turf battle between Colonel Z, British SOE, and General Eisenhower. We're off to see Nigel Marley. We have a couple of days to work things out before Langley returns from his London browbeating and reset. As I see it, if we're to play all three roles—training, tactics development, and support for MI9—our only option is a partnership with Marley's Special Unit 545. If Langley resists, we'll push it through Allied Force Command. I'm sure that since North Africa is over, they will be crossing the Mediterranean. A cross-channel invasion of France will follow. RECON must intensify. Marley will need more aircraft, our aircraft."

"But pilots, experienced RECON pilots, where will they come from? Boss, do you intend to order inexperienced RECON pilots for training? Their Squadron Commanders won't be happy, and the Groups and Bomber Air Marshal will resist."

Engert paused. So, you think both SOE and General Eisenhower will have your back? Ike, if something goes wrong, the Air Secretary will go straight to Churchill."

Ike grinned. "I'm trusting Eisenhower and Churchill are more interested in results than protocol. We'll begin with the most experienced pilots. The carrot to their Commanding Officers is that their best man trains quickly and returns to train his comrades."

"I'll get on it right away. Request one for each plane…"

Ike shook his head. "No. Make it two for each plane per class. The pilots need rest, not the plane. Two missions a day at least. Get a list from Hastings. Get the orders out now. Don't wait for the hangars or the offices. I want men in the air ASAP."

Marley listened patiently to Ike's plan. "I like it. I'm

on board and will stand behind you with Langley, though, you know, he admires and respects you already. When this training command idea surfaced in London, Langley pushed it through with Airey, Crockatt, and Colonel Z. But you realize that most RECON pilots fly high-altitude, pre-bombing sorties. Not our kind of action."

"That's why we start them on routine emplacement missions, pre-invasion surveillance. We get their feet wet on low-altitude and infrared tactics. We let 545 focus on SOE. If 545 needs help, we loan you the best of the class. Oh, and I come bearing gifts. One Master Sergeant Feinberg, Hollywood camera genius, at your service."

Ike turned to the silent Fred Engert. "And get to know my XO, Fred Engert. Great RECON pilot. He's ready to go anytime you need him."

Nigel extended his hand, "Welcome aboard, Fred. I get the impression we're going to get along fine."

Ike stood to leave. "It's good to see you again, Nigel. How are Sharon and your girls, Millie and Penny?"

Nigel smiled. "Doing well. Sharon insisted on coming to the party Saturday night. She would love to meet you—and Rose, too."

Ike smiled and waved as he left. *The party Saturday night! I forgot all about it. Rose will insist on being there. So much to tell her. And Hugh, I need to talk to Hugh. Lord, please don't let me screw this up!*

Ike went directly from the afternoon brief to the vicarage, hoping to catch Rose and Hugh together before the end of her workday. *Workday? Rose makes her own schedule. Makes sense to check for her at Saint Peter and Saint Paul before going to the cottage.* He spotted her bicycle leaning against the vicarage gate as he drove up. The Reverend Hugh Osbourne met Ike at the door. "Rose is in the parish office. She will be back soon. Come in."

Ike stepped through the door as Hugh said, "Is it too early for a drink?"

Ike smiled. "Just one… Hugh, I wanted to talk to you about North Africa…"

"So, that's where you've been. Rose and Dottie figured as much."

"Right, and there is much to tell both you and Rose—I met Arthur. In Gibraltar…"

Hugh sighed, "That must have been unpleasant."

"You knew. Did Rose?"

"Yes. From the beginning. He doesn't approve at all. Rose knows, so does Dottie. It has nothing to do with you personally. It's my brother, and his stubborn insistence on imposing his plan on his daughters. Rose has held her ground since she was a little girl. I thank God that Rose and Dottie remain close despite Dottie being so favored. She never asked for it, and she supports Rose. More than once, she has told Arthur he is unwelcome if he can't be at least civil, if not supportive of Rose."

Hugh walked to the bureau and opened the Bourbon Ike brought the night before. He poured two glasses and handed one to Ike. "Rose will marry you, Ike, that is if you aren't having second thoughts."

"No, nothing like that. I'm just worried about what

comes next."

"I'll be fine. Dottie and Charles will miss her, but then we won't be the first family to see a loved one off across the sea. No, Rose is always up for adventure, and her love is strong even from afar."

"There is something else I need to tell Rose..."

Rose stepped through the door. "What do you need to tell me, Ike? You're not leaving again? Dottie, has something happened to Dottie?"

"Rose! No, nothing so dreadful. First a kiss, then my news."

Ike absorbed the comfort of hugging and kissing someone so dear, someone who made him whole. He smiled. "I came to invite you to a party on Saturday night. Group Captain Hastings is hosting a welcome aboard for my command and staff. Everyone is asking after you. Nigel's wife, Sharon, is coming down. She wants to meet you. And my staff, friends, all. Can you make it?"

"Kiss me again and I'll tell you!"

Their second embrace was more passionate. "Of course! I knew you would ask. Nigel told me the day he learned of your return. I've been dress shopping in London. I can't wait to wear it. But you'll have to wait until Saturday."

"London?" Ike asked.

"I go every other week to Lambeth Palace for my research."

Hugh spoke, "She is one busy lady. Keeps the parish running and still finds time for research. She has become quite close to Archbishop Campbell."

Rose sat on the couch and patted the seat next to her. Ike sat obligingly. Rose said, "He is such a dear man—such a heart for God and people. I know he is wise and a scholar, but he is so warm and open. He says I make him laugh again. He isn't healthy. I think he enjoys a friendly conversation; unlike the correspondence I find in the archives. I know there is politics in everything, but the church—such vindictiveness towards fellow churchmen, seen as enemies. Bishops and Archbishops fighting each other. Ugly. I'm sorry. You didn't need to hear that. But yes, I do like William and look forward to my visits, even if it's only enough to say hello to him. He always asks that I see him before I leave. And always the same question, 'What nuggets have you found today?'"

Ike thought, *First-name basis with the Archbishop of Canterbury? Only you, Rose, so full of vitality and warmth. You don't seek anything from him or of him. You have no need to impress him or ingratiate yourself. You are yourself, and that's why I love you.* "I'd love to meet him. Perhaps when things settle down, I can arrange a trip to London with you."

"And you will," Rose chirped.

Ike took Rose's hand and squeezed." There's something else I need to tell you..." Hugh gave a quick headshake, out of sight of Rose.

Ike continued, "It's about my time in North Africa." Hugh relaxed as Ike explained, "I met someone, very much like Dottie—you know, I was determined to help Dottie even before meeting you. It was the right thing to do."

Rose laughed. "I'm not jealous of Dottie, I'm glad you helped."

Ike smiled. "Well, I had a housekeeper. Really, she owned the apartment, and like Dottie, she was searching for her husband."

Rose nodded. "You decided to help her as well. It's what I've come to expect from you, Ike. You're caring, a true gentleman even if you grew up in the American wilderness."

Ike laughed. "Gig Harbor is not the wilderness, but the old joke is that you can clearly see it from there. Well, anyway, Justine—that's her name, and I became friends. It's complicated, a long story, too long for tonight, but she and her husband were involved in, how do I put it, local political movements; she is the half-French granddaughter of the late Bey of Tunis, like a chief or sheik. He is a French protestant. Both are outsiders and, well, because he disavowed his marriage to join the Free French intelligence, the French authorities refuse to give Justine any information due a spouse or next of kin. It's all very messy. I'm telling you this because, like Dottie, I went out on a limb for her, and it has been reported to my superiors. You know how rumors spread. Justine is an attractive woman. Alluring and mysterious. We're friends—close friends, but never lovers. It's you I intend to marry once this war is over."

Rose buried her eyes in her lap, trying to take in what she heard. "I'm glad you told me. It means you trust me. But must you help every good-looking woman in distress? Like Dorothy, another beauty. But you chose me. Aren't we close, Ike? I mean, not just an attraction, not just love, but friendship too? Do you need her to be your friend? I guess close friendships don't just happen; there must be a connection. Do you keep a connection with her, Ike?"

"She left to look for her husband, the night before I returned. She never said goodbye or said where she was going. But, yes, I guess a connection remains. We both have wandered in a wilderness not of our choosing, trying to understand what God is teaching us."

Rose looked up, smiled, and kissed Ike's cheek. "You said you recovered your faith—that you are 'Stayed on Jehovah.' What happened?"

Ike chuckled. "I heard bells in the wilderness."

Hugh studied the young man engaged to his niece. *There's more to this story. Lord, this is your work. Thank you!*

CHAPTER 15
THE PARTY

Maeve Hastings enjoyed the party life. Group Captain Hastings saw monthly parties at his stately residence in Churchstanton as a morale builder in an otherwise gloomy business. He tried his best to find reasons to celebrate, so the return of Ike Curtis was the celebration of June. Not that Ike wasn't popular, indeed he was, but even Maeve Hastings was surprised at the turnout for Ike.

Ike was grinning from ear to ear as he entered with Rose on his arm. Rose was dressed as she had never been before. Her strawberry blonde hair was styled into a Chignon, with a wave on top rolled into a curl above her right eye. Her long, silky hair was pulled back off her ears and twisted into a low bun at the back of her slender neck, resting on her bare shoulders. A corsage of three simple red wild roses with jubilant yellow centers was pinned above her right ear. Her late mother's earrings glittered as she moved. She removed a white, sheer scarf that protected her from the cool night air, revealing a simple yet stunning red sleeveless gown of soft lace that crisscrossed her decolletage and rose to shy, understated bows on her shoulders. A simple red belt encircled her small waist before the dress fell below her knees. No lady would dress without white gloves, nylons, and high-heeled shoes. Makeup submerged her freckles. Deep red lipstick, dark eyeliner, and a hint of rouge on her cheeks were made perfect by her honest and open smile, which radiated her youthful, joyful heart. No Vogue magazine cover girl ever looked as enchanting.

A whistle from across the room focused Ike's eyes on his Czech friend and RAF ace, Karel 'Kut' Kuttelwascher, his smiling wife, Ruby, by his side. "Kut!" Ike called. Kut waved them over. Ruby kissed Rose. "Darling, you have finally come out of your shell!"

Rose beamed. "Ike, Ruby helped me with my shopping in London. She insists on joining me on my visits."

Kut grinned. "They are great friends now. So how could I miss this celebration?"

Ike gave Kut a bear hug and replied, "You have no idea how happy I am to see you well, my friend. I miss our time together. By the way, Kut, there is something I would like to talk to you about."

"Yes, yes, of course, but who is that with Colonel Langley? Is he married? A date? She is attractive—sophisticated, I didn't think the old devil had it in him. Work, only work for that man."

Ike turned around and gawked. "Maybe Colonel Z wasn't his only reason for those trips to London."

After greeting the Hastings, James Langley guided

the young woman to Ike and Rose. Langley turned to the woman and said, "Ladies, gentlemen, may I introduce my good friend, Miss Peggy Van Lier. My dear, this is the man of the hour, Colonel Ike Curtis, and his lady, Miss Rose Osbourne."

"Fiancée." Rose added."

Langley smiled. "Fiancée, and this is Squadron Leader Karel Kuttelwascher, the famous RAF Ace, and his wife, Ruby."

"Squadron Leader Kuttelwascher, how pleased I am to meet you, a national hero—to both Czechoslovakia and Britain. And Colonel Curtis. Such a pleasure. James talks of you often. And Rose and Ruby, I hope we can become great friends as we spend more time here."

Group Captain Hastings guided Nigel Markley and his wife, Sharon, to the group of friends. Ike called out, "You must be Sharon. It's so good to meet you at last. Who's watching Penny and Millie?"

Nigel greeted his friends and said, "Sharon insisted on coming. You brought faith back into my life and happiness to my family."

Sharon, an unmistakably proud wife and mum, smiled. "The Reverend Osbourne is putting us up at the vicarage…"

Rose interrupted, "There isn't a decent room to be had for miles."

Ike turned to Rose. "You knew about this? And young children with Uncle Hugh?"

Rose smiled. "We all wanted it to be a surprise, a

real welcome. And as for Uncle Hugh, he was delighted. When asked, he replied, 'Two young girls? What a blessing! Perhaps their energy will shake some of the dust from the place."

Kut smiled as the ladies circled in a friendly chat. "Mic, (Kut was Ike's only friend who still called him Mic after his initials), you mentioned that we should talk. What is on your mind? It sounded urgent. Perhaps, we all should hear it. Let Ruby keep the girls engaged while we talk."

Ike began, "Yes, it's something you all should hear…"

Rose interrupted, "Not so fast! You brought me to a party, not a war meeting. You are going nowhere, Ike Curtis, until we dance a, no two dances, and even then, I will come looking for you when I'm ready."

Peggy Van Lier exclaimed, "Hear, hear! That goes for you, too, James."

Sharon needed only to look at Nigel with raised eyes and a knowing smile. Nigel nodded to his wife, message received.

Maeve Hastings said to her husband, "Isn't it time to introduce the guest of honor and invite them to the first dance?"

Ruby laughed as she said to her new friends. "We're going to make a good team. I'm up for dancing. Come on, Kut, time to cut the rug!"

Ike was not a good dancer. Being the first couple on the floor made him all the more self-conscious, but when Rose took his hand, smiling with pure joy, his self-doubt dissolved, and though ungainly as ever, his joy overtook him, and soon the whole room was clapping and cheering them along. Soon, the floor filled with couples, but Ike and Rose saw only each other. As Rose moved with her characteristic exuberance and ease, Ike managed to ask, "Where did you learn to dance?" Her face aglow, she replied, "Why, Dottie, of course. We taught each other. Sisters do that. But I see you're getting the hang of it. Stick with me, mister."

From the side, Maeve spoke to the leader of the small band, a combo really, and soon a slow dance began. Ike mumbled, "I thought the slow dances came at the end of the evening."

Rose chirped, "Thank you, Maeve Hastings! She isn't going to let us go without at least one! Now be quiet and hold me." Ike drew her close, kissed the top of her head, inhaled her rose cologne, closed his eyes, held her tight, and danced. Ike only stopped when Rose stopped and stepped back. "Ike, it's time for your meeting. Please don't tarry but return to me."

Ike followed Hastings and the others to the study, his mind clearing with each step. Once inside, he said, "Gentlemen, I've been told by high authority to make this brief."

Nigel chided, "And would that authority be the lovely Rose Osbourne?"

Ike blushed as the others laughed. "Right. I'll be quick. Since we're all here, I want to share my thoughts and hear your advice. General Eisenhower wants results. He sent me here on loan to MI9 and to train RECON pilots and crews. That includes developing strategies to stay one step ahead of the Jerries. I aim to make this work for all of us. Kut, this may be new to you, but we need a pipeline of new technology. Cameras, I've got. It's weapons. Planes—the latest in RECON and Night Intruder—wing tanks, weapons. You know the trade, as Chief Test Pilot, I need you to get me the best tools for our trade—night intruder RECON, and SOE ops."

Kut smiled. "You can depend on me, Mic! Of course, I will need to instruct your pilots in an operational environment."

"I've never been foolish enough to stand in your way, my friend. Now, James, my staff has requested pilots, but we all know how Commanders can delay or work around an order. They see their mission as their priority. I would, too, if I were in their shoes. I'm going to need help with the RAF training command. Political issue—not under Allied Force Command—Eisenhower can't order the support we need. We need those pilots and flight crews at RECON Training before their initial squadron assignments."

Langley nodded. "Right. RAF Commanders are protective of their Bailiwick. I see, no need to have the PM come down heavy, a word to Colonel Z should suffice. You plan on more than RECON training. And how long will this RECON training take? These pilots are needed replacements."

"Let's say, the final exam may be over the channel—but low risk. You and I can sit down and figure out the timelines. We'll need to coordinate with Nigel's Special Fight Unit 545. We can fill in the details later."

James Langley nodded. "And my payoff is a steady stream of trained pilots. Ike, they're welcome but…"

"James, your payoff is that we go after Adder. Think Operation Mongoose, but on a far grander scale. Not three but scores of false flags to entrap our Abwehr moles, dirty agents, and informers. We must learn from the Jerries. We don't pick them off one by one. There are too many to ferret out before the inevitable invasion. We take out Abwehr lines just as they waited until they could take down the Comet Line in Belgium and have nearly destroyed the Oak Tree before it delivered a single Allied airman."

Kut muttered. "Traitors. They are worse than the enemy. There is some honor due an enemy in serving his country, but for traitors, there is no honor, only death. Yes, we will make this happen!"

Langley had listened without expression. "Ike, I believe, if this is successful, we will make both Colonel Z and General Eisenhower happy. A just payment to the Abwehr's friends and a clean French countryside for our downed airmen. We'll get to work on this right away. We can talk after tomorrow's luncheon."

Ike responded, "What luncheon?"

Nigel Marley replied, "The Vicar, Reverend Osbourne, is hosting us after tomorrow's service."

Hastings chimed in. "Well, that's settled. Gentlemen, I remind you that there are lovely ladies waiting who came for a party."

They found their partners gathered in the living room, drinks in hand, laughing uproariously. Their host, Group Captain Hastings, remarked, "Something so amusing must be shared with us."

Maeve, smiling broadly, said, "Darling, we were just sharing anecdotes—stories—girl talk."

Kut, the bold, laughed. "At our expense, no doubt. Ruby, what did you tell them?"

"Me?" She laughed. "You know me too well. I confess. I told about the time we were shopping in the ladies' boutique, and…"

"And that's enough. Yes, my English can be amusing to others."

Ruby chuckled. "Not just your English."

Peggy Van Lier took a sip of her drink and said, "James can ferret out nazi spies but can't find anything in a ladies' boutique. He bought me lingerie that…."

"Peggy, darling, I think they have the picture."

Maeve followed, "What is it about men? My husband has fought off three Messerschmitts but will not even pick up my undergarments."

Hastings shook his head in shame. "I do have my plusses, dear."

Maeve grinned. "Yes, you do." Winking at the others, she quipped, "A sizeable plus that keeps me satisfied."

Laughter erupted, followed by giggles and finger pointing.

Rose stopped laughing, turned to Sharon Markley,

and asked, "What about Nigel? He seems so nice and mild-mannered. How does he make you smile?"

Sharon gazed at Nigel. "He makes me smile in so many ways. But the joy he has when playing with our Penny and Millie—well, even the thought brings me a smile and assurance. Look, he is blushing. My sweet husband is embarrassed."

Rose squeezed Ike's hand as she listened.

Ruby called out. "Rose, it's your turn to embarrass Ike. Is he really that straight-laced gentleman from the American back woods?"

Rose smiled at Ike. "Well, Ike, should I tell them about the silk experiment…"

"Please, no."

Rose chuckled. Yes, that will always be our secret. But the roll in the hay…"

Ruby chimed in. "Now this sounds good."

Nigel laughed. "I do recall him returning somewhat disheveled and grass stained."

Ike was beet red. "Yes. It was all innocent. Rose and I climbed a hill to visit a ruined castle. I slipped and rolled down the hill. There wasn't anything up there to see anyway."

Rose chirped, "As I recall, we rolled down together. What's the word? Intwined. And you loved every second."

When the laughing ended, Ike managed a smile. "You have me there, Rose." *You've had me ever since.*

When the evening ended and Ike dropped Rose off at the Osborne cottage, following her to the door, he watched the confident, feminine sway of her hips. He remembered his night out with Justine. *So different, yet both attractive. Justine is mature, capable, and proven in hardship. Rose is full of youthful exuberance and fun. Am I good enough for her? Can she withstand life's toughest trials yet to come?*

At the door, he took her hands. "Rose, tonight, the dress, the makeup, and banter—is this a new Rose?"

"It can be if you like. But I am still the Parish secretary, and I still search the ancient scrolls and enjoy climbing hilltops to see ruined castles. And I love rolling down hillsides with you. Now, kiss me goodnight!"

"Rose, there is something I must tell you…"

"You feel guilty about Justine. I know. I heard the rumors. Not tonight, Ike. Tonight is about us."

CHAPTER 16
THE VICAR

Sunday morning, with a smiling Rose on his arm, Ike made his way up the aisle of Saint Peter and Saint Paul Church. As the centuries-old bells rang out their call to worship, Ike recalled his dreams, watching first Linda and then Rose, resplendent in their wedding gown, walking up the aisle. *Funny, I can't recall who walked Rose up the aisle in my dream. Was it Uncle Hugh, not her dad? In my dream, I couldn't see Arthur Osbourne. Was it telling me his stubbornness will keep him away? It must be just that. Does Rose know?*

They sat in the Osbourne family box. Sharon Markly and little six-year-old Penny and four-year-old Millie scrambled about the box in pretty sundresses and bonnets. "Where's Nigel?" Ike asked.

"He's here. You'll see," she said with a wink to Rose.

The bells went silent, and the organ began the processional. Ike could hear Nigel's clear baritone rise above all others. He turned to see Nigel in a white robe with a simple rope cincture around his waist, walking behind Hugh Osbourne. Rose whispered in Ike's ear, "He's our new cantor. Wait until he sings the Psalm and chants."

Sharon shed a few happy tears as she watched her husband. The girls stopped fidgeting and pointed to their daddy. "Look, mummy, papa is the singer!"

Ike bowed as the cross passed and sang along to the old hymn. *Good for him! He put all that hurt behind him and found a calling—leading in praise. I know we will never understand the hurts—war, death, and suffering we encounter, but I still ask, Why, Lord? Why is this man separated from his family, flying into danger? Never knowing if he will return. I just don't understand.*

Voices joined the hymn:

Courage, brother, do not stumble,
Though your path be dark as night,
There's a star to guide the humble,
Trust in God and do the right.
Let the road be rough and dreary,
And its end far out of sight,
Foot it bravely; strong or weary,
Trust in God, Trust in God,
Trust in God and do the right.

When it was time for the sermon, Hugh Osbourne walked to the pulpit. "Friends, we have all heard good news at last. Our boys were victorious in North Africa. Most of the Axis Africa army is in prisoner-of-war camps awaiting transport. I heard there are a quarter of a million prisoners. We have hope—hope the tide of war has turned. But speaking with many of you, I hear something else—fear. Fear that loved ones may not make it to the end that is coming into view. Ironic how increased hope goes hand in hand with increased fear. Now I need not remind you that our hope is eternal, that the victory is won in Jesus. But fear is natural. We do not live in heaven, and Christ's Kingdom is not of this world, so we fear. Jesus said, 'Love casts out fear.' However, there is a fear that we struggle to overcome, a sinful fear. A fear that grabs us, shakes us, and will not let go. Foolishly, we cling to our fear. The prophet Isaiah instructs us: 'You are not to fear what they fear and be in dread of it. It is the Lord of Hosts whom you should regard as holy and should be your fear, and he should be your dread.'"

Hugh paused, then smiled. "Skeptics do not understand the fear of God. It is not a servile fear. No. God loves us. Jesus proved that on the cross. Our fear of God is filial, a loving fear like the loving fear a child has for his parents. You say, Hugh, you're preaching platitudes. I'm struggling. What can I do?

Courage. We counter fear with courage. Courage is the father of all virtues. What is courage? Courage is taking action—bold action—in the face of adversity, fear, or uncertainty. We live in a time of great uncertainty and danger to ourselves, but even more so to our loved ones at war. In a sense, they learn courage; they act as they are trained and fight when ordered, despite their fears, despite having witnessed death and misery. We need their courage.

We can learn to practice courage in our daily lives. I

said courage is the father of all virtues. Our nation's beloved teacher, C.S. Lewis, recently said, '*Courage is not simply one of the virtues, but the form of every virtue at the testing point.*' Courage enables us to confront whatever challenges us, to push beyond our comfort zone, and to stand up for what we believe in. Where is honesty and integrity if not accompanied by hard consequences? Where is kindness if it does not stand against injustice? Must not every virtue, to be true, be tested by trial?"

Hugh paused and scanned his congregation. He closed his eyes for a moment, perhaps in prayer, before continuing. "We can't be truly kind without courage. Without courage, we can't be truly honest, faithful, or good. When Christ saves us, we become new creatures. He lives within us. The Holy Spirit whispers in our hearts, '*Fear not, for I am with you.*' Friends, make courage a habit. Do not succumb to fear; rather, let your courage lead you to stand against all fear. Courage is not just for warriors, nor is it the stuff of heroes, but it is a part of our daily walk. We can't go back. What comes will come. If we live courageously in the little things of life, honesty and kindness, humility and love, daily, it will strengthen with every step and will enable us to rise to bold action in times of peril."

At dinner, Nigel commented. "Hugh, what you said about courage—it makes sense for those away from the war and waiting, and I agree. I never before considered that courage underlies every virtue, but in the air, at least for me, it is different. When I'm flying a mission, I'm focused. I'm prepared, and most importantly, there is nowhere to run. I pity the infantry, ordered to advance under fire."

Sharon smiled and put her hand on Nigel's.

Hugh replied, "How is it different for our bomber crews? They fly into flak and enemy fighters and stay in formation."

Kut spoke up. "They have no choice. They are trapped and fight back. They are no different than a Royal Navy seaman hanging onto debris in the ocean as the sharks circle."

Ike replied, "They have faith. They are not alone. God loves them."

Kut nodded. "Perhaps. But I have no fear in battle. None. I am there to bring justice to my family and nation."

Ruby interrupted, "Darling, that is what worries, no frightens me. Your courage, your determination is—it's overbearing, beyond normal. I fear I will lose you. So, yes, I need courage."

Peggy Van Lier, feeling ever so much the stranger, looked up and said, "I thought I was the only one who does not sleep at night for worry and fear."

Rose piped in, "Dottie, my sister Dorothy, has tremendous courage going where she is sent. She told me before she left that prayer helps put her fears behind her. Then she said, 'The bravest people she knows are the women, and children, the farmers and doctors, postmen and policemen who rush to the parachutes of our airmen, not knowing if they will get them to safety before the Nazis arrive. And then they must hide them, clothe them, and feed them. They buy food without ration cards, not knowing whether a neighbor, acquaintance, or an Abwehr agent will turn them in. Half, she tells me, they know that half of all who help are arrested and sent to Nazi concentration camps. Bold action. That is taking bold action. So if I ever falter in my courage, I remember them and Dottie, and though my head worries, my heart says God is sovereign and I am His. Ike, what about you? Where do you find courage?"

"First, let me say, I fear, as Hugh preached and Ruby and Rose expressed, for others—for Dorothy, for my family, and for the pilots I send out in unarmed planes, and fears make me question every decision I make..."

Langley added, "Amen to that."

Ike continued, "But I have recovered my faith once lost, that God has saved me and has set before me an escape route from all fear and evil, and an escape even after death. But the greatest fear I suffered in this war was flying to Tunis on an unarmed transport attacked by Nazi night hunters. I was afraid because I had no control. I was sitting in the back watching. However, it occurs to me that control can bring a false sense of courage; in the end, we control very little. Not to say we should not act boldly, but act knowing that God knows our beginning and our end, not in a fatalistic sense but in simple, childlike faith."

Kut asked, "Tell me, my friend, how did you escape?"

"A little evasion and the two British Mosquito night

hunters on the tail of the Heinkel."

Nigel asked, "Algiers, Eisenhower's staff. Tell us about North Africa, and why you were promoted and sent back. Rumors that you upset the apple cart?"

Rose interjected, "And the sultry Berber woman and spy, Justine."

James Langley added, "Yes, and about the German POW you tried to protect."

Ike grinned. "All of it true—to an extent. I was transferred to AFHQ because the RECON in North Africa, well, frankly, wasn't doing the job. Deception—the Nazis and their Fascist friends were playing games—they created false targets which led to our bombers leaving only holes in the sand. Easy enough to straighten them out. A challenging terrain required some dangerous flying, but it paid off. I brought a good man back with me, Fred Engert, my XO. Eisenhower was happy, but I ran afoul of Elliott Roosevelt, FDR's second son and an Air Group RECON officer. He was out in Hollywood partying—womanizing as he bragged in the O Club. Seems he set his goal for the lowest lost planes. A spoiled child, he would complain to Eleanor, who, in turn, prodded FDR. Eisenhower had to placate the president while babysitting his problem child. Once my changes were in place, Roosevelt was free to resume his cowboy escapades with RECON functioning properly."

Langley nodded. "His so-called escapades in Africa are widely known in SOE for all daring and no payoff."

Rose jumped in. "And Justine?"

"Right. Justine Samson du Rochelle, a fascinating woman and devout Christian, was officially a housemaid in my quarters. Unknown to the staff, she was the owner of the apartment, the niece of the Bey of Tunis. She was married to a French diplomat who had a family shipping business. A protestant and colonial dissident. He is serving in the resistance. Justine—no word from the French on his whereabouts, was looking for him. She asked for my help. It seems I stumbled into internal French Intelligence and was told by Eisenhower to have no dealings with her. Too late for that. It all blew up on me when Justine and I followed a lead to the Priory of the Lady of the Atlas Mountains. Long story short, a German soldier was hiding there. I convinced the Prior to persuade the soldier to surrender to me. It turns out he was a seminarian who studied under Bonhoeffer at his Confessing Church seminary. A good Christian, forced to enlist when the Nazis found and closed them down. He was no Nazi. A victim, more than willing to fight for the allies. I let him write letters—sent on to his family. Justine and I were required to provide statements—we urged that he be treated well and noted his desire to fight. An honest desire, I am certain."

Ike sighed. "Our statements caught the attention of Intelligence and made their way to Eisenhower. The French were watching Justine. Her persistence, no doubt, but also her history with the Berber Liberation Movement. Simply put, I had to go. Eisenhower's aide, General Smith, agreed to my offer to train and update air RECON for Allied Forces.

Churchstanton was chosen as I requested to maintain ties with MI9. I convinced him that MI9 and SOE provided the best training and tactics laboratory for air RECON. It also gives the General a…"

Ike looked around at the civilians at the table. James gave him a quick shake of his head. Ike turned to Rose, saying, "Fearing Free French Intelligence, she left without saying goodbye. She left no note. I have no idea where she went."

Ike smiled at Hugh and finished. "And it brings me back to my friends."

Hugh raised a glass. "Hear, hear, welcome home, Ike!"

The celebration was joined by Penny and Millie, who returned with muddy shoes and dirt-stained knee socks. Little Millie held up a pail. "Strawberries! We found strawberries."

The older sister, Penny, turned to her mother. "I told Millie we shouldn't, but she didn't listen, so I had to stay with her and pick them too."

Hugh laughed. "Well, those are the two best pails of strawberries I've ever seen. You must take them home with you. Now, if you wash your hands, we can all have dessert—you do like strawberry pie?"

James Langley said, "And then, ladies, the gentlemen will leave you in the good company of the Reverend Hugh Osbourne. We should be no more than an hour or two."

Chapter 17
Making Plans

At the nearby Otterhead House, James Langley's field office, James asked Ike, "Your proposal is on the table. What do you need and when? And tell us how you plan to take down Abwehr chains?"

Ike stood and paced. "Thanks to you, Group Captain Hastings, work is moving quickly on the hangars and offices, and I have four planes now and more coming this week. Kut, you will get us in the pipeline of new equipment and upgrades. But Pilots, I need pilots. Requests have already been sent to RECON and Night Intruder squadrons, but no airman has been ordered in yet. James, you are my best hope for a fast start. You need to grease the skids."

James replied, "A quota, how many trainees can you handle at one time, and training duration. I need to know before I see Colonel Z."

"We talked about requiring all graduating RECON pilots to be sent to AFCRECON Training…"

"Right. Start with the graduating pilots. I can handle all that you can send. Let's start with thirty days for the training break-in period. That gives me time to shuffle them through flight, strategy, and technique—ground school. I'm sure we will need to adjust as we evaluate competency."

James cocked his head before replying. "That will be a hard sell. The uncertainty of time and curriculum. Yes, development. Your Command has a development mission, no different than aeroengineers or strategy. The key is results—ASAP. The timelines for doctrines are yours to develop. I can sell that."

"Good. Now, as to the pilots I'm looking for…"

Kut interrupted. "You are looking for lone wolves, pilots with an independent streak. Perhaps not the best fighter in terms of flying skills, especially for RECON, but hardworking, eager to learn, and bold. The best are the Night Intruder Pilots, with exceptional navigational and flying skills, and, of course, courage. I'll help you select them if need be. I know graduation is at the end of the week."

Langley replied, "Thanks, Kut. I may hold you to your offer. Now, what planes are they piloting?

Ike rattled off, "Spitfire, Mosquito, Hudson, Expeditor, and Lysander."

Hasting spoke, "Spitfire and Mosquito pilots are in great demand. The Expeditors and Hudson pilots typically score lower and are usually assigned to transport squadrons. Lysanders, well, they are all RECON. And you must remember, Ike, that these men are in training status. They must live to report to their squadrons—that is, within an 'acceptable' loss rate."

Kut grinned. "My credentials and the installation of new equipment require me to evaluate your program, especially training across the channel."

Ike smiled. "I'm sure we can find the right training scenario for you to participate—safety observer, of course."

Langley spoke, "Ike, you're telling me between Nigel's 545 and your green trainees that we can have two squadrons in the air, doubling the current force, but hardly the hundreds of missions you suggested."

"I'm suggesting we update our strategy. We'll need you to get Colonel Z onboard, a joint program with MI6 SOE on the ground in France. Every mission is an SOE-coordinated mission. We blitz the Jerries with false missions, many more than Operation Cobra. Every contact, participant, and Jerry responder is identified and recorded. We let Colonel Z's puzzle masters put together the suspects and their contacts until we have a solid line, not just of our friend Adder, but all traitors and their turned helpers and informants. Our radio operators are the weakest link. The easiest to capture and impersonate, every contact they make must be reported."

Langley replied, "A coordinator on the ground in France can minimize radio transmissions, as you say, the most vulnerable operatives, but the coordinator's contact with the radio operators would be even higher risk. And the puzzle masters, as you call them, must be at Aston House."

"Not Wilton Park?" Ike asked.

"Right. Colonel Crockatt may have to give

something to Colonel Z. But the good news is that Airiey Neave is currently in theatre. He continues to fly back and forth regularly. We must be careful not to expose him in this endeavor.:

"Of course, we'll update and share our mission reports as well as all RECON," Ike added.

Langley stood up. "Right. I'll take it to Colonel Z. There is much to be resolved. In the meantime, we train our pilots and get the program up and running. Now, some of us have ladies waiting, and goodbyes to offer. And Ike, congratulations to you and Rose on your engagement."

Langley paused and grinned, like Ike had never seen before. "I heartily thank you, Hastings, for putting this weekend together. Miss Van Leer confided in me this morning that she was pleased to meet you and your women. She felt a bond to each of them and felt included in my life. Yes, I think she is the one."

Hastings nodded and followed Langley out the door. Nigel noticed Ike waiting and said, "Is something bothering you, Ike?"

Ike slowly blew a deep breath between his closed lips before replying, "It's the engagement. Mine, not Langley's—so happy for them. No, Rose. She is so happy and open—we talked, promised—to get married after the war with our families' blessings..." Ike paused.

Nigel asked, "And? Has something happened that Rose isn't aware of?"

"I met her father in Gibraltar. Let's just say it did not go well."

"And you haven't told Rose. Ike, it's a conversation that you must have. Delay will only make it more difficult."

Hugh was in the garden with Penny and Millie when the others returned from Otterhead House. The women were laughing and chatting happily as the men and children came in. Hugh remarked, "I'm sorry to disturb your fun. I've heard quieter hen parties at the pub than you ladies. Maeve Hastings quipped, "Ah! The guilty have returned! We've got your numbers now—each and every one of you. Little boys in men's clothing."

Hastings replied, "Now Maeve…."

Ruby laughed. "My Kut is Czech, his English alone makes him an easy target. Brave in the cockpit but in the bedroom…"

Kut was beet red. "Ruby, honey, please stop."

Sharon smiled at Nigel. "What can I say. Nigel is sweet, thoughtful, and loving. Such a tender heart. But I remember the time when Penny was born…"

Nigel smiled. "Yes, but let's keep that between us."

Peggy Van Leer joined in, "James is shy. Always polite and sweet. But now I've seen another side of him." She beamed at James Langley— "And I love him all the more."

Ruby and Rose exclaimed simultaneously, "Ooo. Love!"

James blushed, "My dear, I must get you home. I'm anxious to hear more on the drive. Reverend Osbourne, Hastings, my friends, we bid you adieu."

Nigel followed. "Father Hugh, thank you for putting

up Sharon and the girls…"

"It was my pleasure. Sharon, you and the girls are welcome any time." Hugh squatted down and hugged the girls. "Don't forget your strawberries. When you come again, we'll see what other goodies are in the garden."

When all the goodbyes were said, Hugh went into the house and settled into his chair with a bourbon. Rose stood beside Ike, watching the sun settle over the hillside. She took his hand, leaned over, and kissed his cheek. "Something is bothering you. Is it Justine? You explained what happened. I trust you. What are you afraid to tell me? You should now know that you can trust me. Please. Ike, please, what's eating at you?"

Ike squeezed her hand. "It's our engagement—I, we agreed to wait—after the war and with the support of our families. I was surprised that you announced it so publicly. Why, I haven't even found a ring. What if—I said I didn't want to leave you with the stigma, the girl the Yank never came back for."

"Yes. However, the war is turning in our favor. I see a future for us. I want to savor our time together. I want to share my joy. I can handle the rumors because I live in joyful hope."

Ike shook his head. "I know, and the rumors don't deter me either." Ike sighed. "We agreed, family. I met your father at Gibraltar. He was…"

Rose stiffened; her feminine softness was gone. "Arthur Osburne is not family! Uncle Hugh, Dotty, and Charles—they're my family. Just what did that bitter, selfish, disgusting old man say? He doesn't approve? I would never ask for his blessing, or allow him in my house, let alone attend our wedding. Now, if there are any other reasons we should not be engaged, please tell me. I won't be led on. It's all or nothing with me."

Ike froze, Rose thawed. "I love you, Ike. It's bad enough that I must share you with the army. And I support what you do. It's important work, and I know you are honorable, and I would never try to take you away from doing your duty because it's your duty, and I love you all the more."

After their kiss, Rose walked with Ike to his car. Ike opened the door, turned to Rose, and said, "Does Hugh know?"

"Of course, he knows. He never speaks of Arthur in my presence."

After one more brief kiss, Ike drove off. *Poor Hugh, as if losing his wife and child was not enough. No wonder he drinks.*

Ike put down the report he was reading and rubbed his tired eyes. *What have I gotten myself into?* He glanced at the pile of unopened letters still waiting on his desk. *Lord, forgive me, but I'm tired and homesick. Just one, maybe two, and I'll get back to work.*

His thoughts were interrupted by a knock on the door. "Colonel Curtis, telegram."

Ike retrieved the telegram and tore it open.

With condolences, I regret to inform you that your father, Earl Curtis, is dead. Accident on the water. Young Earl is safe. You are executor of his estate and controlling owner of Point Defiance to Gig Harbor Ferry. More by mail.

Ole Olson

"Dead? Dad is dead. No. No, it can't be! An accident on the water? His whole life was the short ferry run from Gig Harbor to Point Defiance. An accident? How? Why, God? Why dad? He loved you, Lord. He loved you, just as Linda and Mom did. Why God? Why now?"

Ike did something he hadn't done since Linda died. He cried. He covered his face in his hands and sobbed. "I love you, Dad. I never told you, but I loved you so much. Why didn't I tell you when I had the chance? Please forgive me. I know I caused you and Mom a lot of pain and worry. I was, I was not the son you wanted me to be. The only time I remember making you happy was when I went forward in church. You never knew it was because I was bored and wanted to go home to mom's pot roast. I wasn't like Will, the perfect child. I know how I worried you. But Linda, you learned to love Linda, and I'm thankful for that. Yes, I'm thankful for that."

Ike sat up and grabbed the pile of letters. He found the most recent letter from home. He stared at his father's handwriting and imagined him sitting at his worn desk with pigeonhole boxes rising against the wall. Rather than tearing it open, he carefully chose his rarely used opener. This was no ordinary letter; it was a memorial to his dad.

Carefully, he pulled out two pages. Outside was the familiar thin airmail paper with a small, lined notebook page inside. *He never writes without including a letter from little Earl.*

Dear Son,

There was a gap in your letters, so I figure you have been transferred and pray that you are safe. I want you to know how proud I am of you. Growing up, you made choices that your mother and I found difficult to understand, yet you were never rebellious, just different. They were good choices. Integrity, you stood true. What a blessing Linda was; she brought you sunshine and gave you the support and encouragement that were slow in coming from me. And we're all so happy Rose has come into your life—can't wait to meet her. I regret never telling you how proud I am that you stood true to your values—a life-long integrity. We were worried about your faith, but you've shown me what a young man's walk with the Lord could be. I am so proud that you were honest, trustworthy, and loving in your actions, not just in your words. It was easy for Will to say what we wanted to hear, but it took courage to be honest yet loving. It made your mother and me love you all the more. A father's reward is a son to be proud of.

Love Dad

PS: Little Earl's letter is included. I finally agreed to go fishing with him on Ole's boat.

Ike stared at the letter, his hands shaking and his eyes tearing up. "Love you, Dad. I never knew how much you taught me. Never judge, only love."

When Ike was able to control his tears, he read the letter from little Earl.

Dear Papa

I pitched against Artondale. They were in first place, and we won! Coach said my curve is the best on the team, and my fastball is really strong. He bought us all ice cream at Findholm's. But that's not the best news, Grandpa Earl and Grandpa Ole are taking me fishing all the way up in the Orcas. Grandpa Ole has a secret spot for the best Salmon in the sound. I can't wait.

Dad, I know you are busy with fighting and everything, but can't you come home for a visit? I miss you.

Your son,

Earl

Ike closed his eyes and clutched the letters. When his heart stopped racing, he carefully folded them and returned them to the envelope. He picked up the pile and sorted them, putting letters from home on top. He read the second, smiling as reminders of happy moments at home refreshed his soul. He took time to savor each one before carefully returning them to their envelopes. All thoughts of the war and his planning ceased until a knock on the door before it opened.

Fred Engert stuck his head in, "Ike, we need you at the meeting. There are questions— decisions only you can make."

"Sorry, Fred. I lost track of the time. I'm coming now."

Chapter 18
One Step Back

One week after Ike's return to RAF Churchstanton, a staff car waited in front of Base Headquarters. Ike climbed in with Hastings and Nigel and was driven to Otterhead House. James Langley, Norman Crockatt, and Claude Dansey were waiting in the conference room. Langley ran the meeting.

"Gentlemen, we have a problem. This brief does not go beyond this group. All orders and instructions you give shall not identify this operation or its purpose. Airey Neave is missing in France. He was meeting only with our own people—MI9 and MI6 SOE agents and team leaders. The resistance and helper networks were not notified. Two days ago, he failed to check in. Ray Leblanc was the radio operator. An emergency extraction message was sent yesterday. Airey was a no-show

Nigel spoke up, "My pilot circled three times. No response to his code light. No nazi reception party was seen."

Ike asked, "And the photos? The infrareds?"

Nigel shook his head. "Nothing, no one there unless

under deep cover. Nothing at all like their past ambush emplacements."

Ike asked, "Any further attempts to contact Ray?"

"Of course, Ike, but no joy," Langley replied.

"We need to press ahead with trap…"

Claude Dansey interrupted. "No. We extract Airey…"

"And Ray," Ike added.

"Yes, Airey and Ray, and go to school on what happened before we begin what will likely be a lengthy process of elimination in trapping our traitors. We're sending trusted agents to sniff out what happened. The French Comet Lines leaders don't trust radios. They rely on couriers. One agent will offer the money and assistance they turned down in the past. We must convince them that a turned courier is far more dangerous. With all the recent arrests, Comet Line is down until it can be reorganized. A second agent will find and plan the extraction of Airey. We're sending a radio operator and a new radio. Now. This operation, call it, 'Lost Dog,' takes first priority. Marley, you will make the insertion. I want escorts. You'll be given coordinates on the taxiway. No ground lights. No help on the ground. Can you do it?"

"We'll be ready, just give us the time and the place."

Ike asked, "Yes, when? The risk requires careful planning. INTEL makes it clear that a drop near Paris is too risky. We must not use past drops or landing sites. I assume a landing is required after what happened to Ray—his damaged radio on his first parachute drop."

Ike paused momentarily. "One last question. Who was the last SOE agent contacted before Airey went missing?"

James Langley turned to Colonel Z, Dansey, who nodded. "It was Agent Goldenrod—yes, Dorothy Barkley. She reported their meeting, but she hasn't been heard from since."

O Lord, not again. "All the more reason for a new insertion site. Who can we trust?"

The room went silent. After what seemed an eternity, Colonel Z spoke. "No one in France at the moment. All the more reason to want to get our team in theatre ASAP."

Ike winced, "You can't just drop them in, hoping they will find a helper and depend on bed sheets and pennants to communicate. We know the Abwehr has penetrated all our primary escape lines, Comet, Oaktree, and Pat O'Leary. Let me work with Nigel on something new. What about Mithridate? Can Free French Intelligence be trusted?"

Colonel Z shook his head. Not in Paris. But our North African French friends have sent new agents into the south of France."

Ike smiled. "And MI6 coordination—can they get an agent to the Poitou-Charentes? Near the coast? There's a valley—the Sevre Niortaise River, and trains from La Rochelle, Niort, and Poitiers. We've rarely flown RECON below the Brittany Peninsula. Nigel and I can find a landing site. Give us a day, while you coordinate with the

Free French."

Claude Dansey turned to James Langley, who nodded. Dansey replied, "The Jerries have made recent arrests in Pontivy. La Rochelle is further south with trains to both Paris and the Spanish border. I like it."

Langley replied, "Things may be a little quieter outside La Rochelle. I prefer the station at Niort. This could lead to a new line in southwestern France. I'll leave the site selection to you and Nigel."

Ike asked, "Colonel Z, does this mean you're abandoning Oak Tree and the maritime evacuation plan?"

"Options. We must have options. We'll use whatever works."

Langley stood up. "Gentlemen. We have work to do," and left with Dansey.

Nigel and Ike stayed behind. "La Rochelle is over six hundred miles, Ike, and that is the direct overland route. Our pilot would have no reserve getting back."

"I know. I'm depending on your chief mechanic to rig something..."

Nigel slapped his shoulder with a smile. "That won't be necessary, though I appreciate your faith in my flight sergeant. You have a new Lysander MK III SCW with additional tanks installed, nearly doubling the range from 600 miles to 1150 miles. Do you have a landing site in mind?"

"Yes, we fly up the Sevre Niortaise river from its mouth above La Rochelle. The shallow river is made navigable by a series of canals and small lakes. I'm proposing a canal-side road for pickup by car and delivery to Niort."

"Canal side? Are you thinking of a water landing?"

Ike smiled. "Only if you can't find me a remote field along one of the canals. Easy to mark quickly at the sound of the plane and get out within minutes."

Nigel nodded. "Let me get some photos. We'll decide tomorrow."

It was late, and the June sun was low in the western sky when Ike left his office. *I should have called her. I lost track of time. She has an early train to London. I hope she didn't hold dinner for me.* Ike drove up the gravel drive to the handsome stone cottage, its local stone walls a warm honey tone in the late-day sun. Only Rose's bicycle leaned against the fence.

Ike knocked on the door. After a few moments, he opened the door just enough to poke his head in and call. "Rose? Rose, it's me. Ike. Are you there? Sorry, I'm so late."

"I'm up here, Ike, packing. Come up and carry my suitcase like the gentleman you are."

Ike climbed the stairs slowly. He had never ventured up to the bedrooms before. He found Rose standing in front of a suitcase lying open on the bed. She held a blue gown in her hands, staring at it. The red lace party dress was neatly folded inside alongside nylon stockings.

"Hello, Ike. I don't dare wear the same dress twice. Which do you prefer, this blue or the green on the bed?"

Ike mumbled, "They're both nice. You look beautiful

in everything you wear. Are they new?"

"Ruby helped me pick them out."

"They look expensive."

"They were, though far from being top of the line. Oh, you mean, where did I get the money?"

Ike shuffled, "Well, no. It's really none of my business."

Rose placed the blue satin dress in the suitcase. "I meant to tell you, I am working on a grant. A friend of Archbishop Campbell is paying me to research the archives. Dottie had Sir William; now I have a sponsor for my research. Don't worry, he is old enough to be my father, and as I said, a good Christian and friend of the archbishop."

Ike nodded unconsciously. *Why won't she say his name?* "How long will you be gone?"

"Probably four or five days. Don't worry, I'll be back by Sunday."

"I didn't know the archbishop was putting you up at Lambeth Palace. That is very generous."

"Not this time. He has a conference. I will be a guest of my sponsor at his Whitehall townhouse. We're having a small dinner party. And the next night, I am his guest for a night of games and cards at the Banqueting House, White Hall, with his friends from the House of Lords—of course, a gala would not be appropriate when so many are facing the hardships of war. They're very nice, civil, and each has a true sense of duty."

She's met them before! Should I ask Hugh? Would he

know? If he doesn't, would it only trouble him more? What's become of Rose? When did she become so flamboyant? She must know she turns men's heads. Is it love or only desire?

"Will Charles be there? Please give him my regards."

"Charles is too much like you, Ike. He gives all his time and focus on fighting the Nazis."

Ike's head was spinning. "It's late. I thought we could have supper at the York Inn. You always liked their simple pub fare."

"I'm tired. But I have some of the shepherd's pie that I made. I can warm it up."

Ike struggled to hide his trembling. "Thanks. No need to go through any trouble. You have an early start. Ring me up when you get back. I can't wait to hear all about it. I'll see myself out."

Rose was holding two belts, trying to decide between them, and Ike made his way downstairs and out the door. Rose looked up and called, "Ike! Where's my kiss?" Ike did not hear. He drove off to the York Inn for a late supper.

Ike struggled to fall asleep, his mind spinning with worries. *Dottie is off the reservation again, her second missed extraction. Did her luck run out? Is she with Airey, looking for a new helper network, or perhaps hiding in an abbey? A landing so close to La Rochelle—a significant risk. And a canal-side road, can there be an alternate route? Dottie is who knows where. And why do I think of Justine? Yes, Justine Samson de Rochelle, and she, too, is among the missing. But*

Bells in the Wilderness

Rose...Rose...

Ike's thoughts continued in a dream. Hidden inside thick blackout curtains, the great hall of the London Banqueting House, built by King James I three hundred years earlier, is lit by crystal and gold chandeliers, pouring warm light on Lords in formal uniforms and Ladies in exquisite gowns. A few card tables are set along the wall. There is a bar at the end of the room, and tables of hors d'oeuvres and flutes of champagne against another wall. A small orchestra was set up on the balcony, and it seemed everyone was dancing. Ike saw himself standing near the door, looking at his creased uniform. "I don't belong here. Rose has already danced with half a dozen men. She laughs as they peer down her dress, which leaves nothing to the imagination. Wait, she is looking at me, her eyebrows raised and a smirk on her face. She is enjoying this. She is punishing me.

A voice said, "Come, Ike, enough of this."

Ike turned. "Justine! I thought I would never see you again. You never said goodbye."

Justine kissed his cheek. She handed him a flute of champagne, raised her glass, and said, "To no more goodbyes."

Ike is flying a Lysander by the light of a full moon. Even with the city lights blacked out, he can make out the port of La Rochelle. He turns to the left, dropping low into the Sevre Niortaise River basin. Ike followed the river and canal system at 200 feet, looking for the light marking the landing site. Ike grips the stick as he maneuvers for the landing. He rolls to a stop near a small stake lorry. He follows

James Langley out and yells to Nigel in the co-pilot seat. "Take her home, Nigel, I'm tagging along on this one."

Nigel jumped into the pilot seat, turned the plane around, and stopped by the men loading the radio and gear into the truck. "Ike! What should I tell her?"

"I never said goodbye."

The French driver made his winding way through the dark of fields, forests, and a mountain pass. The car climbed a rutted one-lane dirt road and stopped at the bell tower of an abbey, the Priory of the Lady of Atlas.

CHAPTER 19
OPERATION LOST DOG

Ike woke in a sweat. His sheets and blanket were on the floor. He sat on the edge of the bed and wiped the sand from his crusted eyelids, moaned, stretched, and headed for the shower. The hot water eased his tensed muscles and warmed his cold soul. "Lord, what does it mean? Is it just my fears? Where is the hope, the joy that you promise?"

A simple morning prayer, a Jewish friend taught him, came to mind. *God gives. We receive. His mercy endures forever.* Ike chuckled. "Yes, Lord. Thank you. My hope is in your never-ending love and mercy. Teach me to cast my burdens on you and find joy in your love.

Ike dressed. It was 0530. *Enough time for a cup of coffee and a quick bite of breakfast before I go in. It's going to be a long day.* As he grabbed his hat and went through the door, he whispered, "God, keep Rose safe. Protect her, Lord. She is travelling on a new road to a different place, where different rules apply, and agendas are easily masked. And Lord be with young Earl, Ole, and Margaret. And Lord with my brother Will, who it seems I've lost touch with."

Major Fred Engert was an early riser. He was stacking folders of documents on Ike's desk. A green slip indicated a document to be signed. An orange slip indicated an urgent review, and a red-and-white cover indicated secret information.

Fred gave Ike a friendly, down-east, "Good morning, Ike, glad to see you could finally make it. The lobster pots are full this morning. Start from the top—most urgent and work your way down."

"And a good morning to you, matey. One question. When can we start training?"

"Pilots arrive Sunday. School bells ring at 0800, Monday."

Ike smiled. "Fred, give me an hour to get through this pile, and then I want you to ride shotgun with me this morning. I'm going to Otterhead House. I want to introduce you to the reason I dragged you away from 'Randy' Roosevelt. It could be a long day, so please delegate everything you need to complete today to the staff. They need to learn to be self-starters and be responsible for their duties."

"I'm on it. One hour."

At 0700, Fred accompanied Ike to Nigel's office, and they pored over the high-altitude RECON photographs of the Sevre Nortaise River valley. Nigel had circled three possible landing sites. Each is near a road along the canal with distinct navigational landmarks. Ike listened patiently as his friend laid out the pros and cons of each site. When he came to the third site, Nigel briefed, "Now, I had to include this site for its benefits. It is a wide, open field, out of sight from any farmhouse on the south side of the river. Roads out one-half mile in either direction. Trees shield the north side along the bank…"

Ike interrupted, "Sounds perfect. What's the drawback?"

"Finding it may be tough, even on a full moon. The only landmarks are a fallen tree in the river and a small shelter in a penned area with ten to fifteen sheep."

Ike nodded. With an infrared viewfinder and the full moon, I believe it's our best option. Who is your pilot? I want him to get with my camera expert on the latest in view finding."

"You're looking at him."

Ike smiled. "Now, let's talk aircraft. I figure at least two drop-offs, a radio kit, backpacks, you'll need a co-pilot, and my sergeant. Too hard a stretch for the Lysander, a Beech Expeditor has enough room, half the weight of a Hudson, and a shorter take-off capability. Their range is 1200 miles, more than sufficient even with an evasive offshore route. The Hudson has more room, a better configuration, and a range, but it runs slower. Winds over the channel will affect your decision if you want to avoid a cross-country flight. Your choice, Nigel."

Nigel stared at the map. The shortest air route to the landing site is 314 miles. Round-trip of 628 miles. I will go with the Expeditor, which is half the weight of the Hudson and is fitted with balloon wheels for soft ground.

Lighter is better on an unproven landing site."

Ike tapped the photograph. "We need to be together on this. You will need the escort of your best night hunter, a backup Expeditor in case of an emergency extraction, which we can use as a decoy on a parallel flight, and an overhead Mosquito equipped with radar and infrared capabilities. Something tells me James will be one of the agents dropped."

Ike stood up. "You ready? Let's go."

Fred Engert wasn't the only new face at the 0800 Operation Brief at Otterhead House. A young Canadian RAF Pilot Officer entered with James Langley and sat down beside him. When the room became silent, Langley stood and addressed the assembled officers. "Gentlemen, I need not tell you of the hard straits we find ourselves in. First Comet and now the Pat Line have been penetrated. Oak Tree has less than a fifty percent chance of getting off the ground. Hundreds of Belgian and French helpers, scores of agents have been arrested or gone to ground with the Abwehr in hot pursuit. But we do not have the luxury of backing off. We must fight on all the harder. We must keep our eyes on the prize, the men who return from Nazi occupation or prisons, steadfast in the determination to fight on. I've asked our comrade, Pilot Officer Gordon Carter, to tell you in his own words his experience finding his way home. And if his story fails to inspire you—shame—he brings great insight and intelligence into our final plans for Operation Lost Dog. Pilot Officer Carter."

The lanky young officer stood. "Thank you, Lieutenant Colonel Langley. I was shot down over Brittany on February 12. Within moments of my touch down, a French woman arrived and took my parachute and uniform—I took it upon myself to wear civies under my flight suit. She rushed me to a nearby farmhouse and immediately hid them. It was clear she knew what she was doing. I was born in Paris and speak the language fluently—no Canadian accent. Truth be told, I was raised in upstate New York. I didn't wait for America to join the Allied cause and rushed to enlist in the CRAF. I learned my helper was Janine Jouanjean. She lived with her older sister, Lucette, a courier in the Pat O'Leary Line."

Carter paused. "I was one of the lucky. I didn't need to wait for a guide and a column of fellow Allies, nor did I have to endure the long journey over the Pyrenees. Janine accompanied me by train to Carhaix, where she had arranged two bicycles. We pedaled to Soursin, where she bought a fishing boat, the Dak'h Mael—I learned later that our SOE agents deliver money to helpers and resistance alike. By the bravery of Janine, not yet twenty years old, and Lucette, and by the mercy of the Almighty God, I sailed North and arrived in England on April 9…. God bless you all. You're mission is the hope of every airman."

Carter sat down. The silence reflected the impact of his simple story. Langley stood and spoke. "What Mr. Carter did not tell you is that Janine and Lucette are sisters to Geo, Head of Mithridate in Paris. I know Geo. He's tough. He was an artillery officer in the French army. Nor does

Carter know that Geo was arrested and is likely on his way to a German concentration camp. I would bet my life that Georges Jouanjean would never betray his sisters. We also know that the Pat Line helpers arrested in Pontivy were guides taking our airman to Paris by train. Our best intelligence suggests the Jouanjean sisters were not among them. Why do I tell you this?"

Gordon Carter looked up, puzzled as to why he was here.

"Mister Carter is going to sit with RECON until he finds the house, near Carhaix, where he was hidden. Colonel Crockatt has agreed to connect our Marseille Mithridate friends with the survivors of the Pat O'Leary line via Lucette, the courier, and Janine, who will operate their safe house. With luck, we shall not need to ask neighbors and risk another betrayal. If we lose radio contact or Marseilles Mithridate fails to show, give us a week and find us there. Flying Officer Carter, you will prepare a note, in your hand, that I can present to Janine. Something she will recognize, since she will not be expecting me. Now, I'll hear your briefs."

With plans in place, Ike joined Nigel and Gordon Carter in reviewing both day and night images of Carhaix. Carter was quick to identify the location where he was shot down and the small field where he landed. A simple scan of nearby houses, and he pointed out the Jouanjean home. When Nigel pulled up an aerial view of Carhaix with street names, Carter was quick to respond. "Yes, this is their house. This is the road we biked out to Soursin on the coast.”

“I'll make a silk map of Carhaix. Likely, they'll enter by train. The house is not three streets from the station. The house number—not sure I can work that out,” replied Nigel.

“Thirty-four. I remember the house number is 34.” Said Carter.

Ike nodded. “The note. Make it short, something she will recognize, but nothing the Abwehr could use.”

Carter wrote in French:

Cherie,

How I long for another night with you as on the Dak'h Mael. Promise me you will love me as I will forever love you.

Yours smitten,
Gordon

Ike read the letter. *I suspect there is more truth in this note than in the name of the fishing boat he used to escape.* “Short and, I believe, sweet is the right word. I'll get it to Colonel Langley. You're welcome to sit in on tonight's mission at the OPS Room, Carter, if you wish. I'll drop you at the visiting officer's quarters.”

Carter blushed when he heard “sweet.”

“Thank you, Colonel. I'll take you up on your offer.”

At midnight, the Hawker Hurricane night hunter was the first to take off. An experienced pilot kept the airspace clear for the two unarmed Beech Expeditors that followed. They made for a known safe gap on the Normandy coast where they would take the shorter route to the landing site near Niort, avoiding cities and known Nazi air defense positions. The fast Mosquito RECON plane was last in the air and quickly passed the smaller Expeditors for forward eyes on the air and ground ahead.

Night Hawk, the Hurricane night fighter, was first to radio in. "Night Boss, Night Hawk One. Clear skies, full moon, and quiet seas. Strong shadows, over."

"Hear you load and clear, Night Hawk. Check in on the hour or in the event of enemy contact. Night Boss, out."

The squawk box in the OPS Room sounded, "Roger, one hour. Night Hawk out."

Gordon Carter sat calmly and listened. "Night Boss, Night Eagle, at the crossing. OPS Normal. Making my turn, clear to proceed, over"

Ike replied, "Roger, Night Eagle, safe to proceed. Report as necessary. Night Boss, out."

Carter asked quietly, "The Mosquito?"

Ike nodded.

"Then it's a go."

"Night Boss, Night Owl One, following on the right, over."

"Roger, Night Owl One, proceed on the right. Night

Owl Two, take the left. Good luck. Night Boss, out."

"Night Boss, Night Owl Two taking the left. Night Owl Two, out."

Ike found a chair in front of the OPS board and sat down. "Now we wait." *And pray. Oh Lord, bring them back safe. And please, Lord, keep James safe. He asked for a week; Lord, give him a long life to enjoy his grandchildren.*

A long, slow hour passed before the squawk box broke the silence. "Night Boss, this Night Eagle, the objective appears clear. Safe for approach, over."

Ike took the mike. "Night Eagle, this is Night Boss. What was your search altitude? Over."

There was no reply. Ike tried again, "Night Eagle, make a circle at 2000 feet and report. Over."

The squawk box returned to light static. Seconds passed."

"Night Eagle, Night Boss. Circle at 2000 feet, over."

"Night Boss, read you loud and clear, wait.... Night Boss, I've got company. First picked him up on radar, but now have visual. He's framed in the moon, not very clever. Appears to be Heinkel 219, likely radar-equipped, over."

"Night Eagle, Night Boss. Do not engage. Repeat, do not engage. He can't catch you. You've done your job. Bring her home at all speed. Over."

"Roger, Night Boss, outrun the Jerry and return to base. Night Eagle out."

"Night Owl One, Night Boss. Time to target. Over."

"Night Boss, Night Owl One. On approach. Have light in sight. Signaling 'King' received 'George.' Going in.

Night Owl One out."

"Night Hawk, Night Boss. Status, over."

"Night Boss, Night Hawk, I'm on the Heinkel. He may have firepower, but not much speed. Without the element of surprise…. hold one, Night Boss……"

"Night Owl Two, standby until Night Owl One is in the air and report. Over."

"Night Owl Two standing by. All quiet on site, friendlies only. Night Owl Two out."

"Night Boss, Night Hawk. Heinkel 209 in flames, going down approximately five miles west of Poitiers. Will resume cover for Night Owls. Over."

"Night Hawk, Night Owl Two, this is Night Owl One. I want two sets of eyes on the wreck. I want the kill confirmed. I'll make my way back to base. Night Boss, insertion successful. Coming home. Night Owl One out."

Ike sighed in a breath of relief. "Good work, all. Bring her home, Nigel. Night Hawk and Night Owl Two, don't linger near Poitiers. Confirm if you can and return to Base. Night Boss out."

Carter spoke softly. "This is the part that bomber crews dread. We let go our bombs, and mayhem ensues. Every Jerry on the ground and in the air now looking for us. The job is done, but the return is even more dangerous than the flight in. I'll never forget the silence, No chatter. The entire crew quietly praying, worrying, remembering family, and making promises to God."

Ike nodded. *Funny how Colonel Z and James himself put on stoic faces and declared success when the mission was complete, regardless of the cost. Good men, their wives and children—they don't see the success. They live with the pain. I know Jim well enough to see him on his way to a safe house or train station. His only thoughts are of the mission. I wonder, has Peggy changed him?*

Ike's thoughts were interrupted by the squawk box. "Night Boss, Night Owl Two. Kill confirmed. Burning wreckage photographed. Returning to barn. Night Owl Two, out."

"Roger Night Owl Two. Return to base. Night Boss out."

Nearly an hour of silence passed before the next report. "Night Boss, Night Hawk, and Night Owl Two have cleared the coast. Skies clear. Over."

"Roger, Night Hawk. Bring Night Owl Two along safely." Night Boss, out."

Ike waited five minutes before making his call. "Night Owl One, Night Owl One, Night Boss, over."

"Night Owl One, Night Owl One, Night Boss. Report, over,"

Radio static filled the quiet room.

The RECON Mosquito, Night Eagle, landed safely. Ike was back on the radio. "Night Owl One, Night Owl One, report status, over"

Again static.

Ike closed his eyes; his chest collapsed. *Please, Lord. Not Nigel. How will I face Sharon, Millie, and Penny? Three good men lost. Men with families.*

The Officer of the Watch sat alone in the OPS Room listening to the squelch coming from the squawk box.

CHAPTER 20
PRAYERS

The Bells of Saint Peter and Saint Paul rang on schedule Sunday morning, calling the faithful to worship. The change ringing was the same, but Ike did not hear the defiant joy and victory in their peal. This morning, his heart could only hear a mournful requiem. Tears welled in his eyes when he saw Sharon, Millie, and Penny sitting in the Osbourne family stall. *They came down. Yes, of course they did. Hugh is acquainted with grief—gifted with tender mercy —and Sharon will want to be near the base, waiting for news.*

Group Captain Hastings was there, his wife, Maeve, sat close beside Sharon, with an arm around the visibly shaken wife and mother. Ike, accustomed to sitting in the stall, quietly slipped in beside Hastings. When the bells finished their call, the organist began the processional hymn, 'O Worship the King.' Heads turned when Nigel's strong baritone voice was absent to lead them. Slowly, the congregation looked at their hymnals and began to sing:

Bells in the Wilderness

O worship the King all glorious above,
O gratefully sing his power and his love:
Our shield and defender, the Ancient of Days,
Pavilioned in splendor and girded with praise.

O tell of his might and sing of his grace.
Whose robe is the light, whose canopy space.
His chariots of wrath the deep thunderclouds form,
And dark is his path on the wings of the storm.

Your bountiful care, what tongue can recite?
It breathes in the air, it shines in the light.
It streams from the hills, it descends to the plain,
And sweetly distills in the wind and the rain.

Ike closed his eyes. The words were stirring in his heart. He knew the next verse. It welled up from inside him:

Frail children of dust, and feeble as frail,
In you do we trust, nor find you to fail.
Your mercies how tender, how firm to the end,
Our Maker, Defender, Redeemer, and Friend!

O Measureless Might, unchangeable Love,
Whom angels delight to worship above!
Your ransomed creation, with glory ablaze,
In true adoration, we'll sing to your praise!

Ike sniffled and blinked away a tear. A smile crept across his face. *It's true. God is greater, stronger—sovereign. He will never abandon us. Thank you, Lord, and thank you, Hugh, for giving us the words we need to hear.*

With the choir in their stall and altar candles lit, the Reverend Hugh Osbourne stepped forward for the welcoming. "Brothers and sisters, this is the day that the Lord has made; let us be glad and rejoice in it. I remind you of this, knowing that some of you here today do not feel like rejoicing. Our guests today include Sharon, Millie, and Penny, the wife and children of our beloved cantor, whose strong voice is missing in today's worship. Squadron Leader Nigel Marley and two of his comrades, Flight Lieutenant Russel Davis and American Master Sergeant Feinberg, are missing in action. They are only the latest of the congregation we will pray for and whose families we will comfort. Now, let us confess our sins against God and our neighbor."

When it came time for the Gospel reading, Hugh lifted his Bible high above his head and walked to the middle of the congregation and said, "A reading from the Gospel of John, chapter 15, beginning with verse 4: Abide in me and I in you. As the branch cannot bear fruit of itself, except it abide in the vine; no more can ye, except ye abide in me. I am the vine, ye are the branches: He that abideth in me, and I in Him, the same bringeth forth much fruit. For without me, ye can do nothing.... Herein is my Father glorified, that ye bear much fruit; so shall ye be my disciples. As the Father has loved me, so have I loved you:

continue ye in my love.... These things I have spoken unto you, that my joy might remain in you, and that your joy might be full. This is my command that ye love one another, as I have loved you."

Hugh silently walked to the pulpit. "Please be seated." When the room was silent, Hugh began his sermon. "Numb. So many of us are numb to the horrors of the day. We go on, working, eating, meeting, and trying hard to sleep. The daily BBC reports are simple facts, gruesome things that have happened to others. They no longer surprise us. We are numb to the grim news. We can bury our emotions, or so we think they are buried. And then the telegram comes to our door, and even the numbness that has calloused our emotions is overwhelmed. Why? Try as we do, we can't understand why. There is no why, there is only Jesus who proclaims with loving, open arms, '*Abide in me.*'"

In these three simple words, he tells us, do not be paralyzed by your fear, or grief, or failure to understand: abide in me. God cannot give peace outside of Himself. Our faith must remain steadfast against every challenge of emotion and circumstance of this broken world. Abide in me.

"We've learned much about pain. C. S. Lewis reminds us that pain insists on being attended to. God whispers to us in our pleasures, but shouts in our pain. It is his megaphone to rouse a deaf world: Abide in me.

"If you think God does not answer your prayers in grief, it's because God is the answer. Before his face, questions die away. What answer would suffice? Jesus gently calls us. Abide in me. Friends join Jesus in the upper room, with his closest disciples, where he speaks to each of us. Abide in me."

Ike was not alone as he kneeled before the altar for communion. The words, '*Abide in me*,' connected him through the elements and the Holy Spirit with Sharon, her beautiful children, fellow parishioners, all the saints, and with Jesus' disciples in the upper room, in the unity of the Father, the Son, and the Holy Spirit.

When the last parishioner left the rail and the elements returned to their sacred place, Hugh walked forward and sang. The choir did not join in. The congregation remained silent as he raised his bass voice in praise:

> *O God our help in ages past,*
> *Our hope for years to come.*
> *Our shelter from the stormy past,*
> *And our eternal home.*

> *The choir joined in as they began the recession.*
> *Under the shadow of Thy throne*
> *Thy saints have dwelt secure;*
> *Sufficient is Thine arm alone,*
> *And our defense is sure.*

The voices of the congregation rose, even as they bowed to the cross as it passed by them.

Bells in the Wilderness

Before the hills in order stood,
Or earth received her frame.
From everlasting Thou art God,
To endless years the same.

Now all heads were turned toward the narthex. The choir spread across the rear. Hearts refreshed, the good people of Churchstanton joyfully praised God:

A thousand years in Thy sight
Are like an evening gone
Short as the watch that ends the night
Before the rising sum.

Time, like an ever rolling stream,
Bears all its sons away.
They fly forgotten as a dream
Dies at the opening day.

The choir was silent. Hugh shouted out, "Brothers and sisters, join me in praise! Sing from the depths of your heart so that all in Churchstanton can hear you!

O God, our help in ages past,
Our hope for years to come,
Be Thou our guide while life shall last,
And our eternal home.

Hugh raised his hands. "Now receive the benediction. *'Now the God of Hope fill you with all joy and peace in believing, that ye may abound in hope, through the power of the Holy Ghost. Amen.'"*

A beaming Hugh greeted his parishioners as they left, many with beaming faces and eyes reddened by tears. Sharon was hugged more times than she could count before guiding Millie and Penny to Hugh.

Ike watched as Hugh hugged Sharon, then kneeled to greet Millie and Penny. "Go along, girls. Find something sweet in the garden for your mother."

When Sharon walked towards the vicarage, Hugh, the guest, smiled at Ike and asked, "How are you holding up? You know you're always welcome, with or without our Kentucky friend. I don't say that I can fully understand the burden of sending men and women into harm's way, but I am a good listener."

"Thanks, Hugh, I know that. I see you invited Sharon. I'm glad you did. Well, I have a war that will not wait for me…"

Hugh interrupted. "Stay for lunch. Sharon will be happy you did, and the girls, well, who can lift our hearts like children? Oh, and Rose, rang me up yesterday…"

Rose! She wasn't here. How did I not notice?

Hugh continued, "Yes, she has gone north with her friend. She mentioned a private library. She says not to worry, but she may be gone for a week or two."

Ike was shaken. "Hugh, has Rose ever told you who this friend is? Did she mention the party and the dinners she attended?"

"No, Ike. She keeps it all a mystery."

"Like the expensive clothes, gowns, and nylon stockings. She doesn't have the money to buy these things."

Hugh sighed. "Ike, I believe Rose loves you. But Rose has always had her secrets."

CHAPTER 21
IN COMMAND

Ike sat at his desk, a cup of coffee to his right and a schedule in front of him. The first day of his first training class, and now the schedule was unworkable. Ike knew this training course was unpopular with the squadrons who needed a steady stream of replacement pilots. Ike looked at the roster. Twelve sergeants direct from flight training and eight Pilot Officers from active squadrons. Not one man with more than six months of flying. He closed his eyes and thought: *Every one is a junior officer, each in their first assignment or anxious to get there. No doubt their Squadron Commanders have directed them to report back, looking for any excuse to curtail, if not cancel, this program. We planned a week of basic RECON techniques before putting them in the air. Now, with Feinberg, God bless his soul, MIA. Where do I start? I brief them after morning colors. What do I say?*

Ike's mind was blank. He rubbed his tired eyelids; they ground like sandpaper. In the absence of thought, Ike heard the song of a bird. He opened his eyes and watched a small brown and gray songbird. There, behind the back of the building office (designed to give him as much silence as possible), the small bird flittered between a small tree and the underbrush.   A little bird with a strong voice. He watched, engrossed by its exuberance and joy. *I guess that no one told him about the war. Not to say he's oblivious to other dangers. He must know he has many predators, storms, and misfortunes, yet he sings. Or is it she sings? How like Rose, my English songbird. She's aware but unbowed. But I worry, I don't understand this new Rose in luxury clothes, partying with nobles, and new secrets. She never said who her new benefactor is, what their relationship is, or even made a phone call to tell me where she is. Not even a word about her extending her stay. Stay? Where? With whom? Please, Rose, don't fly singing into the snare.*

Ike picked up his coffee and stared out the window. He knew what he had to do.

"Ten-hut!" Major Fred Engert shouted at Ike entered the hangar, where twenty young fliers jumped to attention and saluted. Ike returned their salute but did not say, 'At ease.' Instead, Ike silently walked before each man and asked, "Name, squadron assignment, and flight hours." After they answered, he would follow up with questions, "Why are you here?" or "What are your expectations? Is this a waste of your time, Pilot Officer? Where are you from? Would you rather be with your squadron? Do you think you're ready to face the Luftwaffe, or a sky full of flak? Did you learn anything about Jerry night fighters?"

Ike returned to the front of the rows of chairs in

front of several RECON planes and said, "At ease. Seats, gentlemen. You have each been given a notebook and a schedule. If you read it, I'm sure you have already decided what you expect. Well, you're wrong. Despite knowing how desperately ignorant you are of special RECON, my staff, Major Engert, and our instructors will have one day. To give you enough information to hopefully survive a cross-channel training mission."

Ike paused as murmurs crept through the class. Ike continued, "I'm glad you have found friends to grumble to. You'll need to learn to depend on each other to survive. Here's the ugly truth: your instructor in camera technology and operations, Master Sergeant Feinberg, is missing in action. Hollywood Feinberg is the best camera expert in the Allied Forces. He is missing, along with the Special Duty RECON Squadron 545 Commander Nigel Marley and Flight Officer Russell Davis, who are missing after a successful MI9 agent insertion. You heard me right, three of the best in the business MIA, yet MI9, score it a successful mission."

Ike paced in front of the silent class. "Men, your time here will not keep you from the war. General Eisenhower has not sent me here to teach RECON 101. Hell, no doubt you got a dollop of that in basic. My job is to teach you the very latest techniques and proven tactics. This command is a laboratory to put Allied RECON one step ahead of the Jerries. You may think the Nazis are evil and brutish, but never think they are stupid. They are smart and resilient, fiercely dedicated to their cause, and adaptable, always changing, always improving in tactics."

Ike looked into the eyes of the young men before him. "For the next month, you men belong to MI9 and SOE. When you leave here, you will be prepared to take what you've learned and experienced to your squadrons—if you survive. Major Engert and I will do our best to see you take the message to your squadrons, but you damn well better do your best. If anyone here would rather proceed directly to their assigned squadron, please see me. I'll sign your papers. But if you want action, if you want to fight the silent war, stick around, you can be one of the best. Major Engert is one of the best. You cross him, you've crossed me. Major, they're all yours."

Fred shouted. "Ten-hut!" as Ike left the room.

At lunch, Ike sat with his staff. "Give them as many of the basics as you can fit in this afternoon and tomorrow morning. This week, half and half. Friday night, navigating across the channel. Keep them short of France. I'm hoping a view of Normandy will give them the inspiration they need."

Fred nodded. "I need to see if they can fly in twos. We need the experienced pilots to lead their less skilled mates."

Fred paused. "Ike, any word on the MIA?"

Ike shook his head. "No, but day seven is coming up."

Fred replied, "I'm ready if you need me."

"I know you are. But right now, I need you with the trainees."

Ike returned to his office upbeat. If his pep talk

convinced not only his class, it buoyed his own spirits. He adjusted the revised training schedule and reviewed each trainee's records. Fred's question about the MIAs, Nigel, Feinberg, and Davis haunted him. He circled the date of Langley's extraction if no word is received in the meantime. *Could Nigel and the others also reach the extraction site? Are they alive? They must be, I can feel it. If alive, are they with the helpers? Lord, I pray it is so.*

Ike went through his in-box. A letter. Army Post Office. Ike picked it up. *From my brother, Will. He's never written me before. Happy enough to leave that to Dad.* He opened the letter and read:

Ike,

I'm sure you heard Dad died and left you the managing owner of the ferry. I don't know how you talked him into it. I did everything the old man wanted. Evidently, it wasn't enough. I saw the way Dad looked at you. He stared, but he was never angry. I could see that he cared. He never looked that way at me. Mom always liked what I did. She was so proud. But they never knew what I was thinking or how I really felt. Now you stole my reward, and I'm going to have what I deserve. The old man was lucky when the New Tacoma Narrows Bridge collapsed. It was sure to kill the ferry business.

Now, here's what you're going to do. You're going to buy

me out at my price, and with luck, you will recover the cost before a bridge is built over the Narrows after the war. It's going to happen, the steel, the concrete, the welders, and fitters are all here at the Navy yard. The state will move quickly while the resources are plentiful. Refuse this offer, and I will provide you with no help, nothing, while you're gone.

Decide quickly, big brother, before some Nazi gives you what you deserve. You are dead to me.

Pay up.

Will

Ike crumbled the letter and threw it in the trash. *Was I that bad a brother? I never thought Will wanted anything from me. He just gloated about Mom and Dad's approval. At school, we never talked—different friends, different interests. I thought he wanted it that way. First Dad's letter, now Will's. How could I be so blind? I'll deal with this later. I have twenty green pilots who need me.*

Ike turned to the twenty personnel files on his desk. He opened the first one and stared down at the page. The joyful sound of the small bird outside his window drew his attention. Another small bird replied, and a duet, an Ode of Joy, pierced his heart. Ike listened. He smiled, and he picked up the file. Sergeant Saunders, Edward, nineteen years old, Home, Easingwold, North Yorkshire. Education,

University of Durham, three terms, engineering. Entered service 1 March 1943. Next of kin, Ida Saunders, widow. He turned to the training page. Fight hours, 12.

Ike sighed. "So young. Left school and his mother to fight."

Then Ike did something he had never done before. He bowed his head and, with folded hands on the file, he prayed softly: "Dear God, You know young Edward. You've counted the hairs on his head. Before he was born, you knew him. You know his widowed mother, Ida. Father be his shield. Guard him and, please, Lord, send him home from this war safely to his mother. Grant him a long and blessed life. Amen."

Ike prayed over each man's file. When he finished, his peace was made stronger by a cheerful hymn sung by two tiny songbirds outside his window.

Ike's moment of peace was interrupted by a knock on his door. "Come through," he replied.

His aide opened the door, quickly poked his head into the room, and said, "Group Captain Hastings respectfully requests your immediate presence in his office. Word is there is news from Carhaix."

Hastings saw Ike enter the building. "Here, Ike. In the OPS Room. Close the door."

Hastings quickly briefed Ike. "Langley made Carhaix. The safe house remains secure. Lucette is carrying a message to Airey. Next contact 48 hours with number to be extracted and landing site."

Ike nodded. "Good. Any word concerning Nigel and

his crew?"

"No. Nothing,"

Ike replied, "This is my extraction. Don't try to talk me out of it."

Hastings smiled. "I know better than to try. I'm only your landlord. That's between you and Crockatt."

Two nights later, Ike took off in a Twin Beech Expeditor into broken clouds with a waning three-quarter moon. A Hawker Hurricane night hunter provided cover, and a second Expeditor would follow and wait off the coast of Brittany. Langley reported three people for extraction. Ike wanted a safety margin. Each radio transmission was getting shorter, evidence that the Abwehr was closing in on James. The skies over the channel were now overcast. Ike cast a worried look at his copilot and navigator. "Fifty percent chance, partly cloudy over the target. Elevation at the landing site is 1260 feet. We'll follow the Hyeres River between the mountain ranges. What could go wrong?"

"Just find us the mouth of the river, sir. We'll be good."

"Night Owl One, this is Night Hawk, over."

"Read you loud and clear, Night Hawk. This is Night Owl, over."

"Night Owl, small breaks in the ceiling over your slot. Find your slot and you're good to go, over."

"Roger, Night Hawk. Glad you have my back. Night Owl One, out."

"Night Hawk, out."

Night Owl Two, Night Owl One, did you copy last? Over."

"Night Owl One, Night Owl Two. Roger. Broken ceiling ahead. Operation is a go. Night Owl Two, out."

Night Owl One cruised at 150 knots towards the coast, looking for a river between the peaks of the Arree Mountains to the North and the Black Mountains to the south. The river valley rose steadily to a narrow plateau at 1200 feet near Carhaix. Ahead would be two strong flashlights pointed straight up to the sky, a mere 500 feet apart. The moon broke through the clouds five miles off the coast, showing a slight course adjustment to the right.

Ike piloted Night Owl One between the shadowy mountain ranges, gradually climbing with terrain holding about 300 feet above ground. The copilot spotted it first. "Major, two white lights five degrees to the left."

Ike replied, "Five degrees to the left. I have them in sight. Flash 'Victor.'"

"Aye, flashing Victor. Ground replying Uniform. Repeat Uniform safe to land."

At a fifty-foot altitude, Ike turned on his belly light and followed a hardened dirt road to a landing in a dark field. As the Expeditor came to a stop, Ike spun the small plane back into the wind for take-off. His prop just began feathering as a car pulled up. Ike recognized James Langley, who was followed by another man and…and a woman! "Dorothy! Thank God."

Before they could reach the plane, machine gun fire rang out as Night Hawk came in for a strafing run on a blacked-out vehicle speeding towards the Expeditor. The car kept driving, but a flashlight from the car signaled Uniform, Uniform, Uniform.

Night Hawk squawked, "Sighted signal Uniform, repeat Uniform, friend. I'm withholding fire. Will respond on your command."

"Roger, Night Hawk. Team armed will confirm friend."

The car drove forward. "Hold your fire, Squadron Leader Marley, Flight Lieutenant Davis, and Master Sergeant Feinberg. Request permission to extract."

Langley replied, "Well, get them on board, Nigel, we haven't all day." He then looked into the car, "Thank you, Janine. Where did you find this lot?"

"They were found on the edge of Carhaix just after Lucette drove off with you. I knew it was a risk, but it was better to get them out quickly. And James, please tell Gordon I will wait for him. Au revoir."

Ike radioed the OPS Room. "Night Boss, Night Owl One, over."

"Read you Night Owl One, over."

"Extracting six souls. Nigel's crew is coming along for the ride. Night Owl One, Out."

Ike yelled, "I hate to break up the party, but we need to leave—now!"

Nigel and his crew clambered aboard. Ray Labrosse, then James, helped a small woman climb aboard. Ike saw jet black hair coiled beneath a scarf. She looked up and flashed a smile of recognition. "Hello, Ike, it's me. Justine."

CHAPTER 22
OLD FRIENDS REUNION

Ike could see the black staff car waiting on the runway as he landed. One glance back at James, and he taxied to the car. As the single door opened, Ike said to Langley, "A quick word, James, before you leave."

The co-pilot stepped out of the cockpit, and Langley took his seat. Ike spoke softly. "I need a few minutes with the French woman, Justine."

Langley nodded. "Your landlady, the Berber noble woman, looking for her husband. Your friend? I thought she might be the same, but what were the odds? I'll give you ten minutes to escort her to the staff car."

Ike greeted Airey Neave as he deplaned, "Any word from Goldenrod, Airey? And Ray?"

"Safe, Ike, as far as I know. Went to cover when the Abwehr arrests went down. It had to be Cobra working off captured Comet Line helpers. We need to consider that Cobra is still alive—we eliminated the wrong man. I'll see that James keeps you informed. This crew pow-wow is about a potential new line south,"

Airey paused for a smile. "Thanks for the lift," and

jumped out.

James called out to the cabin. "Mademoiselle, please wait in the cabin. You will be escorted off. Thank you."

Ike gave Ray a firm handshake as he made his way out. "Welcome back, Ray."

Ray smiled. "You know me, Ike, here today, gone tomorrow. Putting out the word about Val. We'll find him."

Nigel Marley was the last in line. Ike stopped him. "You're return is the answer to many prayers. Sharon and the girls are staying with Hugh. Get some sleep, we'll talk in the morning."

"You coming personally confirms everything I've thought about you, Ike. Thanks,"

Ike quipped, "Hugh sang for you Sunday. The man's got a strong voice but be assured the whole parish will be glad their cantor is back."

With the passengers and crew off, Ike walked back and sat across from Justine. "I am so relieved you are safe. I feared never seeing you again. How did you end up on this airplane with British Military Intelligence?"

Justine brushed tears from her eyes. "I am so happy to see you, Ike. You understand—my only true friend. I will need your help. You are my angel sent from God. You will help, won't you?"

Ike stepped across and Hugged Justine. "Yes, yes, of course. We have only a few minutes before they take you away. Not prison, don't be afraid. Tell me what has happened?"

"I took a boat to our smuggling dock in the South of France and sought out the Resistance. They listened, interested in our smuggling operation. I asked about Jaques. I'm certain they confirmed his identity with Free French Intelligence. They told me he was sent north to Poitiers to penetrate the local Abwehr. They wanted me to wait—I feared it might be a trap from Algiers. When they needed someone to go north to re-establish contact after the arrests, I insisted. I convinced them I was expendable and had no knowledge of the Resistance in the south, so here I am?"

"What have you learned? It's been reported that the traitor we call Cobra, or Captain Jacques, has been eliminated. But the recent mass arrests could only have come from his inside information."

Justine's face contorted. "Captain Jacques? Do you think…?"

"No. Don't give up hope. I will ask James and Airey to send you back to me I will see you again. I promise. As you say, it's God's doing. Now, you must go."

Justine hugged Ike. "Yes, you are my guardian angel. Ike, one more thing. Take my father's rifle. I won't have it taken from me."

As Justine pulled the rifle case from her bag, Ike asked, "Is he still in prison? Your new friends can do something about that."

Ike gave her another hug and walked with her to the staff car. "James, this is one special lady, capable and fearless. Treat her right."

Langley nodded. "We know, Ike. Trust me."

Goodbyes said, the long hours and stress hit Ike's weariness hard. He returned to the plane for his flight gear and Justine's gun case. His co-pilot was waiting. "I'll put her to bed, skipper. Get some rest."

In his quarters, Ike dropped his depleted body into the chair at his desk. He put his head back, but too much adrenaline remained for him to sleep. Ike opened the gun case and pulled out the exquisite double-barreled hunting rifle. He left the double barrel in the case and lifted the burnished walnut stock and receiver. The engraved silver was polished bright. "Hmm. Not your typical hunting scene. Of course, that is not permitted of Muhammadans. Beautiful geometrical design."

Ike turned the stock over. "Only the best—the etchings are alike, yet different."

As he admired the detailed, perfect craftsmanship, Ike spotted a point in a swirl. He ran his finger from the point, following the etching. Amid the beautiful patterns, Ike followed a single line. Hidden in the design was a script. A word now jumped into view, "Jesus!" Soon, a simple phrase in French bore a strange proclamation for a Berber, "Jesus is Lord."

Ike sat dazed. "A son of the Bey of Tunis gifts his daughter with a rifle inscribed, Jesus is Lord?"

Ike turned the rifle over and searched for the dotted circle. Following another cursive line from the center, Ike read, "Yelli-n-Teydeml, Justine, my beloved gift…"

Ike looked up, "I've heard that phrase before.

Where? The thief, Ahmed, on the road—. His Amazigh name for Justine. Yes, she translated it—Daughter of Justice."

Ike read on from the French, "…grace and mercy from above and love from your father."

Ike nodded and murmured. "Hidden in plain sight. She said how precious this rifle was and how her father and grandmother watched her wedding from the sacristy. I wonder…We have to get him out of prison and to safety."

Smiling, Ike held the gun close and turned it over to see the underside of the etched trigger guard and overlapping stock attachment. Another beautiful etching, but no cursive. Its beauty was two miniature radiating suns at each end. Ike ran his fingers softly over them. He felt the gentleness of a father's love and the bright light of hope. "How deep is the sunshine!" he muttered. Before he put the prized gift away, Ike opened the small toolkit in the case. There, among the cleaning kit and screw drivers, was a key-like thumb screwdriver. Ike picked it up, "This looks like it fits the trigger guard extension."

Ike tried it gently against one of the suns. It fit snugly. He turned it gently. It stopped at half a turn. Not wanting to damage the silver, he tried the other sun. It, too, would turn only half a turn, but as it did, the small silver plate came loose.

Ike lifted the plate, which revealed a tube—a tube filled with jewels. "He loves her. He was forced to disavow her in front of the beys. But he could never disavow his love for their shared love of Christ. I need someplace safer than my quarters. Hugh. Hugh will hold it for her."

Ike awoke to the cheerful songs of the nearby nesting birds. "You're better than an alarm clock, my cheerful flying friends!"

After a brief meeting with his staff, Ike headed to Otterhead House for the mission debrief. He had just enough time to stop by the vicarage. Hugh came to the door. Ike could hear the happy chatter of the Marley family inside. "Come through, Ike. Join the celebration."

Ike poked his head in. "A joyful good morning to you all. Now, if I could borrow Nigel, I promise to get him back soon."

Nigel was already donning his hat and heading for the door. "Be home soon, dear."

Ike handed the gun case to Hugh. "Put this somewhere safe—it's Justine's most precious possession. Its value is more than sentimental."

Hugh nodded. "No need to say more."

Ike was out the door behind Marley. Hugh called out, "Ike, still no word from Rose."

Ike shrugged.

Ten minutes later, Ike and Nigel strode into the MI9 briefing room. Nigel's co-pilot was there, sitting next to Master Sergeant Feinberg and Ray Labrosse. Ike eyed a civilian—likely an agent, whom Ike did not recognize. Langley's staff milled about while his aide waited at the door. No sooner had Ike and Nigel found their seats than the call for attention rang out. Ike stood and watched

James Langley enter, followed by Airey Neave, Norman Crockatt, and Justine. *I expected she would be taken to Room 900 in London or Wilton Park, Beaconsfield. Where are they keeping her?*

The three MI9 leaders sat at the table. Justine was seated off to the side. Usually, Norman Crockatt sat silently and let James do the talking at Otterhead House. Today was different. Crockatt began, "Gentlemen," he turned to Justine, "Mademoiselle…our initial attempt to establish Oaktree line has failed. The penetration of the Comet Line helpers and failed communications necessitate changes. And since the Pat O'Leary line is also struggling to establish new leadership, we cannot rely on only one or even two lines. We need alternatives, options that can respond with agility when, by intelligence or betrayal, the Abwehr closes in."

Looking at Ray, Crockatt continued, "Ray understands the problem communicating with our gunboats. He will work that out with the Navy. With Val Williams captured, Ray will lead Oaktree from Brittany. A small beach near Plouha has been chosen for beach recovery. They will deliver our evacuees to Dartmouth. But Navy gunboats can approach only with little or no moonlight, and only small numbers can be carried in each extraction. We will still need what is left of the Comet Line and a rebuilt Pat Line from Paris.

Our first efforts have begun. Couriers have helped us find who's left of Pat Line leadership. We are supplying new radios to coordinate with MI9 and Mithridate in

Marseille. With North Africa won and the western med open, unpenetrated Marseille is now key. Our new agent, Justice, will be our link between the North and South of France. She brings not only local knowledge of Mediterranean extraction sites, but also boats, civilian North African crewed boats, like those so successfully crewed by Norwegians. I'll let Agent Justice speak for herself."

Justine stood. "My friends, we are not alone, we are not few, we are many! We are brave, we are right, and therefore we are strong! Many thousands, now free in North Africa, await the call to help. Many ships, most small and of shallow draft, whose pilots and captains know every secluded beach, dock, and inlet in the South of France, will come to our aid. Many Free French agents from North Africa are entering France. I tell you this to give you hope in the knowledge that there will be no end of helpers in France, no end to the resistance in France, and with the help of Almighty God, every bell in every church in France will one day soon chime joyously in an Allied victory!"

The room stood as the gathered shouted, "Hear, hear!"

A blushing Justine sat down. James Langley stood up and said, "Right. Now, Agent Justice will coordinate contacts with the Mediterranean extraction routes while Ray returns to Rennes and continues with Oaktree and Comet Line. We have agents in Paris reconstructing the Pat Line. In the meantime, the number of our men in safehouses continues to grow. I want you, Nigel, to put every Lysander to the task of bringing our men back, even if it's only three at a time. Rennes will coordinate extractions. Questions?"

Ike commented, "My Lysanders and pilots will be available for the Rennes airlift within a week."

Norman Crockatt stood and led Justine out of the room. Ike whispered to Langley, "A quick word, James—in private."

Ike followed James to his office and shut the door behind them. "You know, James, that Justine went to France to find her husband, an agent, and they both have ties to the Berber Liberation movement."

"Ike, we've done our homework. Yes, we know, and we know that the Free French authorities in Algeria want her back. They see her as leverage over her husband, even though they had him deny their marriage. Double agents are always a risk. But if she can deliver on escape routes by civilian boats less gun-shy than the Royal Navy, we want her."

"Where are you keeping her?"

"For now, she has a room upstairs. Norman is still de-briefing her."

"I can confirm her husband's shipping business included smuggling. The crews, mostly Berber, are not afraid to take risks for the right money. Her father-in-law is in prison and has other sons, likely serving somewhere. The ships are in Tunis. The French government hasn't yet released them. I'm sure Eisenhower's staff can make that happen…"

"Ike, you're telling me what we already know. So, unless you've anything else, I have a very busy schedule and so do you."

"You won't see those ships or crews unless her father, the son of the last Bey of Tunis, is released from prison. He must be brought safely, and his mother, the widow of the late bey, a French woman, is not safe in Tunis—they must be rescued."

"Are these Justine's demands or yours? Just what is your relationship with her?"

"My relationship with her is simply supporting a friend in need whenever possible. This is how we can give back to someone who can help hundreds. The releases can be arranged up the chain of Command. Extracting her grandmother. It's what we do."

James stared past Ike to the window. Nodding his head, he said, "All right, I'll do my best. But I make no promises. Is that all?"

"One last favor, allow me to take Justine to the vicarage. A room there with the Reverend Osbourne is a far better environment than being locked up here—it's a damn office building now, and you forget that Justine is an intelligent, educated, and sophisticated woman. But you probably don't know of her underlying faith. Hugh can help her in ways MI9 cannot."

"I can arrange that. Now, I will tell you something in confidence. We have reason to believe that Cobra is alive, and the dead man thought to be Cobra is her husband,

Jacques. We are trying to confirm what we believe. We want to keep this information from her for now. If it is Jacques, he was betrayed by a woman believed to be his wife. The question is which one of them was the Nazi?"

CHAPTER 23
ADAPT AND SURVIVE

Ike stopped to see Hugh on the way back to the base. Penny and Millie were playing in the garden. Nigel had also stopped by. He was upstairs talking to Sharon. Hugh opened the door to Ike and cheerfully said, "Welcome to Churchstanton Station and Hotel. May I help you with your bags, sir?"

Ike was surprised by his own smile, "Why, thank you, my good fellow. A fine lady will be checking in this evening. You may indeed help her, though she travels light—that is, if you will have a private room available?"

Hugh sighed, "Come through to my study. Ike. Justine, I assume?"

Ike followed Hugh into the study. Hugh reached for a bottle of bourbon. "Too early for a drink, Ike."

Ike stared with a furrowed brow. Hugh put the bottle back. "Yes, I suppose it is. The case you gave is safely hidden. Sit down and tell me what this is all about."

Ike sighed, "Not much I can tell you—secrets act and all that. Let's just say Justine joined the team to look for her husband. She was there when needed and provided help. And she offers more help. They have her in Otterhead House now. The place is all offices. Men everywhere, around the clock. They will need her until… well, she will be staying awhile. It's no place for a vulnerable woman."

Ike sighed deeply. "It's complicated. There is information they are withholding until confirmed. It could devastate her. They need to get it right. I am ordered to secrecy. Hugh, Justine is a fine woman. She's strong. She's smart. A woman of faith, but even Paul had Barnabus as an encourager. It's a gift you have. That's why I want you with her when she needs a good listener."

Ike looked up at the ceiling. "I know you have a full house. Perhaps Sharon and the kids could stay over in Osbourne Cottage? Give them some privacy with Nigel and…"

Hugh interrupted. "Say no more. This house is here to serve God and the parish. As for the Marleys, I fully agree. I am trying to convince them to stay for a while. But I've received some troubling news as well."

"Same risks, different family. Encourage her to stay for a while. She can't keep dragging those dear children back and forth. Wait. Rose. Is Rose not returning?"

Hugh shrugged.

Ike's staff and the students were gathered in the hangar classroom. "Men, you know what we've been training you for. I hope you've been paying attention. There have been some setbacks with our network of helpers in Belgium and France. Your comrades, fellow aviators, are waiting, their numbers growing, as the Abwehr has penetrated our escape lines, and our efforts for a new sea route have been derailed. Until MI9 agents can green-light these and new escape lines, the orders have been given for night extractions. With a limit of two to three being airlifted at a time, every Lysander and, with some luck, Expeditor and possibly our Hudsons, will be required. Before I continue, I'm offering any man here who is unwilling or unhappy with the mission of landing a plane in occupied territory, will be immediately transferred to your assigned squadron, with no adverse comment on your record..."

"Colonel, we know what we've signed on for."

"Colonel, what if we go down?"

Ike smiled. "Get in line. We'll know where to pick you up."

After the laughter, Ike summed up. "Right. Night navigation. You've been taught the concepts. Here are the facts. Most insertion/extraction missions are scheduled for maximum moonlight to aid in navigating by landmarks. That means you must know the landmarks to look for, their positions, and their orientation to other landmarks. Study the recon photos. Memorize the lines of position between them. If possible, see them at night before the mission. This requires constant RECON. Learn to work as a team. Trust your Night Fighter escort and the high-altitude RECON Mosquito above you. The weather over the channel rarely cooperates. Winds are strong and variable, and cloud cover is nearly constant. Your compass can help you find France, but you'll need to adjust your course by using landmarks.

Memorize the coast. Study the infrared photos for Nazi emplacements. You will be taught safe corridors. You must not use belly lights to find the ground from above 100 feet. Fifty is far better, and learn to look for vertical torches lighting the landing strip. A proper off-load/load turnaround is three minutes. None of this should be new to you. Prove to Major Engert and me that you can do it. From now on, night navigation and turnaround drills will be conducted every night until further notice. Questions?"

"Colonel, will we RECON the coast of France before our first mission?"

"Let's hope so,"

Ike turned to Fred. "Major Engert, RECON, photos the rest of the morning. Turnaround drills this afternoon. After chow, night navigation of the Dorset and Devon coastline. They're of little good to us if they can't find their way home."

Fred saluted. "Yes, sir! Squadron, Ten-hut!"

Ike left through the open hangar door.

Fred commanded. "Reconvene in five minutes. Dismissed."

Nigel Marley was seated at his desk when Ike tapped the door and stepped. "Is this a good time, Nigel?"

"I've always got time for you, Ike. Please, sit."

"I like what you've done with the place, Nigel. Real pictures on the wall."

"Thank Sharon, summer holiday pictures with the kids."

"I saw your car at the vicarage. Will Sharon and the children be staying for a while? It would give them a chance to recover and restore."

"You've been talking to Hugh. But yes, for a few days anyway. Ike, you didn't come here to ask about the family, Ike. What's really on your mind?"

"It's the airlifts. I'm preparing my students. Starting them on night navigation and turn-around drills. I need them ready. I'm proposing pairing my strongest night pilots to co-pilot your men. Fred and I can be on the roster, and if you've some hot co-pilots ready, they can step up in my planes as well. I want to take a maximum roster to Langley."

"Make sense to me, Ike. But I know you too well. You're holding something back."

Ike leaned forward. "Our Lysanders can only extract a maximum of three men at a time, while only flying with a near full or full moon. One or two flights a month won't do the job. I say we send every black bird we have on each of four nights a month."

"It will require coordination with every agent and helper we have in the region. With all the arrests, it's a risky plan, Ike."

"We're taking a risk in this blitz of airlifts. I want to up the reward. Not just more men lifted quickly, but a test of who we can trust—the trap we all want for Cobra—yes, James now believes we got the wrong man. Look, if we ever want to rebuild and increase our escape lines, we must root out the rot."

"Okay, Ike, let's lay it out—start with the communications..."

Langley listened intently as Ike laid out his plan. Ike was finishing his argument. "James, I know the risks are great, but this is not the time to withdraw and lick our wounds. When you've been knocked on your heels, it's time to stand boldly on your feet and become the aggressor. What is the pool of our men known to be hiding in western France? 200? 300? We can't bail them out two or three at a time. I say unstop the drain and let the pool run free."

Langley was never slow in making decisions, so Ike struggled to wait for him to speak. "Ike, your preparations for the airlift are spot on. Colonel Crockatt is expecting a two-stage operation: first, withdraw those we can as a reassurance of our commitment, and let MI6 SOE handle the counterespionage. I'll see if I can take your plan to SOE."

Ike sat back and let his tense muscles relax. "I've arranged for Justine to stay at the vicarage. This is no place for her to stay. What can I tell her about Jacques? She knows he came north to Poitiers, where a traitor betrayed so many. No doubt, she has heard of the hit on Cobra. She is far too intelligent to be kept in the dark."

"I know you're right. Ike. Crockatt wants time to confirm..."

"All the more reason to greenlight operation large net."

"Give me a couple of days. I'll tell her we're close to

confirming and that she may need to go to London in a couple of days. Take her shopping. She came with only the clothes on her back. Is there any woman who will say no to shopping before a trip to London?"

Langley picked up his phone. "Ask Agent Justine to join me in my office." He hung up the phone and said, "I'm doing this for you, Ike. We have fully vetted her. Betrayal is everywhere in France right now. Don't lose her. And most importantly, I expect you to share any new information you learn."

Ike nodded. "What about her relatives in prison? We sure could use another sea route."

"We're working on it."

Justine appeared outside the door next to a soldier. "Come through, Justice. I believe you know Colonel Curtis. He believes you would be more comfortable in a quiet home away from base. You've been through quite an ordeal. Take some time. Buy some clothes while we go through channels on the Mediterranean escape plan. We may yet need you in London."

Justine eyed Ike, who nodded his assurance. "Thank you. That is kind of you. I look forward to my return to France, where I am needed."

James watched from his window as Ike opened Justine's car door. He kept his concerns to himself.

Driving off, Justine snorted, "Did he really say, go shopping? Is that his understanding of women? Shopping in London is our greatest pastime?"

"Justine, never take James Langley as patronizing.

His comment may have been clumsy, but he is painfully aware of the courage and resourcefulness of women agents, many of whom served as radio operators —the most hazardous of all missions. He lives knowing few will return alive."

"You have my hunting rifle? Is it safe?"

"The rifle and all of its secrets are safely hidden away."

"You say, it's secrets?"

"Jesus is Lord, daughter of justice. A glittering gift for a beloved daughter."

"So, you found them. An escape line in dangerous times."

"Truly." Ike sniffed. "Justine, you need to burn those clothes."

"I am a strong woman!"

"Yes, a little too strong for polite company."

Justine laughed. "You are right. I do smell. A good shower, a clean shirt and pants and I will feel much better. What a blessing from God, when I saw you on the airplane. It is just as I said, He has joined us in a bond. I pray your Rose will not be upset. I promise I will never take you from her. Are we going to meet her? Please, not like this."

"Rose is away."

"Rose away? Where? I so much want to meet her before I must leave."

"I believe she is in London."

"You believe?"

"Rose has taken a temporary position as an

archivist. She is quite talented. She counts the Archbishop of Canterbury among her strongest supporters."

Justine studied Ike's face. "And you are not happy about this?"

Ike was slow to answer. "We are going to the vicarage. Rose's uncle, the Reverend Hugh Osburne has opened his home to you. He's a good man. A good listener, a man of God like Prior Michael."

"Yes, your good friend. You have spoken of him before."

Hugh came to the door when he heard Ike's car on the gravel. Ike opened Justine's door as Hugh approached. "Good afternoon, you must be Justine. Welcome. There is a shower upstairs if you wish to freshen up. I don't see a bag..."

Justine smiled. "Father Hugh, so Ike calls you. I am pleased to meet you, a great encourager of my friend, Ike Curtis. No. No bag. Could I trouble you for a clean shirt and a pair of pants until I can buy some clothes?"

"Of course, with two nieces always about my garden, there should be something we find."

Ike asked, "Have Sharon and the children left?"

"I convinced them to stay a while at the cottage."

"Great! Once Justine is dressed, I shall take her to meet Sharon. Together they should find something in the local shops."

The shops close early, even in the long sunshine following the summer solstice. Justine returned with two dresses, shirt blouses, and black pants, basics to get by until her return to France. English clothes arouse instant suspicion with the Abwehr.

Hugh welcomed her. "Madam Justine, you've traded your workhouse wardrobe for—well, shall I say how gracious you look. Not that you… I mean…"

Justine smiled. "Thank you, Father Hugh. I do feel much better. Can I repay you with dinner?"

"Please, come through. Ike is in the kitchen about to warm up leftover shepherd's pie. Nothing fancy, but hearty English fare."

"Ike is in the kitchen? No, that will never do." Justine marched to the kitchen. "Ike, please stop what you are doing. Bring a bowl and join me in the garden. I insist on making a real dinner."

She turned to Hugh standing behind her. "I saw chickens in the yard. Do you have eggs?"

"Yes, half a dozen or more."

"Onions? Root vegetables?"

"Of course."

"Cumin?"

"I believe so, in the spice drawer."

"It's too early for tomatoes. Come Ike. Bring scissors, or a knife."

Hugh stood and watched Ike and Justine walk to the garden. "I have some bottles of stewed tomatoes we put up last fall, if that helps."

"One should be enough."

They returned with fresh parsley, peas, radishes,

and peppers. Both men stood silently as Justine went to work dicing the onions. "God blessed us with five senses to enjoy His creation. He graciously gifted us in His image as creators. Every meal should be a creation to be enjoyed with thanksgiving and praise for His goodness."

Hugh bit down on his pipe. "Ike, care to join me in a drink?"

Ike stared as Justine worked. *How many times have I watched her cook? Truly an amazing woman.* "Maybe later, Hugh. There are some things that Justine and I must talk about. War things."

"In that case, I have a sermon to write."

Ike sat at the kitchen table. "The ships. The company belongs to Jacques' family; his father is in prison…"

"If you are going to stay, make yourself useful. Shell the peas and chop the parsley very fine. Jacques' family operates the company. They have silent partners. My father was prohibited from giving a dowry at my marriage. He bought a majority interest and distributed 30% to Jacques and me, 30% to me alone, and 20% to himself. Jacques' father was near bankruptcy. He was allowed twenty percent, and salaries for himself and Jacques' brother."

"If the company was nearly bankrupt, how could it continue?"

"Smuggling. There was never a profit to be made without smuggling. The Samsons were eager, but lacked the connections—the crews, the right officials to look the other way. The French Colonial Government barely tried to stop smuggling; it was a centuries-old custom. Who are the smugglers' customers? The colonial officers, the bourgeoisie, the beys, and their families. Open the tomatoes for me, then bring three eggs from the icebox."

"Langley intends to take you to London and lay out your plan. It's one thing to say you have a strong case for ownership—with your father's help, but he is also in prison. And where will you find the crews and the money to operate? The ships have been idle—they will need work. There are so many problems. Do you have any idea…"

"God will provide. And you, Ike. The moment I saw you in the airplane, I knew it could be done."

The aroma of cumin filled the kitchen as the tomato-based sauce simmered. Justine cracked the eggs, one by one, and let them poach in the savory stew. She sprinkled the parsley on top. "Please tell Father Hugh that dinner is ready."

"You are an artist, Justine! It looks and smells delicious. What is it?"

"Chakchouka. And put the bread on the table."

CHAPTER 24
ROOM 900

James Langley found Ike in the hangar, about to step into a Lysander with a trainee. "Ike!"

"How is that your timing is always perfect, James? I was just about to flight observe a turnaround exercise."

"Just a moment of your time. We're taking Agent Justice to Room 900 to make her case."

"We're, James?"

"She insists you come along. She doesn't have the greatest trust in MI9. Be in my office packed for two days, in one hour."

Ike climbed out. "Sorry, sergeant. You'll have to wait for the next instructor."

Ninety minutes later, Langley drove off from Otterhead House with Ike and Justine en route to Beaconsfield, Buckinghamshire, northwest of London. Room 900 was a leftover from the early days of MI9 in the Great Central Hotel in London. Colonel Norman Crockatt's MI9 was now run from a large country house, Wilton Park.

James broke the silence. "Ike tells me that you went

to France in search of your husband, an agent for Free French Intelligence. Our people work very closely with Mithridate in Paris as well as Marseilles. The Englishman, Airey Neave, has met many Mithridate agents. A good place to start would be an accurate description of—pardon, what is his name?"

Justine turned to Ike, who added. "I trust James Langley and Neave Airey with my life. They are good men."

"Jacques. Jacques Samson du Rochelle. He is forty-five years old, average height, 5 foot 9 inches, black hair with a little gray in his sideburns and above his ears. Blue eyes. What else can I say."

"Is he right or left-handed? What languages does he speak, and does he have any scars, tattoos, or distinguishing marks?"

"Right-handed, and as you ask, a gold tooth. He speaks French, English, a little Spanish, and German—a devout French protestant, he pursued work in the American Consulate and attended German Lutheran and Anglican churches."

"His gold tooth, do you remember which one?"

"Just a small one in front of his right eye tooth."

"Thank you, every detail you can remember helps."

Justine replied, "You can end the charade, Colonel Langly. I am no fool. You have already stated your contacts with Mithridate in both Marseille and Paris. No doubt you have a photograph and full reports on Jaques and me. You are holding back? Why?"

Langley kept driving.

"It's a valid question, James. Answer the lady."

Langly briefly looked over his shoulder before responding. "A man, believed to be a German agent in the Poitiers arrests, is dead. He was thought to be a Belgian traitor known as Captain Jacques. A man who met the description of Jacques Samson—even the gold tooth. Continued penetrations of our Comet Line suggested the dead man was not Captain Jacques but another man in league with the Abwehr. Mithridate in Marseille believes the dead man is indeed Jaques Samson. Samson was traveling with his wife, also an agent. We know one of them is in fact a Nazi."

Justine shot back. "Jacques dead? Of course he would meet with Abwehr; he is a double agent—it's his job. And I am his wife! This other woman, an agent, you say, may pass as her wife. What do you and Marseille say about her loyalty?"

Langley answered softly. "Now, that's the issue we need to confirm."

"So, this meeting is not about my offer of a new escape plan via the Mediterranean. I suppose I will risk boats and crew—our family livelihood to…for what? One trip to rescue a few allied pilots, while I determine if my dead husband was the traitor? Insane!"

"You did not mention the Free French government in Algiers looking for you. No, Justine, it is not your loyalty in question, and we cannot afford to turn down out of hand any offer to help our airmen escape. But one agent is dead for lack of confirmation. We must learn from our mistakes."

Justine sighed, "I don't know who I can trust anymore."

Langley replied, "That's the dilemma that keeps us all up at night."

Langley parked in front of the Great House. A sentry greeted them. "Colonel Langley and Colonel Curtis, Colonel Crockatt will see you now. I will escort Agent Justice to the check-in station and her quarters."

"Formalities, Justine. We will expect you at dinner." Langley said as he gave the car keys to the sentry who drove Justine around the back.

Ike looked up to see Norman Crockatt watching from his window. *Observation, one of Crockatt's fundamentals.* When James and Ike entered Crockatt's office, MI9 was bent over paperwork. *Deception. Appear not to observe. Never forget the fundamentals.* Crockatt looked up and said. "Ah, right. Finally, here. I arranged for Agent Justice to complete our check-in process: photographs, fingerprints, the security act briefing, and a signature. Tomorrow she will receive the most basic training—our way, not Mithridate's."

"Colonel, Justine expects a hearing on her Mediterranean Sea escape line, sir, she..."

Crockatt cut Ike off. "I know what she expects. Answers about Jacques Samson—finding her husband is why she was in France and why she came here."

"With respect, sir. That ship has sailed. She knows

he is dead. James was put to the test. Awaiting confirmation, wasn't it, James? She's no fool. Her plan can work. If anyone can make it work, it's Justine."

James added, "Ike's right. She can pull the plug, so to speak, from the pipeline. And we owe her some confirmation and respect."

Crockatt picked up his cigarette and took a drag. "Right. I'll give her the file after dinner. Now, sit down and tell what else you have observed about her."

The last rays of a setting sun reflected off the polished mahogany table as Crockatt, Langley, and Ike waited for Justine to join them in the private dining room. The sparkling chandelier, silver, crystal, and fine china, in the exquisitely paneled room flashed her mind to an aristocratic mode. She stood erect. Head up, smiling, and entered as a refined lady of stature despite the simple dress she wore. The three men stood, recognizing a woman of distinction. "Forgive me if I am late. So much to learn, I barely had time to dress."

Ike slid her chair in as she sat. "There is much to be said for England's great country houses. Tasteful, never gaudy."

Norman Crockatt replied, "Welcome, Madam Samson, or shall I call you Princess Justine?"

"Among so many friends, Justine."

"I am afraid the dinner fare will likely fall short of the setting."

A steward appeared and began serving soup. "First, I must congratulate you on joining our team. I know how tiresome the paperwork can be, but it has its purpose. From now on we can be more forthright in answering your questions. In fact, I have a file to give after dinner. It contains everything we know about Jacques and the events leading to his tragic death. You may read it tonight. I'm afraid it must stay with us once you leave."

After the soup, James asked, "Justine, I would like to hear what you have observed here in Wilton Park. Your comments on the staff, the check-in procedures, the grounds—first impressions from a different perspective."

Justine put down her spoon. "Wilton Park? In many ways, it puts one off guard. Security is very tight, but out of sight. The staff is courteous and professional—collegial—but able to observe and probe as one is processed. Yes, the atmosphere makes one more open and relaxed than one should be around strangers. Colonel Crockatt has eyes and ears everywhere. If you will permit me to bend the rules of etiquette, I propose a toast to your organization."

"Thank you, Madam Justine. We shall drink to your toast."

Glasses down, Justine spoke. "With your permission, Colonel Crockatt, I suggest we discuss going forward with the Mediterranean escape line. My time here is short, and many good men are stranded in France."

Norman smiled. "I suspect it is always business first with you. I would rather you enjoy this evening. Know the men into whose hands you put yourself. Two days. There is someone else you must meet. His support is critical."

That night, Justine absorbed the dossier on the man

accused of being the traitor, Cobra, and his betrayal by a female French double agent posing as his wife. Documents supplied by French Mithridate agents in Marseille included photographs and letters of introduction from North African Free French Intelligence. Identified as husband and wife, both were listed as trusted double agents. Jacques's embassy background and family business clearly identified him as her missing husband. The woman's biography was thin. Helena Coq, age 25, born in Algeria to a French father, a farmer, and his German wife. Her occupation: Journalist. Justine read and reread the reports and studied Helena's photograph until her body slid into a deep but troubled sleep.

Justine underwent two days of intensive training in coding, silent signaling, courier exchanges, and evasion and escape techniques. In the late afternoon, the chief training officer shook her hand and said, "You're a fast learner with quick wits, good instinct, and intuition—let them be your guide. Godspeed. Now, you have an hour to prepare for an interview with MI9, followed by dinner in the private dining room, where you will be given your orders."

When Justine entered Norman Crockatt's office, she was surprised to see Ike and another officer sitting on the side. "Agent Justice, welcome. I'm told that congratulations are in order. It seems whatever training our French Allies have provided has been more than surpassed by your natural abilities. Colonel Curtis, you know. My colleague leads MI6 section Z. You have likely heard of the Special Operations Directorate. You may address him as Colonel Z. I've asked him to listen to your proposal in the hope that his support might push this initiative over the hill, so to speak, with the government. Please begin."

Justine gathered her thoughts. "First, may I say, thank you, colonels, for this meeting. Simply put, I intend to establish a steady, reliable escape by sea line from the Mediterranean via a small fleet of coastal trading ships, crewed by experienced smugglers..."

Crockatt had been watching Colonel Z's face when he interrupted her. "You have control over a fleet of ships? Ready to go and crewed? How many evacuees per passage? How frequently can they sail? How many safe ports have you established in France? Where?"

"The ships are anchored in Tunis and Algiers. The Vichy France interned them. My family owns the controlling interest. I would need help in releasing my father and father-in-law from prison. They would see to repairing the ships after so long a time out of service..."

"And you have the capital to make them seaworthy again? Could this even be done quickly, competing with every other shipping company in North Africa chasing scarce labor and material?"

"A loan would certainly expedite the repairs."

"So you want the King to pay you upfront?"

"I said expedite, but I have resources. The capital can be found. I know the men who sailed these ships. They remain in North Africa. You ask what is most important? It is not money, the ships, the crews, or the extraction ports.

It is political support to move the new French government to release the men I need and to expedite the recovery of the ships. Words. The backing of influential men—leaders whose will cannot be denied."

Colonel Z tapped his pipe in the ashtray beside him. "Indeed, madam, influence, political influence, is dearer than money. Colonel Curtis tells me that you are your father's daughter. He has taught you well. The fact that you are here and we are having this discussion assures me you have the skill and drive to make things happen. I am willing to take this proposal forward and request the necessary message to the Free French in Algiers. We will not provide funds in advance, but we will offer a reward for each man delivered safely to Gibraltar. So, I ask for an estimate—not a promise—of how many men per transit. How many ships, ports, and transits per month?"

Justine considered her answer. "We can begin with two ships carrying 10 to 15 men on the first operation, increasing to five ships in different ports. Each ship makes two transits a week."

Colonel Z made mental calculations. "Such a schedule would go a long way in supporting a reconstituted Pat O'Leary Line and take pressure off of what's left of the Comet line and Oaktree if we can ever get the Navy to take it seriously. I will recommend your plan to my superiors. With such numbers, a reward of 100 pounds sterling for every man delivered safely to Gibraltar."

Justine smiled. "Colonel Z, no doubt you are a better soldier and spy than businessman. What is the cost of flying your aircraft, paying helpers and guides across the Pyrenees? As you say, the need is urgent, and more money must be spent to address it. And the crew must be paid well for such hazardous work. We do this to bring down the Nazis and Fascists, not for a profit but to meet the cost—300 pounds per man."

Colonel Z laughed. "You have practiced in the bazaars. 250 per living Allied man."

Justine smiled. "250 pounds." She paused. The smile drained away from her face. "We must act quickly. So many good men. So many traitors."

Norman Crockatt stood. "Right. Agent Justice, you will return to Otterhead House with Colonel Curtis and await instructions. Do not rest on your laurels. Use the time wisely to prepare. Become familiar with what our operatives there can teach you. Now, I suggest we proceed to dinner. I'm told you enjoyed big game hunting with your father. I'm sure we would all enjoy hearing more about your father, son of the Bey of Tunis and the family shipping business."

CHAPTER 25
DOUBTS AND DELAYS

Justine was silent, reflecting on the past days' events, as they drove back to Churchstanton. Ike asked softly, "You must be exhausted. I can't imagine absorbing so much in two days—like drinking from a fire hose. But you succeeded. They're taking your plan forward. You have some time to relax and recharge before things can move forward in North Africa."

Justine sighed and did not look up. "Then why do I feel the entire operation is on my shoulders. No support, no money, only payback if I succeed."

"The political support they can offer—all the way to the top—it can't be bought with money. Your father and stepfather will be released, your company will be back in family hands, and besides, you made the case that you have the contacts and the ability to make it happen. They trust you."

"Only with no risk to them. Perhaps, I was trying to convince myself as much as them. I feel isolated and alone."

"Justine, I'm on your side. I can help. This gets you

back in the country. No one will pursue Jacques' loyalty like you."

Ike paused to flash a smile her way. "Justine, where is that unwavering strength built on your faith?"

"That's just it, Ike, wavering."

Ike dropped Justine off at the vicarage. Hugh greeted them warmly. "Welcome back, I trust everything went well? Can you stay for a drink, Ike? A little refreshment after your long drive. The day's near gone anyway."

Ike smiled. "I think I'll take you up on that, Hugh. Justine just proved herself a persuasive ally to the cause."

Justine smiled at Hugh. "Thank you, Father Hugh. But I am very tired and will just retire to my room."

With Justine upstairs, Ike swirled his bourbon in the glass. "Hugh, Justine is having some doubts. She needs encouragement. Not today. Let her rest. She feels like the cat that bit onto a fox's tail, worried about what comes next. Justine is slyer than any fox she'll ever meet."

"Sounds like she found her Goliath but lost her David."

"Something like that. She's strong and determined. Just a little reassurance of where to place her faith."

Hugh sipped his whiskey. "You two are close…"

"Yes. I love her. We have a connection—spiritual and, well, she's like the sister I never had."

"Speaking of love, you missed Rose. She came and went. Said she hoped—assumed you would be here. She was very excited, even more animated than usual. She spoke in riddles, some big secret. She said she found the story she'd been looking for, and that it's now only a matter of confirming each fact. She was off again nearly as quickly as she came. I'm sorry, I don't know any more than that. I'm in the dark as much as you."

"Did she say where she was going?"

"She caught the train to London."

"Hugh, which Rose was it? The old Rose with hair tied back and simple pants and blouse, or the new Rose…"

Hugh nodded. "Hair styled and up, make-up, nylons, and a dress I could never afford for my Jane."

Ike sighed and swallowed his drink.

The next morning, Ike arrived at his office early, only to find Fred Engert busy updating training files. "Good morning, Fred. How are they doing?"

Fred grinned. "Down East, the day begins better than two hours before dawn; obviously, you west coasters prefer to sleep in."

"Now, Fred, I can't speak for fishermen; the Gig Harbor ferry's first run was 0630. Now, are they ready for an extraction?"

"They're motivated. They'll be ready. Every one of them has met or is near the turnaround time, and their navigating skills are coming along. They won't hold up the show; the weather, no, it's the weather that isn't cooperating. Winds and clouds on the French Coast. Low ceilings over the channel and coast crossings. If we miss the moon window, we'll have to send these men to their units before we can try again."

"The moon is waxing. It will be three-quarters full in

a couple of days. Then we have five nights until it wanes to three-quarters. Meteorology doesn't see a break."

Ike shot back. "Seems they never do until it comes. How much light are you giving the men in night flight visual returning from the channel?"

"We send them out timed to have them back over our shores ten minutes before full dawn or dusk. If they don't radio in within 10 minutes, we radio them to switch to guidance. They are becoming confident in reading the weather against their compass course."

"But can they read those course adjustments on new courses?"

"I'll get them going on that. But they will only get one crack at the French landing sites."

Ike slapped Fred's back. "We need some early rising down easter to chart that for us in advance. Work with Nigel—his best RECON and Night Fighter pilots. Map out wind directions and speed to as many landing sites as he's identified near Rennes. Chart the course corrections for the Lysanders and Expeditors. I want to know how the weather patterns change for the routes over and back. No landings! Only heading and sight ceilings."

"That should give them a fighting chance to crack through even in marginal conditions. Glad you're back, boss, maybe that little Gig Harbor ain't all landlubbers in dinghies."

Two days later, Ike briefed his students. "Men, tonight you will see the coast of France. You will navigate to your assigned corridor and take infrared photos of the coast. Do not tarry. Find the coast, photograph, and return. Is that clear? You are to make no corrections once you view the coast. If you encounter flak or Jerry night fighters, turn around and leave them to our Night Hawks. Don't depend on a radio beacon when you return. If you can't find your way home by this time, you're in the wrong business. I want radio confirmation at the coast, on your way back, and any enemy encounter. Questions?"

"None. Good. You won't be alone. The radar-equipped Mosquitos will precede you, and an experienced RECON pilot will fly lead to each corridor. Get some sleep. Be in the ready room at 0100. Good luck."

"Colonel, will we be armed?"

Ike smiled. "You've been issued a pistol. RECON airmen make do with that."

Ike could sense the adrenaline in the men as they filed out. Finally, a mission! Fred waited with Ike. "Boss, let me take this one. You have other lines in the water. The photos is great idea. It'll will show how good their navigation is. If we get even a half-open window, with training, I'm sure they'll be ready to slip through."

"Thanks, XO. I'll be in the OPS Room with Hastings and Marley tonight. I want a front row seat in coordinating the Mosquitos and Hurricanes. If this works, we will do a full dress rehearsal tomorrow over France. You'd better get some sleep, Fred. You've got quite the crowd to babysit."

"Schooling cod, Ike. Schooling cod."

After coordinating with Group Captain Hastings and

Nigel, Ike rang Otterhead House looking for James Langley. Still no word on when he would return. *Justine must be climbing the walls. I'll swing by Otterhead House and pick her up.*

Justine was more than willing for an early break. "Ike, have you heard anything?"

"No. Still nothing on Langley's return. How's the training going?"

"So much tactical procedure. Very different from Mithridate. I've noticed they keep internal SOE organization and field chains of command from me. I still don't feel trusted. Ike, if they send me in at all, mark my word, it will be alone."

Ike listened. "Justine, its all the betrayals. We depend on the resistance and our helpers. But with so many willing to help, the French cells are easily penetrated. Jacques' death is a perfect example. A new agent, a double agent there to penetrate the Abwehr, is betrayed, likely by the agent posing as his wife. Who can you trust?"

"Posing as his wife. No. She was his mistress, a woman with no morals. She used Jacques, and now she is in the bed of some Nazi."

Both were silent as they drove to the vicarage. "Please come in, Ike. I will make dinner. Hugh is good company. He is fond of you…"

"It's not just my bourbon?"

"No, and you must help me help him. He drinks far more than is good for him. Come in, please."

Hugh called out when he saw them enter. "Ike! I must have Justine to thank for this. Come in. Let me pour you a drink."

Justine scowled, "Father Hugh, only one drink tonight. Decide—now or after dinner."

Hugh took the bottle and two glasses, "While you cook, Justine. Just one. Sit down, Ike."

Out of earshot, Hugh confessed, "Justine believes bad habits, even old bad habits, can be broken. A wise woman, but as you say, struggling."

"The man or woman who denies they are struggling in these times is either deluding themselves or hiding behind, behind..."

"A bottle?"

"Alcohol, parties, fantasy, or some pointless diversion."

"You think Rose is chasing after a diversion from the war?"

"I don't know what or who Rose is pursuing. Since I returned from Africa, I'm not sure I know who Rose is anymore."

Justine stepped in and said, "Dinner is on the table."

Ike followed Hugh to the dining room, took one look, and said. "Looks like shepherd's pie but smells different, exotic."

Justine chuckled. "Spices. You English and Americans know so little of spice."

Hugh said grace, and with the "Amen," Picked up his fork and cut through the crusty top. "Don't tell Dottie, but Justine could teach her a few things about cooking."

Ike nodded as he took his first bite.

Hugh noticed Justine staring at her food. "Another hard day, Justine? You look like you have the weight of the world on your shoulders. You know who can and earnestly desires to take your burdens and give you peace."

"My head knows, Hugh, but my heart struggles."

"When you arrived, Ike compared you to David facing Goliath. But you are looking at Goliath as Saul and his army did, through human eyes—daunting and unbeatable. The opposite of David, who saw Goliath through God's eyes, a man blaspheming God. A man insignificant against almighty God."

"I am not David. I do not have his heart for God."

Hugh reached across the table and put his hand on hers. "Justine, you do. Remember God chose David. The least of his brothers. David himself wrote, 'According to your own heart, you brought all this greatness.' So, when we read that David was a man after God's own heart, in Hebrew, the same phrase as 'according to your own heart,' It was God who set His own heart upon David. David was given a new heart, filled with God's love, His choosing, His will, and His purpose."

Hugh gave Justine's hand a gentle squeeze. "Justine, God has chosen you. Everyone who puts their faith in Jesus is called by God. His calling is one of love. He gives every child he calls a new heart; the same heart he gave David. It's a heart that finds peace and joy despite the world's brokenness. The heart he gives is one of strength to face any Goliath, any evil, knowing His own heart is given in love and victory over every trial and tragedy. Who is greater than God? Look for that mustard seed of faith. It's there. Nourish it and it will grow. Do you doubt that what you do is the will of God? Is it done in His love? Then trust Him, remembering, according to your heart, God, bring forth your will."

Justine sniffled. "Thank you, Hugh. Thank you. Now eat before it gets cold."

Ike silently said amen, smiled, and ate.

The Operations Room was dark except for the light on the board. Six Lysanders and four Expeditors, in three tight formations, navigated their way to the three safe corridors on the French Coast. The three Mosquitos that preceded them reported eighty percent cloud coverage over the coast, with a ceiling of 500 feet. Three Hawker Hurricanes flew high cover over the small, unarmed RECON planes.

Fred Engert's voice crackled over the squawk box. "Night Owl One, five miles out, going down to 500 feet."

"Roger, Night Owl One, going to 500. Report arrival."

A few minutes later, Nigel reported. "Night Owl Two. 500 feet broken clouds. Going to 400. Will report on arrival."

Roger, Night Owl Two, 400 feet, out."

"Night Owl three, 450 feet, broken clouds. Will report arrival."

"Night Hawk One, No sign of enemy. The Jerries

must be in bed."

Night Hawks Two and Three also reported no imminent air threat. Followed immediately by Night Owls One and Two reporting arrival, no shore lights, returning to base. Five minutes passed. "Night Owl Three, Night Owl Three, report."

The squawk box crackled with a broken reply. "Night…three,,, cloud ….200….barn…"

"Night Owl Three, repeat. Night Owl Three repeat."

The silence was broken with a clear voice on the radio. "Night Barn, this is Night Eagle Three. Two Jerries en route to intercept Night Owl Three. Repeat, send help to Night Owl Three.

"This is Night Hawk Three, intercepting Jerries."

"Night Hawk Three, Night Hawk Two, right behind you."

"Flak! Night Owl Three, drawing coastal artillery fire. Looking for Jerries."

"Night Owl Three, Night Barn. Is Night Owl Three in sight? Report visual on Night Owl Three. Over."

"This is Night Hawk three, engaging Jerries, out."

"I'm with you, Night Hawk Three, I'm coming behind the follow-on Jerry."

The OPS Room team sat in silence, waiting.

The squawk box nearly whispered, "Night Barn, Night Barn, Night Owl Three in cloud cover coming home."

Again silence. Three minutes later, "Splash one Jerry, correction, splash two Jerries. Night Hawk Three Out."

"Night Eagle One, Two and Three, return to base, over."

"Roger, Night Eagle One, returning to base. Out."

"Night Eagle Two, returning to base, Out"

Night Eagle Three, returning to base. Out."

Ike stood up and said to the Ops Officer. "I want the photos on my desk first thing in the morning, and all pilots in the briefing room at 1000," and walked to his quarters.

CHAPTER 26
RETURN TO ACTION

The last pilot was finishing his oral report when James Langley walked in and sat down. Ike stood. "We'll start with corridor one." A detailed daylight photograph appeared on the screen. "Sgt. Haskins, come forward and point out where you crossed the coast." The young pilot hesitantly pointed. Ike nodded. "Do all of the corridor one pilots and co-pilots agree?"

A low buzz came from the seated men. One spoke out. "Colonel, the photo you're showing is daylight. We had on-again, off-again moonlight. We saw it only once. How can we be sure?"

Ike replied, "Corridor two, can you do any better?" Corridor two's coastline appeared on the screen.

A corridor two pilot replied, "Colonel, I, we agree with the corridor one pilots. The sea was black, and the coast not much different."

Ike asked, "Corridor three pilots," their daylight photo appeared on the screen. "Take a quick look, now look at a night photo, any better?"

"Sir, it's pretty much what we saw. Pretty hard to

identify any landmarks."

Ike flashed a new infrared photograph on the screen. "This is your RECON photo of the coastline." Ike projected the daylight photo above the infrared. "As you can see, you were two miles south. Good navigating if you can find your landmarks. Corridor one had the closest, one-half mile, corridor two had one plane within two-thirds of a mile. Everything considered, you applied wind and speed very well. You can study the photos after this briefing. Now, takeaways?"

"Colonel, we have to know landmarks to look for above and below the corridor route."

"And?"

"Sir, we must be able to follow landmarks all the way to the target."

"And?"

Master Sergeant Feinberg spoke up. "Were you all asleep in Camera techniques? Know your equipment. Each plane is equipped with a handheld infrared in addition to the installed beast in the belly. What? Cat got your tongue?"

A quavering voice spoke slowly, "We can use the infrared handheld viewfinder at the coast and along the corridor to the target?"

"Very good, sergeant. And it never occurred to a single one of you last night?"

"With respect, we depended on the corridor leaders and our experienced pilots."

Ike responded, "Thank you, Master Sergeant. Men

remember that you have been trained to think and act on your own. We provided experienced pilots to evaluate and prevent any unsafe situations. I want better results tonight —right to the target. You will have the same leaders; they are there as a resource. You call it, they'll advise."

Langley waited until Ike was alone. "Are you sure they'll be ready before we lose the moon?"

"They'll be ready. Where have you been all week?"

"Selling the Mediterranean Sea escape Line. The requested diplomatic support is underway. Agent Justice will be sent to Algiers within the week."

"Justine will be glad to get back; waiting has not been her strong suit."

"I'm glad she hasn't lost her nerve. One more thing. You're briefing Eisenhower on the operation. Seems he wants a report on your progress here."

"How much time do I have?"

"Five days, maybe six. If you want in on the air extraction, you'd better make it happen soon."

"And my plan, Snake Charmer, will I get a crack at trapping Cobra, Adder, and any other fascist reptile?"

"Let's get some airmen out first. Airey is taking your plan to the resistance. We'll discuss it when you get back."

The next night, Ike sat in the Group OPS Room listening to the reports. He smiled as the three team leaders reported successful crossings of the three French Coast corridors. He listened as one by one the nine Night Owls found their landmarks and vectored off to photograph their assigned fields. His chest swelled. *Good. The radio contact between the Night Hawk leaders and the three Night Eagles and three Night Hawks is disciplined and professional. These guys are ready! They accomplished, in three weeks of training, skills that often take many months to attain.*

When the last plane reported clear of the coast, Ike told the watch officer, "Have all crews report to the briefing theatre upon arrival."

"Yes, sir."

"I'll be in my office. Call me when they're assembled. I'm not waiting for tomorrow. And, yes, get the film processed ASAP."

Ninety minutes later, Ike entered the Briefing Theatre. He strode quickly to the podium, anxious to speak, he called out, "Ten Hut!" The room became silent. "At ease, gentlemen. But before you sit down, give yourselves a round of applause. You've proved you can find your target. And in two days, you get your final exam—extracting pilots and airmen who went before you. Are you ready?!"

"Aye! We're ready, sir!"

"Did all of you hear what I said? I want to hear it like you mean it. Are you ready?!"

The theatre erupted. "Aye, sir. We're Ready! We're Ready! We're ready."

Ike smiled. "That's more like it. I knew you had it in you. Take a seat."

When the room was quiet, he continued. "Tonight,

no one was expecting you. Pray that it's only friendlies next time. You men are to fill your planes. You've been shown how to squeeze men inside. Now, something you did not know. You're being sent in because traitors have compromised our existing escape lines and have torpedoed our operation for a new sea route. An identified traitor is dead. Unfortunately, he was the wrong man. My point is that he's still out there, as are others. You will be given signals for a friend and a wave-off. Don't hesitate if you see the waive off. Return immediately—report, report, report. You have radios, use them. You've drilled on turnaround time. Remember, a Jerry welcoming party may show up unexpectedly. Load up and get out. Now, get plenty of sleep. Dinner. Report to the hangar at 2000 to review your photographs. Study them. Learn from them. Any questions?"

"Colonel, the Jerry Welcoming party, what are the odds?"

Ike nodded. "You're taught to beat the odds. But considering coast watchers, ground sighting alerts, and Nazi collaborators, I would hope they're less than one in three that Jerrys will be waiting. But I believe you men signed up, not worried about the odds, but focused on doing your part. I fully expect every one of you to return. You won't be alone. You'll have Night Eagle top cover and ace Night Hawks looking after you. All the same, be careful and be quick about it on the ground. 1600 tomorrow. Good night."

Ike was asleep when the knock came on his door at

1100. "Colonel Curtis, Colonel Langley has asked me to drive you to Otterhead House ASAP. He insists the matter is of some urgency. The Colonel said to pack a bag."

Ike wiped the sand from his eyes and headed to the shower. "Give me 15 minutes, Lieutenant. You'll find a bag in the closet and clean uniforms. Leave one for me and pack two others."

Ten minutes later, Ike, showered, shaved, and dressed, added a few personal items to the bag. He scratched his head. "Any ideas where I'm going, son?"

"No, sir, but there is a transport flight to Algiers today."

"Figures." Ike grabbed a flight suit and field dress. *These may come in handy. It's got to be Justine's trip back. Just like James to spring a surprise.* "Let's go," Ike barked. The young intelligence officer grabbed Ike's bag and led him to the staff car.

Ike marched into Langley's office. "James, what the hell is this all about? I'm supposed to brief 15 flight crews on the most complex air extraction ever attempted. I've been planning my operation for weeks…."

James interrupted, "Pipe down, Ike. Take a seat. First, it's not your operation; it's an MI9 operation. You're not a one-man show. Ike, you're good, tops, at what you do. You told me these men are ready. You've boasted about the abilities of Nigel Marley and Fred Engert. You told me you trust them with your life. Well, unless you've been blowing smoke, they can handle it. If you want a chance to send them off, stop complaining and listen."

Ike slowly exhaled his frustration. "Right. What's this all about?"

"Justine is going back tonight. Operation Privateer is greenlighted. The prison releases have been arranged. Her father and father-in-law will meet her in Algiers to plan with an MI9 Agent. Expect Airey to be there. They want your expertise as well…"

"I thought we were all replaceable."

"General Smith made it clear that Eisenhower wants you. You meet with him tomorrow."

"Eisenhower?"

"Ike, I don't make this stuff up. Claude Dansey and Norman Crockatt put together a report for General Eisenhower, with letters from the PM. Very private—back door."

"What time is the flight?"

"1600 in front of Group Headquarters."

"What about Justine?"

"She'll be there,"

"Where's that driver?"

James laughed. "He's waiting. Good luck, Ike."

Ike instructed the driver to stop at the vicarage. "I won't be long. I need a word with Agent Justice."

Ike found Hugh in his study. He could hear soft footsteps from upstairs. *That would be Justine, packing.* "Hugh, just wanted to let you know I'm headed out for a few days in case Rose asks. Justine will be gone for some time. You might want to pray with her before she leaves. It's, well, you know, Dottie and Charles. It's dangerous."

"She told me as much when she came in."

Justine heard Ike come in and bounded down the stairs. "Ike, you heard."

"Yes. It seems we'll be traveling together. I have a briefing to give. You might want to get some sleep. It's going to be an all-nighter."

"I know. I'm treating Hugh to dinner before I go. You're welcome to join us. We plan a quiet afternoon—time to visit—reflect with my good and kind-hearted friend." Justine smiled sweetly at Hugh."

"I'll try, but I have one last duty before we go. See you at 4 o'clock. You know your way to the Group Headquarters?"

Justine laughed. "I'm sure the driver will get me there in time."

Ike paused. "I'll leave you to your landlord-to-landlord chat." He caught the gleam in Hugh's eyes and the soft smile on his face, nodded, and saw himself out.

The driver dropped Ike off at the Officers' Mess, where Ike had his first and likely last meal of the day. He paused over his coffee to let the day's events sink in, then hurried across the base to his hangar office. Fred was in the ready room, reviewing the latest RECON photos and marking the landmarks and fields. Ike looked up at the clock, nearly three. "Glad to see you're already at it, Fred."

"If you don't update your wind and weather, your nets come up empty."

Fred looked up. "Why the bag, boss?"

"You're on your own on this one, Fred. I'll be gone before the boys show up."

"Whoa! Gone?"

"Back to Algiers, I am now a back-channel courier. Listen, tell the men how proud I am of each one of them. They're going to make this operation a success. The biggest air extraction attempted. With luck, I'll be back before they move on to their new squadrons."

"Rocks and shoals. Gotta hurt. I'll pass it along. When are you leaving?"

"1600. Do me a favor, feed the results and the out briefings to me via Don Shelton at AFHQ. I'll check in with him. Ask him to set aside a copy for me before he sends it up the chain. Beetle Smith scheduled me to see Eisenhower."

"Why would they pull you from a critical mission to carry letters? There must be something more."

"Justine is going back. She's been green-lighted to establish a Mediterranean Sea Escape line. But I still don't understand why I'm needed. Oh, Airey Neave will be there too."

Fred nodded. "Before you go, boss, let me run through this with you one more time. Two sets of eyes are better than one."

Forty minutes later, Ike picked up his bag and headed for the door. "You got this, Fred. See you in a couple of days."

"I'll keep the porch light on."

Ike had five minutes to chat with Group Captain

Hasting before a staff car dropped off Justine. "I'll have sea rescue and two additional Hurricanes on standby. I'll handle the OPS Room myself."

The Hudson transport took off on time, destination Algiers via Gibraltar.

Chapter 27
Sand, Sun, and Sea

It was after 10 PM when the Hudson taxied to RAF Gibraltar base check-in. The other travelers, AFHQ staff officers, climbed off the plane as the door opened. Ike stared at the small gate. *No Archie here to greet me. Maybe he's right and she won't marry me. But it's not likely he'll ever see the inside of her gentleman friend's Whitehall Townhouse.* He saw Justine standing, waiting for him to deplane. *No time to be maudlin. Rose would never run off with an old aristocrat.*

Justine whispered. "Ike, we need to talk."

"Yes, of course. Let's get something to eat. We only have an hour before we leave for Algiers."

Over two plates of Fish and Chips, Justine spoke softly, not to be overheard. "I am not safe in Algiers. There is a man on the French High Commissioner, General Giraud's staff—I have seen him with the Gestapo."

Justine, the entire North African French leadership fought with their German occupiers until the very last."

"After. Yes, after the surrender, after Giraud was chosen High Commissioner."

"You saw him with the Gestapo after the liberation of Algiers?"

"I saw him with Louis Pagnon and Raymond Monange, two traitors from the North African Brigade. Intent on joining the Carlingue, thieves and underworld traitors in collaboration with the Gestapo, the aide, a French Colonel, arranged their passage to Marseille."

"Do you know his name? Why not report him?"

"I don't know his name. I saw him again, watching me when I inquired after Jacques at the ministry. He tried to follow me. I easily lost him; the man has no skill. Friends who watch and listen have told me that he has offered a reward for my capture."

"You should be safe on the base."

"He will be watching, following my father."

"How can I reach you if you must disappear?"

"The café. My friend…"

"The man with the key, the Maître 'd."

The jolt and screech of landing gear on the runway shook Ike out of his half-sleep. He glanced at Justine, her eyes fixed on the window, staring out into the darkness. He smiled at her. "If you need me, Major Don Shelton at the Allied Forces RECON office will know how to contact me. Remember, Major Don Shelton."

The plane taxied to the gate for check-in. Ike noticed a dark figure standing at the gate. A shadowy man in civilian clothes. Ike was concerned about the irregularity of a civilian meeting the plane in the middle of the night, staring and watching. The man struck a match and lit a cigarette, and, in that flash, Ike smiled. Airey Neave was waiting.

Ike turned to Justine. "Airey Neave is waiting. He's MI9. You can trust him. Tell him what you told me."

Outside, Ike led Justine to Airey. "Airey, glad that you are here. Justine, Agent Justice, is in danger…"

Airey stomped out his cigarette. "I know. That's why I came to meet you here. Agent Justice will be going with me, now. A safe house. I'll be in contact after your meeting tomorrow."

Ike nodded. "Major Shelton in RECON. He'll know where to contact me."

Airey turned to Justine, "Please come with me, my car is waiting."

Ike went inside and was given a room key and a packet of instructions. As he walked to the senior officer's suite, he opened the envelope and pulled out the schedule. Schedule for Colonel Montclair I. Curtiss: Meeting with General Smith 0630. Meeting with General Eisenhower 0645. Briefing AFINTEL and AFRECON 0730. Meeting with General Smith at 1030. Field Work 1300. Ike glanced at his watch—0215. *Should I even try to get some sleep? Yeah, I can't afford to be off my best.* Ike set his alarm for five thirty. *Fresh fruit and juice. At least I won't go hungry.* Ike peeked in the small refrigerator. A small, covered dish contained a sandwich and salad. He opened his bag and hung up his uniforms. Undressing, he spotted silver items on the dresser—silver eagles. *General Eisenhower never forgets—the promotion to full Colonel that he promised me must have come through.* Ike glanced at the envelope. "There it is, Colonel, not Lieutenant Colonel."

Ike drank a cold juice and went to bed. The day's events and the schedule, Airey's appearance, and the promotion swirled like a whirlpool pulling him down to the depths of dreamy sleep.

Beetle Smith was his direct, no-nonsense self. "Colonel, General Eisenhower must focus on Sicily, not France, and not North Africa. Do you have the letters?"

"Yes, General. Do I give them to you, now?"

"He is expecting you, Colonel. You will give them to him, sealed—to preserve the chain of custody. He will question you on an alleged infiltrator on General Giraud's staff, and he may ask for a report on your Training Command."

Beetle Smith reached for an envelope on his desk. "Lieutenant Colonel Shelton sent these. MI9 Reports from France last night. Seems they extracted 25 airmen. No losses. Well done, Curtis. That will be all. You're dismissed."

Remembering Eisenhower's punctuality, Ike walked across the hall to Eisenhower's anteroom and announced himself to the adjutant. He took the remaining seven minutes to scan the report and view the photographs. Two sites were compromised, but the resistance forces neutralized them at the approach signal. The two-source communication, first by radio, and then revised by courier, was successful. Sadly, it was confirmed that two MI9 radio operators had been captured. Cobra. Ike stopped and looked up. *Why wasn't Airey in France for this operation? Why is he here?*

"Colonel Curtis, the General will see you now."

Ike nodded to the adjutant and walked into the Allied Forces Commander's Office. Eisenhower said from behind his desk, "You have something for me, Colonel?" Ike handed him the sealed envelope and stood at attention. "Take a seat, Curtis."

Ike sat with eyes straight ahead as Eisenhower read the letters. The General put the letters down. "What's in the other envelope?"

"Sorry, General. I was just catching up with the report of last night's MI9 extraction in France."

"MI9? Let me take a look. Spoke to an MI9 man yesterday, Airey Neave."

"Yes, General. We work together. The plan is to establish a sea escape route from southern France to Gibraltar. Our escape lines in the North have been infiltrated."

"And that is why I was asked to obtain the release of a brother of the Bey of Tunis and a smuggler here in Algiers. The woman involved…"

"Justine Samson."

"The landlady who drew the attention of General Giraud. Yes. Since the request to release the two prisoners, he's been eager for information about her arrival. Colonel Neaves warns that she is at risk and that there's a collaborator on Giraud's staff. Damn French. How many times will they trade sides? You and Neave will out the traitor and get on with the sea escape line."

Eisenhower scanned the report and looked at the photos. "Clever operation. Good work, Curtis. And how's the RECON and Strategy Training Command coming?"

"General, you're looking at their work last night."

"Outstanding! I have something, Curtis. The invasion of France will be coming. Sicily is a grind, but we've got them on the run. I want heavy RECON over the Pas-de-Calais. Let the Jerries know what you're doing. However, keep up to date on Normandy, from Cherbourg to Le Havre. No explanations to anyone, use MI9 missions as cover."

"Yes, General. I'll make it happen. Claude Dansey and Norman Crockatt's support would help."

"You'll get it, now, I have a field commander's staff brief to attend."

Ike got up to leave. Eisenhower commented, "Congratulations on your promotion, Colonel. And remember, you report to me."

Ike made his way to AFRECON to meet Don Shelton before the scheduled 0730 brief.

Don was sitting in his office when he heard Ike enter. "XO the coffee and two cups. Ike, you look none the worse for wear. That was some operation your boys pulled off last night. Rumor is they were students."

"You look comfortable behind the desk, Don. I see it's now Lieutenant Colonel. Congratulations. And yes, students with three weeks of training in night navigation, low-level photography, and rapid turnaround for field landings at light. Good men, still eager to do their part. So, what's the scoop on this brief with INTEL?"

"You're the star witness. Eisenhower wants to expand joint missions, RECON, SOE, artillery spotting, and personnel extraction. He sees agility and wider use of assets, particularly light aircraft. He wants to take some of the load off the mosquitoes, probably the Allies' most versatile aircraft. He'll want to know of any new tactics and getting the latest out to the squadrons."

"Thanks, you've just given me twenty minutes to organize my thoughts. How about a sheet of paper and a pen?"

"Make yourself at home in your old chair. I'll see what's keeping that coffee. Oh, there's something else. Colonel Johnson in INTEL may take you aside regarding a need-to-know-only operation. He's been spending a lot of time with OSS."

Ike's engineering and business experience prepared him to quickly organize and outline his thoughts. He had time to join Don for a quick brief on the Sicily campaign.

Ike didn't need his outline. He covered the mission, training program, and coordination of RECON with MI9 and SOE. He took questions on tactics and equipment. He was free to discuss the partnership between Allied Forces, the RAF, and the British Intelligence Directorates. Colonel Johnson stepped forward to close the session after 90 minutes of engaged discussion. Ike watched as Randy Roosevelt, silent the whole brief, was first out the door.

Such a little man. No questions. Skulking off.

Colonel Johnson shook his hand. "Great job, Ike. If you have a couple of minutes…"

Ike nodded as he scanned the briefing room again. *Where the heck is Airey? This is as much his baby as mine. Justine. Where's he taken Justine?*

Ike followed Johnson to his office. He recognized Airey Neave talking to a civilian Ike didn't recognize. "Where's Justine, Airey? And who is your friend?"

Airey replied, "She's safe. You'll be joining her soon. Ike Curtis, meet Jasper, Office of Strategic Services."

Ike studied the young man with tanned, athletic, and penetrating eyes. "I've heard of you guys. Good to see Americans finally get into the dirty war."

Jasper said nothing. His face unchanged, but his eyes locked onto Ike. Colonel Johnson replied, "Americans, OSS has been busier than you realize. Jasper was here before the landings. Hell, he mapped them for us. OSS has been pursuing French collaborators embedded in General Giraud's High Commission and Army."

Ike asked, "Collaborators? French North Africa stood and fought alongside the Nazis until the end. What French Officer isn't a suspect?"

Agent Jasper replied, "If I may, Colonel, you misunderstand the position the French found themselves in. The French had hard memories of World War I, and when Britain abandoned them at Dunkirk, they were left to deal with Germany alone. Who in Europe remained with them? Not Italy, not Spain, or Portugal. Belgium and the

Netherlands had fallen. Russia was allied with Germany, and President Roosevelt declared that the United States had no interest in joining the war. Marshal Pétain made a deal with the devil to spare further deaths in the face of assured defeat. The Vichy Government played along as it had to, but it delayed and dragged its feet. America recognized the Vichy Government and was permitted an embassy, where our diplomats and agents were fed crucial information. And there is the French character. Their military was patriotic to France and its civil government. General De Gaulle, for all of his noise, did not sway the French Armed Forces. They viewed him as disloyal to the legitimate government of France. His attempt to persuade the French Forces in North Africa to surrender fell on deaf ears. Only when the North African campaign showed progress did they decide to join the Allies. Even so, with rare exception, they refrained from going on the attack. Remarkably, for some anti-fascist French, they chose to die for the French flag rather than defy their crumbling Vichy government."

"Which begs my question, Jasper, how do you separate the wheat from the chaff, the truly loyal French from the fascists, the Carlingue thugs and sell-outs?"

"We've made good progress in mopping up the brutal thieves and thugs of the Gestapo-led Carlingue. What remains are the French fascists, one or more Gestapo agents, and officers, more than willing to take Nazi money. We're closing the net, but they have a high-ranking officer providing them both intelligence and safety."

"Justine's Colonel."

Colonel Johnson nodded. "You got it, Ike, and that's why we're here."

"Count me in. What now?"

Airey Neave slapped Ike's shoulder. "We'll go catch a dirty French Colonel."

CHAPTER 28
NEW RECRUITS

Ike sat in the back of an old, beat-up Citroen as Jasper drove along the harbor. The mid-July sun was hot, and the sea breeze was lost in the maze of warehouses. The car turned alongside an old two-story colonial stone building fronting a long warehouse pier with small coastal trading vessels rafted three deep in the shallows and American Liberty ships lining the piers on both sides. Ike thought of Tacoma as he watched William Kaiser's miracle ships unload. America's industrial might enabled shipyards to build Liberty ships from the keel up in just weeks. Newsreels reported one Liberty built in 5 days. A pair of cargo booms serviced each of the five holds. A wire rope from the boom, positioned over the hold, joined the wire rope from its twin over the pier, attached at the cargo hook. Working two winches together, pallets of crates were lifted from the hold by the first and pulled and lowered by the second into the guiding hooks of longshoremen working the pier.

Airey called Ike away from his memories. "Ike, are you coming?"

Ike had to dodge a steady stream of trucks as he made his way to a rear door of the stone building. Inside was a busy office filled with store clerks and Stevedores. Jasper led them through a side door to a stairway. Upstairs, there was an open office and a reception. Jared nodded to the receptionist, knocked on the door, and entered. An elderly Frenchman sat behind the desk with his face buried in papers. An impeccably dressed gentleman sat calmly in an easy chair, sipping tea. Ike marveled at the contrast between the busy, dirty pier and the quiet mahogany-paneled office.

Ike did not notice Justine quietly step in behind him. Jasper asked, "Where's Justine? Ah, there you are. Shall we begin?"

The man behind the desk pointed to a conference table at the back of the room overlooking the harbor. The American agent, Jasper, spoke as they made their way to the table. "We know there is a collaborator on General Giraud's staff. Justine is our only eyewitness, having seen and overheard his plan to send two traitors, French Gestapo-led police, the Conques, across to Marseille. Justine informs us that he is a Colonel and has attempted to follow her after recognizing her from the café rendezvous. This Colonel is close to General Giraud, who has passed French interest in finding Justine. Justine has volunteered as bait to capture the Colonel. How do we do that without alarming the French before we have sufficient evidence?"

Airey replied, "We must catch him in the act."

Paul Samson pointed to the small ships tied up below, "As we speak, my engineer is inspecting the fleet. You can see from here that the two outboard boats have clean hulls and greased pulleys and wire rope on the cargo gear. They have been in service while supposedly impounded. No doubt they've been smuggling. Something I admit to knowing of, but I was in prison for smuggling, betrayed by someone in authority."

Justine's father spoke. "Gentlemen, who has charge of purchases? Food, goods, supplies? Who oversees all that is impounded and sits on the command staff? The supply officer. Have we not heard it argued that tactics win battles, but logistics win wars? It seems to me your traitor is either the supply officer or a senior in the supply chain with close ties to General Giraud. I do not see the general himself as a traitor, but French generals become accustomed to fine wines and goods hard to come by in a war. It is easy for them to accept without asking how or where these goods come and appreciate their provider."

Ike thought, *like the bourbon smuggled on every new plane flown in from America.*

Airey replied, "How do we entrap him. He may be more interested in money, selling what we need to get the shipping company running quickly, and smuggling, or he might be more interested in silencing Justine before risking any new scheme."

Again, Justine's father advised, "They are not mutually exclusive. Greed has a voracious appetite. Our man has done well so far. With the opportunity for money and eliminating Justine's threat, he will surely act on what he sees as a win-win opportunity."

Justine smiled. "Papa is right. I can be bait and offer something better than francs or jewels. Here is how I can make it work…"

Paul Samson sat across from the Colonel in a small café on the waterfront. "Thank you for meeting me here. I can imagine how valuable your time is. In fact, I trust you know the true value of everything Algiers, no, French North Africa requires. And with the Americans and the Allies moving on to Sicily, and hopefully, soon, France, supplying the needs of millions is no easy task."

"Yes, I am here. What are you offering?"

"I'm offering those supplies that Allies cannot. The same special goods I supplied to the embassies and the consulates that were made available at prices affordable to those whose positions entitle them to a certain degree of perks."

"You are a smuggler."

"Such a crude word. I ran a coastal trading company. Small ships, serving quiet harbors in France, Spain, and Italy. Of course, I could offer my ships to the allies for cargo from Gibraltar, but as I say, I have developed a niche business importing smaller, more precious cargo."

"You want something from me. What?"

"My ships are to be released from impound. There is a small issue of control. My sons know my business well and are safe here in Algiers, all except one. Jacques. No one has heard from him. He is serving in France with Free French Intelligence, an idealist like his wife, Justine…"

"Justine Samson?"

"You know her?"

"I've heard her name. She is not trusted."

"Well, then, I am not alone—half Berber, and no friend of we French in North Africa. Sadly, she can persuade a silent shareholder to deny this lucrative opportunity. She brings wealth, not in francs, but in jewels to buy my interest. Now, what she does not know is that Jacques is dead. With no Justine, the shares and the jewels, you know she is the granddaughter of the late Bey of Tunis? Her father's favorite, he hides his wealth with her."

"You want me to fix this problem?"

"I'm sure you can persuade her. She has agreed to meet you to discuss an official government contract."

At three o'clock the next afternoon, Justine sat alone at a table against the back wall of the café beneath her apartment. Two men sat a table away, sharing a bottle of wine and a baguette. She watched a clean black sedan park in front. A uniformed Colonel stepped out and walked into the café. Justine smiled despite the tingling in her spine and the tightening of her neck. *It's him.* The sedan drove off.

The Maître d' stepped outside and watched. He returned and busied himself as the Colonel addressed Justine. "Good afternoon, madam, are you Justine Samson?"

You know exactly who I am. "Yes, and you must be from the High Commissioner's procurement office? I am waiting to speak with an official regarding a government shipping contract."

"May I?"

"Please."

The colonel sat across the table from Justine. "Indeed, we need vessels of all sizes to keep North Africa fed, clothed, and healthy as the Allied Army moves on to Sicily and hopefully the continent. Tell me about your ships and their capabilities."

Six are at a pier here in Algiers, and six more are anchored in the impound at Tunis. Coastal trading ships. Very versatile and capable of shallow water ports. We have established agreements with agents in small ports throughout the Mediterranean. This is especially useful in fresh produce, direct from farms at a lower cost than large port distributors."

"Impounded, you say? Now, that is a problem. With so many of our citizens dead or missing, proving ownership takes time. I could put your ships under contract, but the time... Hmm, I might be able, with some capital, to expedite your claim. Twelve boats, twelve thousand francs."

"Twelve thousand francs are hard to come by. But jewels, my family prepared for war by moving our capital to jewels—portable and always redeemable. I will have my jeweler confirm the equivalent of twelve thousand francs. I live upstairs. I can go now..."

"Now would be perfect."

The colonel stood. "Don't forget your sun shawl, you wouldn't want to burn." As the colonel placed the linen shawl over her shoulders, Justine felt the cold steel of a pistol in her back. "You will go out the back door and say nothing."

When Justine walked to the rear, the two men stood to follow. "They aren't going upstairs!" Before they reached the back door, the black sedan's door slammed, and the engine roared as it accelerated.

The Maître d whistled happily. "Don't worry, my friends, they have nowhere to go."

Outside, cars blocked both entrances to the alley. Agent Jasper watched as his French counterpart made the arrest.

General Eisenhower was brief. "Give this pouch to Claude Dansey—personally. Make it the first thing you do and never let it out of your sight."

Ike took the pouch. "Yes, General."

"You remember my orders regarding RECON?"

"Yes, General, let the Jerries know we're looking at Calais, but stay current on Normandy."

"Right, keep up the good work at Allied Force RECON Tactics and Training."

"Will do, sir."

"That will be all, Colonel. Your flight leaves in two hours."

Ike saluted and turned for the door. "And Curtis, I

had a visit today from General Giraud. He informed me his Supply Officer was arrested for collaboration with the Carlingue and Gestapo, as well as smuggling. The General said that his concerns with Madam Justine Samson du Rochelle were mistaken. The impoundment of her coastal trading ships has been lifted. Operation Privateer is moving quickly. Safe trip, Colonel."

A black staff car was waiting when the transport plane landed at RAF Churchstanton. A young officer greeted Ike on the tarmac. "Colonel Curtis, could you please come with me?"

Ike tucked the pouch under his arm, and the officer picked up his bag. "Let me help you with that, sir."

Ike joined Claude Dansey in the back seat. Once Ike's bag was safely in the boot, the young officer took the driver's seat, started the engine, and drove out the gate.

"Where are we going this time, Colonel?"

"You have something for me, Ike?"

Ike handed Claude Dansey the pouch. "Do you know the contents? Of course not. Tell me, Ike, did General Eisenhower give you any other instructions?"

"Be seen doing RECON over Calais, don't be seen stepping up RECON of Normandy. Use SOE and MI9 ops for RECON."

"And why are you to do this?"

"The general did not say, but a reasonable conclusion would be invasion preparations and planning."

Dansey exhaled a cloud of cigarette smoke. We're

off to Room 600. We need to determine how to carry out the General's orders without arousing too much interest. But I need to make a stop along the way in Westminster."

After circling a block in Westminster several times, Colonel Z reappeared on the sidewalk without the pouch and waited to be picked up. Nothing was said.

At 54 Broadway, Ike followed Dansey to the briefing room in MI6 Headquarters. The room was already full. Dansey walked straight to the podium. "Apologies, gentlemen, I see I am ten minutes behind schedule. Couldn't be helped. What I am about to tell you will be the greatest deception in the history of warfare. Greater than Operation Mincemeat. I've just come from the PM. He will hear of no foot-dragging or command priorities in providing 100 percent support of what you are about to hear. Colonel John Bevan of the London Controlling Section will now brief you. Johnny…."

Colonel Bevan pulled the curtain on a large map of England and France. "Gentlemen, Operation Bodyguard. Within the year, the Allied Forces will invade the coast of Normandy. Every cross-channel invasion has traditionally originated from Pas-de-Calais, the narrowest point of the Channel. Only 22 miles. Crossings from Dover can be quick, and rail and road transport provide rapid movement across inland areas. For these very reasons, it has been used successfully in the past. The Germans are well aware of this, and reconnaissance confirms that they are preparing to defend against Pas-de-Calais as the invasion site. Meanwhile, a few thinking Jerries have been arguing that the history and infrastructure that make it look so inviting make it a perfect distraction. These Generals argue for the continued buildup of defenses along the Normandy coast. The Operation Bodyguard mission is to convince Herr Hitler to pour all of his efforts into defending Pas-de-Calais. For this distraction to be effective, all of our efforts and current operations must be planned and coordinated to align with Operation Bodyguard. Now, let me walk you through our current intelligence and rules for coordination."

After the briefing, Ike was authorized to have a driver take him back to RAF Churchstanton. The rays of the summer sun, with two more hours of heat, cast long shadows across central London. There was hardly a whisper of wind. Even with the windows rolled down, the heat compelled them to head out of London on an open road.

"Driver, I've never seen much of Whitehall, the townhouse homes of the aristocrats. I'd like to see how the upper classes live. Show me the townhouses of Whitehall."

Ike directed the driver down each of the small streets and peered out the window. A few well-dressed citizens braved the heat to take their early evening stroll. *Rain or shine, they abide by their routine.* Ike laughed and whispered, "What's the old saying—mad dogs and Englishmen?" He spoke louder, "You have to admire the dogged determination of the upper class, their sense of duty, yes, it is about duty, not pride, but conformity to the expectations of class. Sadly, that same show does not continue behind closed doors."

The driver said nothing,

"Stop! Stop here!" Ike shouted.

A young woman, strawberry blonde beneath a hat, was climbing the steps to a townhouse. Nattily dressed in a white blouse and a blue and white patterned skirt, she turned for a moment and took in the sun now dropping into the trees of the park. *Is that her? I think it's Rose. Should I call on her? What if it's not her? No harm done. If it is Rose, what will she think? No. It would be a disaster. She's hiding something from me. She is the one who decides.*

"Driver, take me to RAF Churchstanton."

CHAPTER 29
CHURCHSTANTON

Ike addressed a new class of pilots in the hangar. "Welcome to RAF Churchstanton and welcome to RECON Tactics and Training Command. First and foremost, everything you do here is subject to the Secrets Act. No sharing with your girlfriend, no spilling the beans over too many beers. Your instructors are the best in the field, and you will learn by doing. You are the second class. The men who went before you left their mark. As hard as it is for me to imagine, I expect you to do just as well. Show of hands, who would have rather gone straight to your squadron?"

A hand went up. Ike smiled. "Stand up. What is your name?"

"Sergeant McDill, Colonel. No disrespect, sir, but the men and I are ready to fight."

"You're bold, Sergeant. You'll need to be bolder here. Sit down. Now, I mentioned those of class 1. Every one of them flew over the coast of France. Every one of them participated in day and night RECON and SOE operations. Every one of them navigated to and landed at night in a dark field and extracted downed airmen. Who here thinks they will get into the war faster at their squadron? Who here thinks this is not what they signed up for? Speak now, and I'll sign your orders to your squadron—restricted from night RECON. Anyone? Good. Now the XO, that's right, another Yank will lay out your training. When we think you're ready, you'll be briefed on a secret operation. You'll be in it from the beginning. Good day."

Major Engert called out. "Ten-hut!" When Ike was out the door, "Seats."

Ike drove to Otterhead House and joined Nigel and James Langley. "Ike, good that you're back. New INTEL reports the Abwehr operation that took down most of Paris was the work of one Roger Leneveau, aka Roger Le Legionnaire, the same man who betrayed Albert-Marie Guerisse and other helpers in Marseille last March."

"Cobra?"

"Unfortunately, no. More likely, the agent we've been calling is Adder. Jacques Desoubrie is Cobra. Our team was right about the Oaktree traitor's name, Captain Jacques, but identified the wrong man. Both Leneveau and Desoubrie have moved on. The new Mithridate Paris operation believes they have gone to Germany. There is no confirmation that this is true. The whereabouts of both are uncertain."

Ike said, "I would still like to go forward with the trap, after all, we did have a little trouble on the last extraction, and it fits nicely with Operation Bodyguard."

"Bodyguard?" Nigel asked.

"James, I assumed you had briefed Nigel. What are you waiting for? Even my new class is in the loop."

More out of habit than need, Ike decided to stop at the vicarage on his way back to the base. Hugh greeted him at the door. "Ike, you're back! Tell me, how is Justine? Is she safe? You're not putting her in danger?"

Ike smiled at Hugh, "Like I could if I wanted to? You know better. Last time I saw her, she was fine. She had a long-awaited reunion with her father. The apple didn't fall far from the tree. We're not going to change her, so we must pray all the harder."

Hugh laughed. "I'd invite you in for a drink, but I'm saving the one Justine permits me for after dinner. Oh, right. Rose is back. She's at the cottage. Maybe I should skip dinner tonight and give you two time alone."

"Hugh, don't stay away on my account. You go. After all, I've not been invited, and even so, I would appreciate your company."

"Why don't you stop by. You two need to talk."

"I think I will."

A few minutes later, Ike pulled in front of the small honey stone cottage. Rose's bicycle leaned against the fence. He could see a figure bent over in the garden. *How long has it been since I've seen Rose in the garden? Has the real Rose finally returned, or just on holiday?* As Ike approached, Rose stood up and turned to him. *This is the Rose I fell in love with. Hair tied back, red locks peeking from under a farmer's hat, coveralls, dirt on her cheek, and muddy hands.*

"Ike! Finally! Have you been avoiding me, mister? It's been forever! Help me finish weeding this row and carry the peas, carrots, and radishes into the house. I even have our first tomatoes! You're staying for dinner! I promised Uncle Hugh garden fresh tonight."

Rose stopped talking and looked into Ike's eyes. "Aren't you going to kiss me? Didn't you miss me? I missed you."

Ike squeezed her close and kissed her deeply. "I love you, Rose, but I…"

"You what, Ike?"

"I don't know who you are anymore. Since I've been gone, you're different. You dress differently, wear makeup and style your hair, there's the nylons and expensive clothes, and this friend—rich friend that you keep secret."

Rose set down the vegetable basket. "Let's take a walk."

"No shower and makeup before dinner?"

Rose took Ike's hand. "Come on. Let's go sit at the top of the hill. There is something about a horizon that brings a sense of perspective."

Rose continued softly, "Do you remember when we came up here that first evening. I will never forget it. There was no tension, no worry, only peace and joy in each other's company."

"I remember."

"Ike, you tell me you love me…"

"I do. I never thought I could love again, but I love you so very deeply."

"And I love you. Remember the night of the party, and you asked if the fancy dress and makeup were the new me?"

"Yes, you said it could be."

"Ike, I am Rose, me, whether working in the garden, rolling down hills, or dressed for a party with the lords. How are you dressed, Ike? In uniform, I see another promotion, congratulations, full Colonel. Has the rank or the uniform changed the man I love wearing it? Are you not the same man in civilian clothes or sitting with friends? I love you for who you are—a good man with a kind heart. I know the secret I keep from you worries you. I'm sorry, but I must keep my promise…"

"To your mysterious benefactor? Rose, we all know you cannot afford the clothes, and you stay with him in Whitehall. What should I think?"

"You should trust me. You should think I am doing what I know is right. Have I ever been selfish? Have I sought clothes, make-up, those silly nylon stockings? Trust me, they are no fun to put on or wear without snagging… that's my point, Ike. Please, if you love me, and I believe you do, then I ask you to trust me. Trust me because you know you can."

Ike drew her close and hugged her as they listened to the evening chorus of songbirds. Ike brushed the dirt from her cheek and kissed her gently.

Walking down the hill arm-in-arm, Rose laughed,

Uncle Hugh is smitten."

"How so? Not Justine?"

"Absolutely, Justine. Can you believe it? I never thought Uncle Hugh could see another woman as, you know, to have feelings for. I mean, yes, he has a loving heart for everyone, but besides Aunt Jane."

Ike chuckled. "He wouldn't be the first. You know, he turned down a drink this afternoon, saying Justine has limited him to one a day!"

Rose laughed. "I think it's wonderful."

Rose sighed, and her smile drained away. "What is it, Rose? Something else on your mind?" Ike asked.

"I received a letter from my father…."

"And?"

"He's coming home. He wants to speak to both of us."

"Right."

Ike waited downstairs as Rose cleaned up for supper. He paced, wondering what conversation he could possibly have with Arthur Osbourne. *Lord, I don't think I could hold my anger, the man—selfish, arrogant. Perhaps, one day, I could forgive how he treated me, but his disrespect, the way he treats Rose? Never!*

Ike sighed. A new thought entered his mind, a thought that came from outside, not a memory, a truth. *Forgive us our trespasses as we forgive those who trespass against us…Yes, Lord, I know the prayer. And I also remember, for if you will not forgive those who sin against you, neither shall I forgive your sin against me. That's a hard saying, Lord, help me. Help me.*

Rose came down clean and smiling, wearing the white silk blouse which had become a private token of their love. "Uncle Hugh will be here soon. Come help me in the kitchen."

Ike smiled. "You don't have our little red torch handy, do you?"

"Perhaps after Uncle Hugh leaves, tiger."

"Oh! Tiger, not mister?"

Rose pawed the air and growled, "Grrrr! Tonight, my mister is a tiger on the prowl!"

Uncle Hugh's perfect timing had him arrive as Rose put supper on the table. "What is that heavenly aroma, not shepherd's pie, what is it?" Hugh lifted the cover from the serving bowl.

"Something I tried in London, a pasta dish, Italian, simple to make, and delicious. But first the salad."

Hugh stared. "Doesn't look like spaghetti, and where did you find the pasta?"

"London. And not just pasta, but Italian cheeses, bacon, well, it looks like bacon, but it is something Italian, eggs, of course, fresh peas, and, ta da, truffles!"

"Truffles? I've never had them, not something you could find in Gig Harbor. Aren't they expensive?"

Hugh glanced at Ike. "They are—not exactly on our local menu either."

"Please, let me give this to you. Yes, they were a gift from my employer. I commented on how much I enjoyed the dish and wished I could share it with you and Uncle Hugh; well, he gave me the ingredients to take home. I know what you're thinking, he is more than just someone funding research. And, yes, he is more, a friend, a very special friend whom I have come to love dearly, like you, Uncle Hugh. Almost like the father I wish I had. So please, accept his and my gift, given in love."

Hugh blessed the food, the home and two or more gathered at the table. After tasting the delightful food, Hugh spoke. "I come with news. Rose, your father will arrive tomorrow."

"I don't want to see him. He knows I never want to see him again, not until his funeral."

"This is his house. You are his child, and in his way, he loves you. He tells me he has changed. Like a caged songbird, he wants to let you fly free and listen to you sing. I truly believe he is coming to ask for your forgiveness. And if you do marry Ike…"

"When not if."

Hugh chuckled. "When you and Ike marry, his heart will beat with pride walking you down the aisle of Saint Peter and Saint Paul."

"He sent me a letter, too. I'm not ready to forgive twenty-odd years of pain. No, it is too hard, and the way he treated Ike, how can either of us forgive him? He was wrong. He is not worth it to me."

"Are any of us worth forgiving? I was reading Exodus the other day, the Passover story. When the angel of death passed over the houses of the Israelites in Egypt, did he look inside the houses to see if they were worthy to be forgiven their sin, to be saved from judgment and death? No! The angel saw the blood, only the sacrificial blood that we, lovers of Christ, know was a foreshadowing of his blood spilled for us. We do not deserve his forgiveness, yet he grants it. So, when Jesus taught us to pray, 'Forgive us our trespasses as we forgive those who trespass against us,' it has nothing to do with worthiness."

"It's easy for you to say that I should forgive him. You're not the one who was wronged, who suffered. I'm the victim. I'm the one in pain."

"Wasn't Christ a victim? Didn't he suffer? But that's not what Jesus wants from us. He wants to comfort us so we can find peace and joy despite any pain this world or this life can inflict on us. We forgive, remembering we have been forgiven. When we forgive, we do not forget the transgression; we do not pretend it never happened, we do not remove the consequences. We remove the burden of pain so we can live in joy and rebuild relationships on the road to reconciliation. Consider the joy of being reconciled to Christ. There is no greater joy than reconciliation— reconciling with a loved one who was dead to us, brought back to life. Your father can be like Lazarus, once dead to you but brought back into your life,"

Rose closed her eyes and sighed. "I'll think about it."

Hugh replied, "Don't just think, pray."

CHAPTER 30
RESETS

Master Sergeant Fienberg was briefing: We will complete the installation of camera upgrades at RAF Churchstanton within a week. Also, the pilot and co-pilot can begin filming with both the high-altitude and infrared cameras upon crossing the coast and leave them running. The cameras remain filming until manually deactivated after returning across the coast of France."

"Thanks, Master Sergeant," Nigel Marley said. "That was the easy part. Our challenge will be day-and-night RECON of the known Jerry emplacements and strategic defense positions. We are confident that our high-speed, high-altitude Mosquitos can outrun Jerry fighters, but concentrated flak is altogether riskier. The toughest nut will be sending our unarmed small planes low and slow outside the safer coastal corridors. Dangerous enough for my most experienced pilots, but I leave it to Ike to decide if it's outside the envelope for his green pilots still in training. Do you have anything to add, Ike?"

"You called it right, Nigel. A couple of thoughts.

Let's keep the training squadron over the safer coastal corridors for now. When they're ready, we can transition them to entering via the safe corridor and returning over fresh territory. Let's hope the Jerries remain concentrated on incoming traffic rather than outgoing. Hell, we need to test if they even train for low flights from behind their defensive perimeters."

Fred Engert commented, "Maybe, maybe not, Ike. But from what I've seen, they're fast learners. We're gonna need something more, a next step, when they do adjust."

"Any ideas, Fred?" Ike asked.

"You're not gonna like it. Ever fish with lanterns?"

Ike replied, "It attracts the fish."

"Bingo."

Group Captain Hastings smiled. "Finally, a real role for our attack and night fighters. I'm in. Of course, this tactic should only be employed in the Pas-de-Calais region. We don't want that kind of attention over Normandy."

Ike squinted. "Wait! You're not gonna light up a Lysander? It would be suicide!"

"No, not the Lysanders, but small towed gliders, balloons, anything that stays aloft to draw their fire. While the little guys fly below the action."

Ike nodded. "I promised Eisenhower new tactics. Adapt and adjust as we go."

Ike moved aside the pile of personnel files on his new

trainees and attacked the mail in his inbox. A white non-government envelope stood out. A letter from home. Ike instantly recognized Margaret Olson's exquisite penmanship.

Dear Ike,

I hope this letter finds you safe. We pray for you every day. And little Earl does too in his bedtime prayer. He is such a sweet child. You will be surprised how much he has grown. Smart, like his father, curious, and unlike his father, very outgoing. He misses you so much, as do we all. I've enclosed pictures.

I am writing to request your decision regarding the ferry. As you know, your brother can be spiteful. He demands money, not just from profits, but his share. I know, legally, he cannot force you to sell, but I've met with the State commissioner, and the Narrows bridge will be rebuilt. It's a matter of time—after the war ends. He understood the risk we faced. He clearly wants the ferry to continue running until the new bridge is built and proven safe. He made an offer. A fair offer at that. Given your situation and your plans to marry Rose in England, I think it might be the right thing to do.

Please let me know as soon as possible before the

BELLS IN THE WILDERNESS

State's offer is withdrawn.

> All our love,
> Margaret

P.S. Earl has a few words to add

Hi, Dad.

Everybody in town was at Grandpa's funeral. Many men spoke, and even the Pastor said kind things. I miss him. Baseball is going great! Got good grades at school. Still no fireworks on the Fourth of July. I have to go now; Mr. Malich is taking all the kids to Horseshoe Lake for a swim. I miss you. Come home soon. And bring Miss Rose. I want to meet her.

> Your Son
> Earl

Ike put the letter down and gazed at the pictures. *I really miss home. Will Earl even know me when I get back? I've missed growing up with him. And the ferry, Marge is right. I should sell it while I can. But it was Dad's, his life, my life, and now, it won't be around for Earl. Probably a good thing. Outgoing. Good, he'll find what's right for him. Why do I feel my ties to Gig Harbor are being cut?*

On Sunday, the bright and enthusiastic change ringing of the bells of Saint Peter and Saint Paul called the parish to worship. Ike was unprepared to see Arthur Osbourne sitting in the family stall. Rose, walking, holding Ike's arm, whispered. "You sit next to him. I won't, I can't. Not yet. No, please, do this for me."

Ike led Rose to the stall and slid in beside Arthur, who turned and smiled. The organ began, and Nigel's strong voice sang out:

Come, ye sinners, poor and needy,
Weak and wounded, sick and sore;
Jesus ready stands to save you,
Full of pity, love and power.

Come, ye thirsty, come and welcome,
God's free bounty glorify;
True belief and true repentance,
Every grace that brings you nigh.

Come, ye weary, heavy laden,
Lost and ruined by the fall;
If you tarry till you're better,
You will never come at all.

The words melted Ike's heart as he sang. Arthur's voice started strong before fading away. Ike noticed him, eyes closed... *I think he's weeping. Yes, I can hear him quietly sobbing.*

Ike turned to Rose. She stood silently staring ahead. *Not the procession, not the altar, she's staring into her past.*

At the peace, Arthur stood and offered Ike his handshake. "I owe you an apology. It's Ike Curtis, right? Ike shook his hand, apology accepted, Mr. Osbourne."

"Arthur, now, may I give my daughter a hug?"

"Rose, can you forgive a foolish old man?" Arthur gave her a gentle hug. Rose stood motionless until she slowly raised her arms and hugged Arthur lightly. Ike watched the tender moment. *Her eyes, first vacant, are warming. Yes, I can see her face softening. Oh, good, oh, how sweet! Thank you, Lord.*

James Langley walked into Ike's office. Ike looked up and said, "Must be urgent, you didn't wait for me to be summoned."

Langley didn't laugh. "I need you tonight in a Lysander. It will give you a foot up on low-level flights over Pas-de-Calais. I'm using you as bait to entrap whoever penetrated one of the cells in the multi-plane extraction. You and Agent Golden Rod, yes, Dorothy. You'll be carrying money, a radio, and an operator. She is establishing an ambulance service, or rather, a truck line for transporting the injured to the south of France. You're the only one who knows Dorothy. We think…"

"Who's we?"

"The community. We think Dorothy is a prize that will bring out the traitor."

"Dorothy as bait? She's not trained for…"

"She's learned the hard way. She knows the risk and

doesn't need convincing. Now, you'll have two Hurricanes and resistance support on the ground. She'll have documents. Land, make the exchange, and get back."

"When do I go?"

"Take off is 2330."

"Tonight? There's barely more than a crescent moon, if the clouds break over France."

Langley nodded. "I checked the weather, seventy percent cloud cover. Predicted ceiling 200 feet. Good luck."

Ike passed the word to Fred and barked out a few last instructions. "And I want you running the show in OPS."

Spent, Ike held out his hand. "You'll do fine, whatever happens, you're ready."

Fred stood tall, cocked his head, and said, "You got this, boss. Maybe not the next guy, but you got this."

Ike sat down and wrote the letter he should have written much earlier.

Dear Son,

I have loved you since I first saw you in your mother's arms. I can't imagine any other father having a greater pride in their sons than I have in you. Ask Ole and Margaret to give you a hug for me. Keep up the good work, and hey, pitching and baseball are fun but the whole world is going to need engineers and builders to put back what this war has destroyed.

Rose can't wait to meet you. When you do, it's okay to hug her.

Love Dad

Ike looked at his wristwatch. *I should have time to see Rose and still get in a bit of shut-eye before a light dinner, pre-brief, and takeoff.*

There was no one home at the Osbourne cottage. Ike drove to the vicarage. Rose's bicycle was not there. Hugh answered the door. Ike didn't smile. "Hugh, I'm looking for Rose. Any idea where she is?"

"She left with Arthur. They were headed to Bath. Should be back in time for dinner."

Ike paced. "Can I leave a note?"

"Of course, come through."

"I'm off on a mission tonight."

"Something's different this time, Ike. I've never seen you so nervous."

Ike wrote quickly.

Rose,

I love you with my whole heart. You brought love and joy into my once-dead heart. Pray for me. And please, whatever happens, hug little Earl when you meet him.

Love,

Ike

Ike folded the letter and gave it to Hugh. "Make sure she sees this."

"Of course. Ike, I don't understand why this mission, it is a mission? What is so different?"

"I don't know, Hugh, it's just a feeling, a new feeling that I have so much to lose. Pray for me."

Hugh put his hand on Ike's shoulder and prayed, "O God, who know us to be set in the midst of so many and so great dangers, that by reason of the frailty of our nature we cannot always stand upright. Grant your servant Ike, such strength and protection as may support him in all dangers and carry him through all trials, through Jesus Christ our Lord. Amen."

Ike hugged Hugh. "Thanks, I feel better. I must go. Goodbye, my friend."

CHAPTER 31
PAS-DE-CALAIS

Ike, Nigel, and Fred stood around the table map of Pas-de-Calais. They were focused on lines and circles drawn from German air defense radar positions. Nigel explained, "This is the most up-to-date information we have. It plots Jerry's early warning system in the Pas-de-Calais region. The outermost lines represent the range of the Freya radar, including only direction and range. The inner circles represent the range of the Wurzburg radar, which has a much shorter range, but it also measures altitude."

"Nothing new so far,"

Nigel continued, "Allied bombing has made deployment in Germany their priority. Their goal is to cover their territory in box grids twenty-seven miles wide and twenty-one miles deep with one Freya and two Wurzburgs in each. The Freyas detect incoming planes and hand them off to Würzburgs for searchlights, anti-aircraft guns, and fighter interception. We've had limited success in electronic jamming."

Ike nodded. "Right, thank God for the few

remaining gaps, our corridors to the interior. I don't see any gaps over Pas-de-Calais, perhaps a narrow one, here to the south, but there are no significant landmarks. Couldn't we try jamming? I understand it's a black art with only about thirty-five percent effectiveness. They will know something is coming, but it will be harder to detect where, after all, we want an increased interest in Calais, known?"

"We would rather your presence become known after you clear the coast on the way home. Why increase the risk of your plane returning to face a 360-degree revolving fire control radar waiting for you? Here's what I recommend: not a gap in the outer perimeter but an anomaly in the overlap between the two. We need to test two seams in their radar interface. First, the transition from the longer-range 2D non-altitude radar, and second, shadows cast by topological obstructions along the approach corridor. If the Jerrys are improving their coastal air defense system, we expect to see it here. If so, this is where we want it deployed—not in Normandy. Now for the good news…"

"Ike shook his head, "I never thought you'd get to any good news."

"The sites are elevated, enabling you to fly under the radar for most of the approach before entering shadows and seams close to the coast. Also, neither of these radars provides effective fire control for well-directed flak. Their night air defense relies more on roughly directed searchlights to scan for visual detection and directed anti-aircraft fire. That, and the fact that the

Lysander is a small, harder-to-detect target, quite different from the bomber squadrons, which is their primary concern."

Ike shook his head. "We don't have time for a debate. Show me where to look for these shadows and seams."

"We can only estimate, but the coast of France itself is the best shadow, and of course, low altitude."

Ike nodded. "Right. It appears to me that my best bet is to stay low, hugging the coast and flying through bays and river valleys, below their radar horizon. Since this is a start, my thoughts are to cross the channel far to the south, come up the coast behind Pas-de-Calais early warning Freya radar, and below the Wurzburg installations...."

Ike tapped the map. "Here, Bay of Somme, fly up the Somme Valley to the landing site. I will angle-fly the coast and film the cliffsides before leveling for the bottom view over the valley. I will return along the Authie River over Berck and out of the Bay before turning south for my channel crossing."

Ike and Nigel did not hear James Langley approach from behind. "Well, gentlemen, that being settled, this is Agent Martine. She will be your passenger along with her radio."

Ike smiled at the young woman, who was not yet twenty, her face set in determination. Ike said, "Please don't let the planning challenges we discussed discourage you. I'll get you there safe and sound."

"Colonel, I know the risks whether they take me tonight, this week, or a year from now. I'm prepared for whatever is to come."

Fred Engert spoke up. "Ike, I'll get on the horn with Group Captain Hastings. We'll coordinate night hunter support over the Dover channel—should it come to that."

Ike looked at the radio set on the floor. "Can I help you with that, Agent Martine?"

"No, thank you, sir. It's my responsibility, and my lifeline. I don't entrust it to others."

Ike nodded. *Lifeline? More like her death warrant.* "This way."

Low clouds hung over the channel. They could protect Ike from Night Fighters, but not from radar, though a single, slow, low-altitude aircraft was a low priority for the Germans. Ike watched his altimeter as he descended, looking for the bottom of the cloud cover. At 400 feet, he slowed his rate of descent. At 350 feet, he saw only blackness all around him. He said to his co-pilot, "I'm going to try the belly light, see if you can make out the surface below."

Ike turned on the belly-landing light and continued his slow descent. Seconds passed slowly. "Sir, I've got a reflection, yes, sir, I can see the surface. We are below cloud cover in clear air."

Ike replied, "Altitude 330 feet. Now to find the coast before it finds us. How are you doing back there, Martine?"

Ike couldn't see her fingers clutching the bottom of

the co-pilot's seat as she sat on the floor. "Fine, Colonel, just fine."

The next half hour passed in silent darkness. No Jerry night fighter wasted its time on a small single plane hiding beneath two thousand feet of cloud, and no shore guns fired out into the sea. Ike hugged the cliffs until he came to the break at the Bay of Somme; he descended to 200 feet and turned inland. *Thank you, Lord.*

The landing field was outside the small village of Hangest-sur-Somme between Abbeville and Amiens. The town was on the banks of the river and had a railroad station. The river and the church spire provided excellent landmarks for night navigation. Ike's morale improved when the moon broke through the clouds five miles inland. *How good is our God!*

A mile west of town, Ike spotted the torches of the landing field. The code was flashed, and the all clear was returned. The wide wheels of the Lysander touched down, and the plane slowed. The tail wheel found the ground as the aircraft rolled to a stop. Just as Ike took a sigh of relief, gunfire broke out. Rounds passed through the plane. "Hold on, I'm turning around."

Agent Martine unbuckled herself, opened the door, dropped her radio outside, and jumped. "Sorry, Colonel. This is my stop."

Small arms fire erupted all around. Ike heard the engine stop as bullets struck metal. Helpers were at the door. "Come with us. We have friends who will deal with the Jerries. This plane is going nowhere. Hurry, there's little time."

Ike grabbed the bag of francs, joined his co-pilot, and followed the helper to a waiting truck. Agent Goldenrod was behind the wheel. "Dottie! You're safe!" Ike called.

"I will be when we get out of here. Sounds like the resistance has the situation in hand. We now know the traitor. I hope he doesn't live through the night."

Ike asked Dorothy, "You chose the site for the train station, is that the plan?"

"Not anymore. We adapt. It's how we survive."

"The plane can be repaired with…"

"The resistance will burn it before they leave. Everyone, civilian clothes. No English labels! Ike, don't forget to unzip your boot tops. We'll toss them in the river, another mile upstream. Anything that floats should be halfway to Abbeville by dawn. I don't think the train station in Picquigny will be safe, either—too close. We can't risk road checkpoints. We'll drive to the Ailly-sur-Somme station. We'll still have to transfer at Amiens, but we won't have to pass through the terminal to buy our tickets. Ike, make yourself useful. Read the train schedule to Paris."

Ike shielded his red lens night flashlight and read. "First train leaves Ailly-sur-Somme at 0712, connects with the Paris train at 0911. Wait—there is a direct train—yes, it departs Ailly-sur-Somme at 0853. Stops at Amiens and continues to Paris."

Dorothy replied, "Perfect! Same train we planned. Now, we wait and hope our friends at the other end encounter no problems."

Ike whispered, "Haven't many of our airmen been captured at train stations?"

"Most were betrayed, the others unlucky. Follow my lead, I've done this before."

Dorothy and Ike watched the station as time passed. Merchants and workers entered for their commute to Amiens, only eight miles away. Dorothy went over her instructions. "Ike, you're with me in front. Then Martine and then you, Flight Lieutenant. Follow my lead, only I speak or Martine. Understood? Men will carry the bag and the radio. Martine and I will be carrying bags of fruit. We are returning from the orchards with fresh fruit from home. Let's go."

Dorothy and Ike walked to the ticket counter. Dorothy was talking to Ike as they waited, reminding him in French of what they still needed, what to say when they met them, and nagging to the point where the ticket master finally asked, "Madam, are you buying tickets or not?"

"Oui, four tickets to Paris."

Ticketmaster printed the tickets and asked for payment. Ike sheepishly pulled francs from his pocket and paid, with a solid expression of a henpecked husband. The Ticketmaster gave him a knowing smile as they went through to the platform. Dorothy walked towards the tracks and looked both ways, not for trains, before retreating to the others seated outside the station.

The platform soon filled with waiting passengers.

When the train pulled into the station on time, Dorothy waited until they were in the midst of the rush before leading them to the open railcar door. One last glance and Dorothy spotted a German Officer walking quickly toward them. She turned her back to the officer and yelled something at Ike. Then she stepped back and turned, spilling her bag of peaches, pears, and plums onto the platform at the feet of the surprised German Officer.

She wore the sheepish grin of a maiden in distress. Pulling her skirt up as she fell to her knees, she said, "Please, sir. Can you help me? I mustn't miss my train. I promised these to my employer, Colonel Schmidt, at the Constabulary in Paris. Please?"

Martine hurried the others onto the train, and the German knelt to help. Her bag refilled, Dorothy smiled. "Thank you, sir, you are a true gentleman. Please take one—for your kindness."

The German helped Dorothy up, "I'm happy to be of help. Look, you can still make your train."

Dorothy smiled sweetly and handed him a fresh pear. "Please, kindness must be rewarded."

The officer bowed as he accepted the pear. "If you insist. Gooday, mademoiselle."

CHAPTER 32
THE FRANCOISE LINE

As the French countryside passed by her window, Dorothy traded some of her fruit for baguettes, and the four foreigners enjoyed breakfast. "We must save some for Francoise and Jean, our hosts, and for their other guests." The food and the late night made them drowsy. Dorothy stayed awake. She nudged each awake as they approached the station. "Remember, follow my lead and don't speak until we've left the Paris station."

Ike eyed three armed German soldiers standing on the platform, one at each end and one at the terminal exit. A short man wearing a coat in the heat of summer, his face shaded by a large fedora, stood next to the soldier at the exit. *Gestapo and not the brightest fellow.*

Dorothy and Martine stood close outside, the two men's arms out, and carrying the now small bags, talked loudly across the men, "Hurry, both of you. We will miss our ride, and it will be your fault." The men, shaking their heads, walked with their heads held low. No one even glanced at the two Germans as they passed through the exit. Suddenly, a voice in French commanded, "Come with me."

Ike lifted his head. "Airey?" He turned to look. Airey Neave replied, "Two more than we bargained for. But welcome."

He turned to Martine, "Martine, I presume, I see the precious cargo has made it, and two more airmen to extract. Pay attention, Ike, you may learn something."

Once in the car, Ike asked, "Any word on last night?"

"Local issue, looking for downed airmen in the countryside. Haven't even put out a notice. Now that you're here, Ike, you're one of us. Martine and her radio are here to help pick up the pieces of the Pat O'Leart line. Only a few escaped—bringing in new leadership…"

Ike interrupted, "Francoise. Sorry, Airey, go on."

Airey continued, "Aye, Francoise. Dorothy's job is to coordinate with the new French leadership the sea escape route for those unable to cross the Pyrenees without holding up others. Boats to Gibraltar, for the injured and the VIPs, at least until we increase the pipeline."

Ike glanced at Dorothy. "And the money is to pay for all of this."

Airey went on, "Martine will stay in Paris. Francoise is in Bergerac; she will join us in the morning. Dorothy's injured are in the mountains at…"

"Conques, a small village with an ancient abbey, officially closed, Sainte Foy de Conques."

The car was parked behind a barn on a very tired and rundown farm. Airey led the team to a silo. A door opened, and a farmer motioned them in. "My name is Jean Bregi, from the Pat O'Leary Line in Paris. After the betrayal and arrest of Albert Guirisse, the real Pat O'Leary, we are now only a handful, but with funds, a radio, and the leadership of Francoise, we can rebuild. Not the Pat Line, a new line, the Francoise Line. I chose to squeeze you into this small space so you might know Francoise. This is how she lives, and I have never seen her dressed or in like appearance twice. She will come tomorrow to escort you to Conques and plan the route to the sea. She began her service in Marseille and, more recently, in Toulouse. She is as capable as Albert, God bless and keep him, a true patriot and hero of every free Frenchman. Yes, Francoise, is that good, perhaps even more. She is the very best we have! Tonight, we have the barn, fresh vegetables, and eggs. Yes, I am very good at omelets. And please do nothing to put the real farmer at risk."

A farm truck drove into the yard midmorning. A feeble woman, with gray hair, back bent as she walked slowly with a cane, approached the group. She said nothing as she slowly circled them. She straightened her back and spoke in a commanding voice. "You've been lucky, dressed as you are. I grant that the two airmen were not planned. We'll try to get you out on the first boat. But you must do as I say. I will listen after I have spoken. Do not interrupt me. Goldenrod, I know, and, of course, my friend from MI9. The money is safer with me. Now, let's see what we can do with those clothes."

She stopped in front of Ike. "Your watch, American

aviator. Lose it. That goes for you as well, young man. I'll buy you French watches and clothes. I commend you for wearing civilian clothes under your flight suits, but the cut is not French. We'll fix that. What do you say, Colonel Neave?"

Airey answered, "This is Colonel Ike Curtis, MI9 and AFRECON strategist. He is well known to both Goldenrod and me. We must get him back to England; he is a top-level courier. You can thank him for our infrared technology and air support. And this is his co-pilot and fellow SOE airman."

"Well, Colonel, a big fish. You'd better hope your identity is not discovered," Francoise muttered.

Airey said, "He is not known outside a very few among the senior allies. He has shown his courage and ability in North Africa. Colonel Curtis vouched for Agent Justice, with whom he has worked, and he is one of the few who could recognize Goldenrod after Albert's arrest. His plan enabled us to identify a traitor, but it cost him his airplane. He is cut from the right cloth."

"Stay here. I have better clothes for them."

As Francoise walked back to the car, a puzzled look affirmed Ike's question, "She must be at least sixty years old. I grant the infirmity was staged for us, but even so, her hair and her face—her vitality and presence are undeniable."

"That and her intelligence make her the best of French helper leadership. They call her the chameleon."

Francoise returned with common French work shirts and slacks. You may keep your boots; they may save your life. Now, we have a train to catch."

They were safe aboard a train heading south by one o'clock. Francoise distributed baguettes, cheese, and fruit as they settled in for the nine-hour train ride. She had reminded them to speak softly in French or not to speak at all. The Gestapo often rode the trains to and from Paris. No place was really safe. The Paris suburbs gave way to the beautiful French countryside. Green. Not at all like Gig Harbor in the summer when nine months of rainfall stopped like a divine spigot and the earth, grass, and brush turned brown. *Wildfire season. How many thousands of acres this year? How many lost homes—war widows and orphans now homeless? Who am I? Who have I become? Will home ever be the same? Rose tells me to trust her—I want to, but it's so hard. Justine is somewhere out there dealing with pirates, smugglers, the Gestapo, and hardcore Nazi's. What's in it for her? Where is the reward? Some things I'll never know, I guess I just have to give them up to you, Lord.*

Ike sighed and glanced at Dorothy. She smiled—a long, understanding smile. The smile of family, of sister and friend.

Ike nodded and chuckled softly. *If I can't talk, I think I'll try to sleep.*

Ike was standing under the ferry pier in Gig Harbor. It was low tide on a summer day. Little Earl was standing beside him, scratching pictures in the sand with a stick as Ike spoke. "This is a very special place, son, for both me and your mother. Adventure, oh, how she loved adventure. Did I ever tell you about the Polynesian sailing canoe we built?"

"Yeah, only a hundred times."

"Here, we built it here."

Ike laughed. "What a pitiful sailing canoe that was. Mom insisted on sailing—Gosh, it was hard to say no to her. She would give me that look."

Earl looked up, "I remember, yeah, when I asked, and I knew she would say no. I remember she could look cross and happy at the same time."

Ike knelt and drew Earl close, then wiped a tear from his eye. "Well, everything went wrong. Mom fell overboard, and so did the paddles—we needed one for the centerboard to sail. I pulled her up, soaking wet. That's when she became more than my best friend. I was amazed! I saw her beauty. She kissed me..."

"Dad..."

Ike rubbed the top of Earl's head. "She told me she was going to marry me. And she did. And then you came along. A spittin' image of your mom."

Ike's voice trailed off, "That's the day I fell in love."

Ike walked to the water's edge and looked in the shaded sound. Soft ripples rolled through a reflection. Linda spoke softly, "We will share our love forever. Now, give your love to Rose."

"Can we go now, Dad. We'll be late for the ball game. I'm pitching."

Ike slung Earl onto his shoulders. "Don't hit your head." And he ran to the stone steps at the sea wall.

As the sun drew low in the west, hills to the east grew taller. Round peaks were replaced by steep ridges growing into high peaks. The train followed a river valley of small farms and tiny villages. The mountainside was unbroken forest, not unlike the Cascades of Washington. After one more river crossing, the mountains were left behind; once again, hills flanked the river valley. Francoise gathered her things as the train entered the small city of Rodez. Wordlessly, they followed her lead.

Francoise led them to a sedan parked across the street from the station. She opened the door and climbed in. The key was in the ignition. As soon as the last car door closed, she drove off. "Where are we going? Ike asked.

Ike saw Fransoise's scowl. "North, two hours in daylight, perhaps three, as it will be dark soon. We go up the mountain. You are hungry, maybe? We will eat at the Old Hermitage, the Abbey of Sainte Foy."

Now that they were permitted to talk, they sat in silence as the sun fell below the tree line.

CHAPTER 33
SAINTE FOY DE CONQUES

The small slit in the headlight covers provided only enough downward-directed light for the driver and front passenger to see the road ahead. Low boughs of the trees along the narrow road appeared in sudden, gruesome, shadowy gestures. Running water, never seen, occasionally made its presence known. Francoise broke the silence. "It is best to come and go at night. The locals have no need to be on the road in the dark, and the Germans consider it too great a risk. The occasional Gestapo agent will act the tourist and visit the ancient Church of Sainte Foye. They fool no one."

"And no one reports your headlights?"

"They dare not. It would be death. The mountain people of France live by a code. They are a proud and loyal people."

Ike thought, *This ride is worse than any night mission I've flown. I feel helpless. Her voice is strong and assured.* "Tell me, Madam Francoise, who was Sainte Foy?"

"In English, Saint Faith of Agen. A young woman, a virgin, martyred by Emperor Diocletian's soldiers. She would not deny our God and Savior; she was tortured to death with a red-hot poker, impaled, and burned. The relics of Sainte Foy were brought to Conques in the eighth century by monks who established a priory there. The relics were venerated, and soon, pilgrims came. The priory grew into an abbey, and the church was built. Sainte-Foy-de-Conques was for centuries a stop on the Way of Saint James, the pilgrimage to Santiago de Compostela. The abbey closed years ago, and its cloisters were abandoned. The Abbot's chapel, adjacent to the cloisters, also closed."

Francoise turned for a moment and smiled at Ike, "The cloisters, the Abbot's Chapel—it is the perfect place for Allied airmen to mend. The doctor tends their wounds. The chemist provides medicines, the merchants provide food—they shall be happy to receive payment now, and the mayor and Gendarme keep the Gestapo bored. As I said, for one to betray us, it would mean death, but even so, we must be careful."

The car slowly made its way around a narrow curve, with a steep, wooded hillside to the left and to the right, and a deep drop to the river hundreds of feet below. "We are here. As I said, nearly three hours in the dark."

The car found its way, slowly, through the narrow medieval cobbled street barely wide enough for a single car. After they passed the tall church, Francoise turned right and wound her way slowly downhill, turning into an alley behind the cloisters. She turned into a room opened by a fallen wall. Parking the car, she said. "We must cover the car and hang the canvas curtain. Only then, I, and only I, will I light my torch and lead you in."

They walked the columned cloister to the Abbot's Chapel at the end. The oak door was locked and sealed by a heavy iron chain. Francoise grabbed the last link on the left, where it entered the wall, and turned it, then pulled. The door silently swung open. Soft light welcomed them inside. Ike's engineering training got the best of him as he studied the expertly crafted new jam hidden behind the old.

"Step quietly on the stone floor. We must take every precaution," Francoise urged as she led them to the sacristy, through a door, and down to the crypt. She opened another door deep in the bowels of the ancient chapel. Light spilled out. Standing in the center of the room, framed by the light around her, stood Justine.

"Ike!" She muffled her happy surprise and ran to him. She hugged him and buried her teary-eyed face in his chest. "Jesus has answered my prayers! We meet again, safe and secure. And Father Hugh, he is well?"

Ike smiled. "Justine, yes, it's a blessing, Hugh is well. Last time I saw him, he insisted on only one drink, saying he must keep his promise to you." Turning to Dorothy, Ike said, This is Dorothy, Hugh's niece and sister to Rose."

"I am to meet with Goldenrod, who will lead the extraction of the men unfit to cross the Pyrenees. I have a boat waiting near Perpignan. These men will be the first. Seven, and one must be carried in a litter. But Francoise assures me it is possible."

Dorothy shook her hand, "I am Goldenrod. You know my family?"

"We will talk later. Come, meet the airmen."

A helper announced that their supper was prepared. The simple onion soup, cheese, and baguette filled and comforted them. Straw mats were laid out, and sleep came easily.

Church Bells rang. *Is it a dream?* Ike sat up. The bells continued to ring, a second, a third, and a fourth time. They stopped, but only for a few seconds, before they rang one more time.

"Four bells. It is the village fire alarm, but the fifth is a warning—Gestapo. A fire drill will greet them. It is both our warning and a delay, as the street will be blocked and filled with the men of Conques. We should be safe. Just wait quietly."

A car drove into the Abbey yard. A Gestapo officer walked to the door and pulled on the chains. He called to his comrade, "Bring me the crowbar. This will take a while. Go and find the gendarme; if he is not in the town hall, look for him among the firemen. Then wait for me here, but stay outside, do not be fooled, if you enter, they will surely escape past you."

Alone, the officer turned the far-left chain link and swung the door slightly ajar. His heavy footsteps echoed through the chapel as he crossed the stone floor. He went straight for the sacristy, through the side door, and down the stairs. He tried the undercroft doors one by one. Until….

The room was silent. Everyone's eyes were on the door as it slowly opened. Ike stood against the wall beside the door, waiting....

The door slowly swung open. No one. Only an empty corridor. Then a voice called out softly. "Do not fear. I come in the peace of our Lord and Savior Jesus Christ."

I've heard that voice before. Ike replied, "Then show yourself."

Footsteps, the Gestapo officer stepped from behind the wall and walked in. "I urge you to leave here soon. You have been betrayed. A townswoman has reported you. She records your headlights and others buying more food than they need. Food and headlights that come to this chapel."

"Ernst! Earnst Schmidt!" Ike shouted.

"Yes, our dear friend Ernst!" Justine confirmed. "You're safe. Gestapo? Not our Ernst!"

Ernst nodded. "Yes, my friends, and no, not the Gestapo, well, yes." Ernst sighed. "American intelligence, thanks to your help. But first, I must deal with the traitor and the Gestapo officer with me. Please wait quietly until I return. There is more you must know."

Ernst went back outside and waited. He stood with his back to the chain, the door still slightly ajar. Five minutes later, the Gestapo officer returned with the town gendarme and mayor in tow.

"Good work, Peter. I will speak to both. I made a thorough inspection, and there is no one here, just mice. Go with the gendarme and arrest the woman who made this false report. Wasting our time in this worthless village hours from anywhere..."

"Is that wise? It may discourage other informers."

"Arrest her. That is my order! Think! What value is there to the Reich? There is no garrison, no emplacements, and no industry. If it is of no value to the Reich, there can be no resistance. Think! Hours of our time were wasted while saboteurs were left to menace the trains from Rodez and Toulouse. Perhaps that is her true intent. Let the whole village watch as she is marched to jail. Do as I say. Mayor, you will stay. You have authority here, and with it, accountability. I have more to say to you."

After the others left, Ernst said, "Mayor, covered trucks will come and go by night. They are not to be recorded or spoken of by anyone in the village, or they will receive the same fate as awaits your traitor. So long as you keep this order, no Gestapo will bother your citizens."

The mayor's surprised face formed a smile. "You have my word. You will hear of no problems in Conques."

"Good. You may return to your duties…and pray that all goes well in the Abbey."

The mayor folded his hands as in prayer, smiled, and walked off. Emst went inside and closed the door behind him. In the crypt, he met Francoise. "Madam Francoise, it is a pleasure to meet you. I have been assigned to watch and protect you. Even Bergerac is not safe for you. Your new escape line is critical, both by land over the Pyrenees and a new Sea route. I have bought you time here. The Gestapo will not bother you, though you should still maintain precaution. And Colonel Neave, I presume, I am directed to share information with you."

"You have silenced the Gestapo?" Airey asked.

"And we can continue?" Francoise added.

"Yes, and there is more. There are two ambulances hidden in the cloisters, a shame you did not make routine inspections of your perimeter."

"Ambulances! Already procured?"

"And three passes for checkpoints. You will be allowed to pass without inspection. The red crosses are covered. I recommend that you leave them covered while you are in the village. Uncover them only down the mountain."

"Of course. And the mayor?"

"We have an agreement. Now, if you please, I would like to pray for you, all of you, my brothers and sisters in Christ. Please, gather around. If you will hold one another's hand as I pray the first benediction, given when the Lord said to Moses, 'This is how you are to bless the Israelites. Say to them: The LORD bless you and keep you; the LORD make his face to shine upon you and be gracious to you; the LORD turn his face to you and give you peace. Amen"

Francoise asked softly, "But how? How did you pass through the door? And how did you know where we were hiding? We listened to your steps. You did not hesitate but came directly here."

"The door was easy. I followed you and watched. But I knew that if I didn't go directly to you, you would likely escape before we could speak. You were wise to remove the floor plans from the Church and Abbey at the entrance, but I remembered my seminary teacher of exegesis, it is always best to return to the original text. I sent an order to deliver the plans of every building still standing in Conques to my office. From them, I found the safest space in this chapel."

Justine rushed to hug Ernst before he left. "Your family, are they safe?"

"I have no word. I trust God and go on."

Ernst smiled. "You will find the keys and the passes in the ambulances," and he was out the door.

Two German army trucks left Conques at two am. They passed through the sleepy streets and made their way down the mountain. Halfway to Rodez, they stopped, jumped out, and uncovered the Wehrmacht ambulance markings. Outside Rodez, they approached A German checkpoint. The drivers presented their passes without a word and were allowed to proceed. It was another two hours to the Mediterranean coast. The airman on the stretcher was suffering with every jolt and bump. Francoise ordered a rest stop.

"There is another port, closer. It will be easier on the poor fellow. Let me make a call. I can arrange it."

They stopped outside a small village. Justine walked into a café, "Bonjour. A coffee, please. Where is the toilet?" The owner pointed to the back.

Justine walked past the telephone and washed her hands before making a phone call. "Jacques, I will visit you today at the point. A dozen, yes, I'll pick them up on the way. Au revoir."

Justine returned to the bar and sipped her coffee.

She placed a coin on the counter and said, "I'm sorry, but I must hurry. Now I must visit the market on my way. Au revoir."

Back in the ambulance, Justine told Francoise, "Drive to Beziers, there is a village on the point, Agde. The boat will be there."

They drove through Beziers and stopped at the end of a dirt road in a valley cut by a small stream into the hillside, which ran down to the sea below. Justine jumped out. I will lead you down. The path is steep. Ike, you, and Airey should bear the litter. Francoise and Dorothy…"

"We'll wait here with the ambulances. We won't be going."

Justine nodded. "If there is any trouble. Do not wait for me or Airey. Drive off at once!"

At the bottom of the creek, an old, rusted hulk was Mediterranean moored to a two-plank finger pier. Only the well-oiled boom and winch betrayed its current service. Ike and Airey carefully carried the injured airman on board and down below. The others filed on quickly as Justine spoke to the captain.

As the anchor was weighed and the engine started, Justine made her way to the stern plank. A shot rang out. Justine fell to the deck.

CHAPTER 34
TOLL THE BELLS
LOUDER STILL

Ike stood smiling as Hugh walked Justine to church. "You two make the perfect couple. How is the shoulder?"

"Why did it have to be my right shoulder? So much to do! But I manage."

"How did it go in London with Airey and Colonel Z?"

"The Francoise line is working—both by land and sea. Another boat arrives in Gibraltar tomorrow. I won't be there to see them for some time. There is talk that I…" Justine grinned. "We will speak later. Look, Rose is coming. You will want to see her."

Rose approached, holding the arm of a gentleman. Ike fumbled to speak, "Rose, I… it's… You look beautiful as ever, and happy."

Rose smiled. "Colonel Montclair Issaac Curtis, meet my friend and benefactor, Lord Robert James Curtis."

Ike, perplexed, took the outstretched hand and shook it. "It is a pleasure. Rose speaks highly of you."

"It is good to meet you at last, cousin. I've been searching for you. Please forgive Rose. I asked her not to say my name. I needed to be certain, not for myself, I had no doubts, but for the crown's verification."

"The king of England?"

"I'm sure he has people who do the work, but yes, by his authority, you are my heir to the titles Earl of Montclair, Viscount of Berwick, and Baron of Tweed Bridge."

"But I'm an American from a fishing village on the Puget Sound. My father ran the local ferry boat. How can..."

Bright and clear change ringing called them to worship. Lord Curtis smiled and said, "We are being called to worship. Please, allow Rose to take your arm. If you will allow, I would like to join you in the family stall."

When Hugh took the pulpit, he nodded to Nigel, "Did you listen to the processional that Nigel so fervently sang? I heard you sing, but did you listen? How firm a foundation is Jesus our Lord. Absolute truth. We know it in our minds, but our hearts remain uncertain. Recall the stanza: '*When through the deep waters I call thee to go, The rivers of sorrow shall not overflow; For I will be near thee, thy troubles to bless, And sanctify thee thy deepest distress.*' And finally, '*The soul that on Jesus has finally leaned for repose, I will not, will not, desert to its foes; That soul, though all hell shall ever endeavor to shake, I will never, no never, no never forsake!*'

"The promises of God. How easy it is to question

them. Hymns such as these and Bible stories like we read this morning in Chronicles, tell us it is natural to doubt and to wonder, but not to remain in that doubt, but to stand firm on the promises of God, who said, *'You are my sheep, the sheep of my pasture, and I am your God declares the Sovereign LORD.'*

"Recall as David prayed to God, *'Who am I, O LORD, and what is my house that you have brought me so far?'* David went on reminding God of all the promises made to him, *'For your servant's sake, O LORD, you have done all of this greatness...'* And what does David ask? *'Do as you have spoken!'"*

David prayed what his head knew but his heart doubted. "Do as you have spoken! Uphold your promises! A prayer to God to meet the promises he has made, to comfort, to give peace, to forgive, to bless, and to hold us in his hand with an eternal salvation. Brothers and sisters, pray, from your heart, from your fears, and pain and doubt—from your guilt, and listen as he answers you in grace, mercy, and love."

After worship, Ike joined Hugh, Rose, Justine, and Lord James in the vicarage. "It makes sense, Hugh, what you preached. We'll be surrounded by the wilderness as long as we live. But the wilderness is a toothless tiger that can never swallow us up. We know it is there. We know it roars and growls and curses us, but we look through our hearts, by faith, and see the garden beyond. We need only to follow the lighted path where God leads us—to graze as contented sheep in his pasture.”

“I should let you preach sometime, Ike.”

Ike blushed and changed the subject. “Forgive me. Lord Robert, we never finished our conversation.”

Lord Robert chuckled. “You've confirmed everything that Rose has said about you. You are at once humble yet noble in heart. I know of the common American disdain for the nobility. There is good argument for it. The simple difference rests on one word: “The.’ Your history is filled with nobility, not by title but by deeds. Perhaps it will come as a surprise to hear that it has always been the intention of our leading class. But like any human structure, it was corrupted by sin. Examine the ideals of chivalry and their abuses. I had no choice in my birth. I have no brothers and no children. I was born with a title, but I made a choice to live not as a noble, but nobly. And I am honored that our family line has produced a noble successor. I want you to come. I want to show you what will be yours to steward, and to learn that you and I are not alone. Many who have gone before us were truly noble. Most, like me, served as priests, not in authority, but in service, ministering in our hospital, orphanage, and homes for the elderly and infirm. It is our calling—your calling.”

“I should like to do that, Lord…”

“Cousin.”

“Yes, Cousin Robert. Did Rose tell you about little Earl? You would love him.”

“Indeed, she has. I can't wait to meet him. He must visit our old castle, Cutis Tower in Cawmills—a Norman tower. Three stories filled with Medieval treasures."

Robert winked, "Very small, really. It will change your perceptions of the age of chivalry."

Justine cleared her throat. "Now can we eat? Hugh, pour the drinks while Rose brings out the wonderful meal she has prepared."

Rose laughed. "I sliced, prepared, mixed, and cooked exactly as Justine told me, ever looking over my shoulder to be certain I did it right."

Harvest had come to Churchstanton, and it was a special time of celebration. Ike stared at the mostly empty garden. The sound of songbirds serenaded him with their same joyful song of spring. Ike smiled. One bird's anthem carried above the others. *Rose, my sweet songbird.* Ike drew in the fresh air. *It's not dead, it will be reborn. One more lesson from above.*

The bells of Saint Peter and Paul began to chime, the most joyful change ringing Ike had ever heard. He ran into the church. The bride stepped into the aisle. Beaming in her beautiful gown. The music began, and she walked forward, tears of joy in her eyes. Ike's heart was aglow. He turned and whispered, "Isn't she beautiful? And her smile."

Rose squeezed his hand, "Justine and Hugh are a perfect match."

Justine's father escorted her up the aisle, raised her veil, and kissed her cheek. Her grandmother watched joyfully from the first stall.

DAVID MARTYN lives in Gig Harbor, Washington with his wife, Karen. Retired from a career in the Maritime Industry, he can keep watch over the ships passing to and from Tacoma and the Vashon Island Ferry. David believes God reveals Himself and sets us on a journey of discovery that brings us to the revelation of God's Word, to the very heart of God. His love of Scripture, which burns in our hearts, has been strengthened by years of home Bible Study groups which brought him insight on Bible passages and confirmation of God working in the lives of His people. It is David's hope that his stories awaken the seed of revelation God planted in the reader's heart.